101 INVESTMENT LESSONS

from the

Wizards *of* Wall Street

THE PROS' SECRETS FOR RUNNING WITH THE BULLS WITHOUT LOSING YOUR SHIRT

By
Michael Sincere

CAREER PRESS
3 TICE ROAD, P.O. BOX 687
Franklin Lakes, NJ 07417
1-800-CAREER-1; 201-848-0310 (NJ and outside U. S.)
FAX: 201-848-1727

101 INVESTMENT LESSONS FROM THE WIZARDS OF WALL STREET
Cover design by Tom Phon Design
Typesetting by Eileen Munson
Printed in the U.S.A. by Book-mart Press

To order this title, please call toll-free 1-800-CAREER-1 (NJ and Canada: 201-848-0310) to order using VISA or MasterCard, or for further information on books from Career Press.

The Career Press, Inc., 3 Tice Road, PO Box 687, Franklin Lakes, NJ 07417

Library of Congress Cataloging-in-Publication Data

Sincere, Michael.
    101 investment lessons from the wizards of Wall Street : the pros' secrets for running with the bulls without losing your shirt / by Michael Sincere.
        p. cm.
    Includes index.
    ISBN 1-56414-382-1 (pbk.)
    1. Wall Street.   2. Stocks--Valuation--United States.   3. Monterary policy--United States.   I. Title.   II. Title: Investment lessons from the wizards of Wall Street.   III. Title: One hundred one investment lessons from the wizards of Wall Street.
HG4572.S54   1998
332.63'22—dc21   98-45106

To

Chuck, Lois, Alex, and Alice

ACKNOWLEDGMENTS

This book moved from an idea to reality because of the assistance of a number of people.

I could not have completed this book without Joanne Pessin, who kept the project on track, conducted research, offered numerous suggestions for improvements and tirelessly assisted in all aspects of the book. Her efforts were invaluable.

Alexandra Bengtsson came from Halmstad, Sweden, to help check facts, collect background information, and find supporting research for every lesson.

I want to give special thanks to Gloria Fuzia at Career Press for her constant encouragement and superb editing skills. Thanks to Ron Fry for believing in the project from the beginning.

This book would not have been possible without so many experts, the Wizards of Wall Street, who took time from very busy schedules to talk with me about the stock market. I am deeply appreciative to the following individuals for sharing their knowledge:

Ted Benna (401(k) Association), William Berger, John Bogle (Vanguard), Shelby Davis (Davis), Amy Domini (Domini Social Equity Funds), David Dreman (Dreman), Jean-Marie Eveillard (SoGen), Elaine Garzarelli (Garzarelli), Gary Goodenough (Loomis Sayles), Erik Gustafson (Stein Roe), Mason Hawkins (Longleaf), Harvey Hirschhorn (Stein Roe), Sheldon Jacobs (No-Load Fund Investor), Rick Johnson (Columbia), Dan Leonard (INVESCO), Robert Levitt (Evensky, Brown, Katz & Levitt), Paul McManus (John Hancock), William Miller (Legg Mason), John Montgomery (Bridgeway), Louis Navellier (Navellier), William J. O'Neil (*Investor's Business Daily*), Jim O'Shaughnessy (O'Shaughnessy), Don Phillips (Morningstar), Gary Pilgrim (PBHG), Robert Rodriguez (First Pacific Advisors), John Rogers (Ariel), Steven Romick (UAM FPA), Robert Sanborn (Oakmark), Spiros Segalas (Harbor), Morty

Schaja (Baron), Oscar Schafer (Cumberland), Dr. John Schott (Steinberg Global Asset), Jack D. Schwager (Prudential), Bill Stromberg (T. Rowe Price), Ralph Wanger (Acorn) and Martin Whitman (Third Avenue).

I am also indebted to the public relations personnel and staff members for helping arrange interviews and providing background material. In addition, thanks to Paul Wierzba, Jon Roventini, Anna Ridolfo, Luigi Silvestri, and Greg Roventini for making suggestions for improvements.

CONTENTS

PART 6: DECIDING WHAT TO BUY　　　149

PART 7: TRADING TACTICS　　　169

INTRODUCTION

Many people invest in the stock market hoping to find the next Microsoft or Dell. However, I know from personal experience how difficult this really is. For more than a year, I was making hundreds and sometimes thousands of dollars a day investing in the market. It seemed so easy. I dreamed of quitting my job at the end of the year, of buying a small apartment in Paris, of traveling around the world. But these dreams came to a sudden and dramatic end when a stock I owned, a Texas cellular phone wholesaler, fell by more than 75 percent over a one-year period. On the worst day, it plunged by more than $15 a share. There was a rumor the company was exaggerating sales figures. That was when I learned how quickly Wall Street punishes companies that misrepresent the truth.

In a panic, I sold all my stock in the company, paying off my margin debt with cash advances from my credit card. Because I owned so many shares, I lost a small fortune, half of it from money I borrowed from the brokerage company. One month, I'm a genius, the next, a loser. This one big loss was my first lesson in the market.

My father was a stockbroker, as was my grandfather before him. (In fact, he founded one of Chicago's earliest brokerage firms, Sincere and Company.) But like so many things in life, we don't learn anything until we experience it for ourselves. The only way to really understand the inner workings of the stock market is to invest your own hard-earned money. When all your stocks are doing great and you feel like a winner, you learn very little. It's when all your stocks are losing and everyone is questioning your stock-picking ability that you find out if you have what it takes to invest in the market.

You might wonder why you should read a book from someone who lost money in the stock market. I lost, and lost big, but instead of giving up, I got inspired. I began to read everything I could about the market from books, magazines, and newspapers. I sought out professional money managers and financial experts who willingly shared their successes as well as their failures. I spoke with some of the most well-known and respected investors—the Wizards of Wall Street—and created 101 investment lessons based on what I learned.

Included in this book are strategies and inside tips from three dozen experts as well as individual profiles of 20 top investment professionals. I took special care to eliminate financial jargon and complicated formulas or calculations. By reading this common-sense guide to the stock market, you will learn how to do research, build a diversified portfolio, trade stocks, manage money, recognize when to get help, and how to avoid the most common trading pitfalls.

I think you will learn a lot from the men and women included in this book, investment gurus like John Bogle, Shelby Davis, David Dreman, Elaine Garzarelli, Mason Hawkins, Bill Miller, Louis Navellier, William O'Neil, Jim O'Shaughnessy, Ralph Wanger, and Martin Whitman, to name only a few. They will tell you what to look for in an investment, the mistakes they made and what they learned, and the secrets to making money on Wall Street. The people I profile are acclaimed experts recognized by the media and others who work and do business on Wall Street.

The 101 lessons are designed to help you formulate your own investment plan, a key factor for investment success. Some of the lessons are well-known on Wall Street, others might surprise you. Quite a few are contradictory. In a bull market, the lessons will help you to protect your profits. In a bear market or during the next correction or crash, you will learn how to invest with a minimum of risk. Either way, you will come out a winner.

As for me, I eventually recovered everything I lost in the stock market and made even more money along the way. As a result, I wrote this book to prevent others from making the same mistakes I made. I wish you the best of luck. My only hope is that you will use what you learn from the experts to make a fortune in the stock market. If you come close to doing that, then this book has served its purpose.

PART 1

Developing a Winning Plan

1. Choose a successful strategy

Many people, after making the decision to invest in the stock market, aren't sure what to do next. According to professional investors, your first step should be to develop an investment strategy. Nearly every pro agrees that a personal investment strategy is essential if you want to be successful in the stock market.

What is an investment strategy? Very simply, it's a plan that will help you make decisions in the stock market. All the pros, for example, have reasons to believe a particular stock will go up or down in value. These reasons make up their investment strategy, and every decision they make in the market is based on this strategy.

An investment strategy is important because it helps you find quality stocks. Many people are vulnerable to money-losing tips and poor advice from other investors. With an investment strategy, you will be careful about the stocks you buy. A strategy helps you limit the number of stocks you will look at.

You'll learn more about the personal investment styles of the pros after reading the profiles of the Wizards of Wall Street. In the meantime, however, take a brief look at the following successful investment strategies and find out if one of them appeals to you.

Value investing. It is difficult to introduce the value investment strategy without also mentioning the name of Benjamin Graham, the acknowledged father of value investing. The value investor is constantly searching for high-quality stocks selling at a price that is significantly less than what the company is really worth. This investor is looking for companies that are temporarily unloved and out of favor by other investors. The value investor seems to find the best bargains in a slow, flat market.

Although everyone wants to find high-quality, low-priced stocks, value investors spend a lot of time determining what a company is really worth, what they call fair value. They use a number of objective and subjective measurements to calculate the fair value of a company. For example, value investors like stocks with low P/E (price/earnings) ratios. The P/E ratio is calculated by taking the company's stock *price* and dividing it by its 12-months *earnings* per share. For example, if the current price of a stock was $40 a share and the company's earnings for the prior 12 months was $2, you would divide $40 by $2. The result: a P/E ratio of 20. To give it perspective, the P/E of the S&P 500 Index has hovered around 20 for the last few years. Value investors also look for stocks with other characteristics, such as a high dividend yield. This information can be found in most financial publications.

According to value investors, the difference between the value of a stock and its price creates what they call a margin of safety, a key component of the value strategy. Value investors tend to be patient, holding an out-of-favor or depressed stock for years until it reaches what they have calculated is fair value. They believe that investors should act as if they were buying the entire company, not just the stock. To do this, they try to understand the underlying business.

Growth investing. Growth investors look for companies that are growing and expected to grow even faster in the future. These can be large or small companies in any industry as long as they have above-average sales, earnings, or market share. Growth investors especially like companies that are growing at least 15 or 20 percent a year and will continue to do so. It doesn't matter if a stock has a high P/E ratio as long as the company's earnings and sales are rising, too. Just like value investors, growth investors use a number of subjective and objective measurements to determine how fast a company's earnings will grow in the future.

There are a number of different growth strategies. For example, the *momentum* investor looks for the highest-flying, most aggressive stocks, whatever is hot at the moment, like the Internet or biotech companies. They will pay almost any price for these stocks but hope to sell them for an even higher price. Momentum investors have strong stomachs. They are willing to ride out the ups and downs of their favorite stocks for the chance to make a fortune.

Other growth investors want fast-growing companies but will only buy them if the prices are reasonable. These investors are looking for GARP, growth at a reasonable price. GARP investors tend to shun the momentum stocks because the prices are too steep.

Contrarian investing. Contrarian investors, like value investors, look for high-quality companies that are temporarily out of favor and underperforming the market. The contrarian is delighted to find companies shunned by Wall Street but that exhibit superior performance characteristics and excellent prospects for the future.

Unlike many value investors, however, the contrarian pays closer attention to psychological factors. The contrarian believes that investor emotion and perception heavily influence stock prices. According to contrarians, there is a follow-the-herd mentality to the stock market. When stocks have been hit hard because investors panicked or overreacted, the contrarian steps in. He or she sees this as the perfect buying opportunity for high-quality stocks at low prices that have been temporarily abandoned by other investors. Contrarian investors dig deep to uncover these unloved stocks.

The contrarian investor likes medium- or large-sized companies with extremely low P/E ratios. David Dreman, chief investment officer of Dreman Value Management and a strong proponent of contrarian investing, uses a number of objective measurements to determine which stocks have the lowest P/E ratios. Then he picks out the lowest 20 percent from that group. He also looks for stocks with high revenue growth, a high dividend yield, and a low price-to-book ratio. These are just a few of the criteria he uses to find stocks that will outperform the market over time.

To be a successful contrarian, you must be willing to go against the crowd. Many times the contrarian stands alone, preferring to buy stocks that few on Wall Street would even consider.

Quantitative strategy. Quantitative analysts, or "quants," as they are commonly called, rely heavily on proprietary computer programs and quantitative analysis to find the best stocks in specified industries. They are high-tech number crunchers. Quants make their buy-and-sell decisions based primarily on what the computer tells them. They are constantly plugging in numbers and making adjustments, hoping to create a superior computer model. The goal, according to people who believe in this strategy, is to design the perfect computer model that will find the perfect stock. Quants believe that stock picking should be clinical and unemotional. That is why they rely principally on computers to do their calculations.

Louis Navellier, CEO of Navellier & Associates, constantly refines and changes his computer models. It doesn't matter if he buys growth or value stocks as long as they fit the criteria he enters into the computer. Every quant uses a different set of criteria to come up with the best stocks. However, most agree on this guideline: Let the computer determine which stocks to buy or sell.

Dow strategies. There are a number of investment strategies involving the 30 companies included in the Dow Jones Industrial Average (DJIA), the most widely used stock market indicator. One well-known strategy involves buying the 10 highest dividend-yielding Dow stocks and holding them for one year, then repeating the process each year. Michael O'Higgins, an investment advisor and newsletter writer, helped popularize some of the Dow dividend strategies by writing about them in his book, *Beating the Dow*. You can find the dividend yield of any stock by looking in most daily financial newspapers.

David and Tom Gardner, also known as The Motley Fool, made adjustments to the Dow dividend strategies that were introduced in O'Higgins' book. They call it the Foolish Four Approach. Instead of including 10 Dow stocks in their portfolio, The Motley Fool selects only four, rotating them every 18 months. The advantage of this approach is that it automates the stock picking process, and it takes little time or knowledge to implement.

If you're like most investors, you probably want to know which of the aforementioned strategies works best. The answer is, they all do—maybe not all the time in every market, but they all work. Keep in mind that no matter how successful a strategy is for someone else, if it doesn't make sense to you, it probably won't help you in the stock market.

What is most important is that you start thinking about your own personal investment philosophy. The pros say this is essential if you want to be a successful investor. However, don't plan on coming up with your philosophy overnight. It can take a long time to develop a philosophy and strategy that works for you.

2. Create a written set of rules

Nearly every professional money manager has a set of rules based on a personal investment philosophy or strategy. Ralph Wanger said it best in his book, *A Zebra in Lion Country*: "If you develop a set of convictions you adhere to, you can turn your back on thousands of stocks and concentrate on a manageable universe. A set of guidelines—and I urge you to put them down on paper—gives you confidence when times are rough. It helps you make the toughest decision: when to sell. It makes it possible to get better and better through cultivation of a repeated skill. And it keeps you from the folly of the amateur who leaps from fad to fad, usually just about the time the fad is fading."

If you're new to the stock market, you might wonder how to come up with a set of rules. Believe it or not, that's the easy part. If you read the profiles of the Wizards of Wall Street, for example, you will find that many growth investors have a rule to buy stocks that are growing by more than 20 percent per year. Many value investors, on the other hand, have a rule not to buy a stock with a P/E ratio higher than 15.

Consider developing rules for buying, rules for selling, and rules to keep you out of trouble. Many of the lessons included in this book can be converted into rules that will keep you out of trouble. For example, you could make a rule to never go on margin, which means you should never borrow money from the stock brokerage to buy stocks.

Martin Pring, author of *Investment Psychology Explained*, said that rules will not totally eliminate losses, but should help you to trade more objectively. By relying on a set of rules, you will prevent fear, greed, and hope from clouding your judgment. Pring stressed that no matter how many rules you have, they won't do you any good unless you put them into practice. It is essential, says Pring, that you regularly review your rules as your financial position, investment philosophy, or market conditions change over time. He warns against making thoughtless adjustments to your rules, however, because that does more harm than good.

◆ Profile ◆

James P. O'Shaughnessy

Chairman and CEO, O'Shaughnessy Capital Management, Inc.
Portfolio Manager, Cornerstone Growth and Value Funds
Author, *What Works on Wall Street* and *Invest Like the Best*

Although he didn't know it at the time, the biggest mistake Jim O'Shaughnessy ever made in the stock market was doubling his money in options as a young man. "When you are 20 years old and double your money, you think you're Peter Lynch, Ben Graham, and Warren Buffett all rolled into one," laughs O'Shaughnessy. "You think you'll be at the top of the *Forbes* 400 before you turn 25 years old." The mistake, he says, was thinking he was bigger and smarter than the market. The market thought otherwise.

On his next stock, which he bought based on a tip, he lost much of the profit he made on the options. He says he made the same mistake many people make: He bought the stock based on his intuition and gut feeling. "We are programmed by nature to fail as investors because we are programmed to believe in our intuition or gut, and they often mislead us. People run around from stock to stock and story to story, and the results are disastrous." He learned from his mistakes that people must find a good investment strategy that makes sense, and then stick to it. He found that consistency is the one characteristic that unites all the best investors.

To develop his own investment strategies, O'Shaughnessy used computers to back-test Wall Street's most popular investment strategies in every conceivable market cycle to see what worked best. What did he learn? The single best factor to look at when trying to value a stock is the price-to-sales ratio. His extensive research helped him to develop what he calls a core group of winning strategies.

The Cornerstone Growth Fund is one of them. To be selected for this fund, a stock must have a price-to-sales ratio below 1.5. "What this means," explains O'Shaughnessy, "is that the most we will pay for a dollar's worth of sales is $1.50. To provide perspective, the price-to-sales ratio of the stocks that make up the S&P 500 is currently 1.8. So the stocks we buy are very cheap."

O'Shaughnessy uses other criteria for the stocks he selects. He wants stocks whose earnings growth is higher than the previous year. He also wants companies with a market capitalization of more than $150 million. Finally, O'Shaughnessy buys the 50 stocks that have the best one-year price appreciation over the previous year. "Essentially, when you apply this strategy to the data, you find it compounds at more than 19 percent compared to 12.5 percent for the S&P 500. And there has never been a 10-year period where it failed to beat the S&P going back to 1951."

Once a portfolio has been assembled, it is rebalanced once a year. "We equal-weight stocks at the beginning of a portfolio season," says

O'Shaughnessy. "When you are looking at 50 stocks, you are really looking at how a class performs and not the individual stock. We never bet on an individual name. We remind ourselves daily that stocks don't know we own them. We never fall in love with a stock. After we rebalance, if it no longer meets our criteria, it's sold, it's gone, and we don't care. That is how we minimize risk: always equal-weighting the shares at the start."

While doing research for his book, *What Works on Wall Street*, O'Shaughnessy made the following observations: The stocks that make up the S&P 500 are determined by the people who work for Standard and Poor's. "What does this tell us?" he asks. "It tells us two things. Number one, that the S&P is a strategy, not the market. And number two, the reason the S&P 500 beats 80 percent of conventionally managed mutual funds is that it never deviates from the strategy of remaining 100 percent invested in large stocks. The S&P doesn't wake up and say, 'Oh, no, Alan Greenspan is bearish and I'm going to cash.' The S&P doesn't wake up and say, 'I'm going to prove what a great stock picker I am.' The S&P just consistently and methodically stays fully invested in those stocks."

There are other strategies, he says, that will do vastly better than the S&P if used in a consistent and disciplined manner. For example, O'Shaughnessy is a leading proponent of buying the 10 highest-yielding Dow stocks and holding them for one year, the so-called *Dogs of the Dow*.

Can the individual investor learn how to use these strategies? "The individual has never been more empowered to invest than today. Right now, you can take any of the strategies I use, go on the Internet, log on to www.marketguide.com, and find a stock model for $7.95. If you want the secrets to the kingdom, we'll show you how all these models did over the last 45 years and show you how to use them. The individual can take any of our strategies and duplicate them, and we tell them exactly how to do it."

But even with these successful strategies, O'Shaughnessy says individuals will end up losing money. "Remember what Casey Stengel said: 'There is a huge difference between knowing how to do something and doing it.' We know that people are going to go out there and override our system. They'll say: 'These strategies are a good starting point, but then I'll decide which stocks I like.' Human nature has programmed us to think we're better than other people in picking stocks." O'Shaughnessy says our intuition convinces us that we should be able to pick winning stocks.

"What we sell is discipline. We sell consistency. That is the secret to investing. Ninety-five percent of success in the stock market is just being fully invested using a good strategy. The other 5 percent is having the diligence and discipline to never override that strategy." He adds, "This is not rocket science. Whenever the math gets above the algebra level, I am certain to lose money."

According to O'Shaughnessy, good investing hasn't changed for hundreds of years. He mentioned that Isaac Newton, the great English mathematician and physicist, lost a fortune by investing in the South Sea Trading Company in the early 1700s. People poured money into the stock. Even poets wrote about the company. "If there is a better sell signal," he jokes, "it's when people start writing poems about your stock. It was inevitable that the company would collapse and burn."

The South Sea Trading Company was like the Internet company of its day, says O'Shaughnessy. "If I say Yahoo! or Excite, people will pay 5,000 times sales for it because they are so overwhelmed by the story and how appealing it is," he observes. "The stock market pays attention to the laws of economics. People who pay the moon for stocks get burned and people who don't do well." Because the Internet stocks have such high price-to-sales ratios, he avoids them. "I know historically such valuations have led to ruin. I don't know how the individual company will perform. Yahoo! could still go up another 500 percent. What I do know is that the class of stocks Yahoo! belongs to will go down."

At first, it was hard for O'Shaughnessy to be so disciplined. "That was the hardest thing for me to learn," he admits. "I like to joke that I am still in a 12-step program for traders. I say, 'My name is Jim and I want to trade stocks.' I have learned that I am not bigger than the market. We are the Joe Friday school of investing: 'Just the facts.' If I follow just the facts and invest that way, I make huge sums of money." For individuals to make money, they have to find a strategy that suits their emotional makeup and stick with it.

3. Stick with your strategy

It takes more than a strategy and a set of rules to be successful in the stock market. After talking with dozens of money managers and financial professionals, I discovered the secret to being a successful investor. I found out why the best investors make more money, make fewer mistakes, and consistently beat the stock indexes year after year. The secret to successful investing is really quite simple. It can be summarized in one word: Discipline.

Even though successful investors use different strategies, follow different rules, and buy and sell all kinds of securities, the one characteristic they all share is discipline. It doesn't matter if the market is up or down, if interest rates are higher or lower, or if the economy is good or bad, the pros methodically and consistently stick to their investment strategy.

Jim O'Shaughnessy, CEO of O'Shaughnessy Capital Management, came to the same conclusion when he did a study for one of his books. The study showed that the most successful investors never deviated from their investment strategies. Unfortunately, being disciplined is not easy. Says O'Shaughnessy: "It's fascinating how simple it is to be a successful investor. But it is also simple to lose weight, to write a book, or to quit smoking. There are a ton of books that will show you how to do it." Although the secret to being successful in the stock market might be simple, it is incredibly difficult to be disciplined.

Dr. John Schott, a psychoanalyst and portfolio manager of Steinberg Global Asset, explains what it means to be disciplined: "It means you have a plan and you stick to it no matter what. You have a system that controls your emotions that would otherwise be destructive—fear, greed, anxiety. Every fund manager has a set of rules like that."

In other words, after choosing your investment strategy and creating a set of rules, you need to have the self-discipline to stick to the strategy and follow the rules. The top investors rarely switch strategies and almost never make exceptions to their own rules. If you don't have the discipline to stay with the program, the best strategy in the world will not help you. Robert Rodriguez, chief investment officer of First Pacific Advisors, says the worst investment failures he has seen over the years involved people who didn't stay with one strategy. He says that even professional money managers occasionally make this mistake.

What should you do if you aren't disciplined? In that case, the pros recommend you invest in a professionally managed mutual fund, an index fund, or use a Dow dividend strategy. If you have a lot of money to invest, you might consider hiring an investment advisor. Nearly every pro agrees, however, the stock market is not friendly to people with too much money and too little discipline.

PART 2

MASTERING YOUR EMOTIONS

4. Don't let emotions ruin your portfolio

There is an old saying on Wall Street that the worst enemy for investors is not the stock market but themselves. According to the experts, many people lose money in the market because they get too emotional about the stocks they buy or sell. Martin Pring wrote in his book, *Investment Psychology Explained,* that when you commit real money to a financial endeavor, you are also committing emotion. The true battle for investors is not the market, but learning how to control the constant bombardment of emotional stimuli.

For example, the two most common emotional reactions to the stock market are fear and greed. The fear that the market will go to zero has caused many investors to sell their stocks or mutual funds in a panic. Like clockwork, when the market makes sudden drops, nervous investors call the brokerage or mutual fund company and sell everything they own. Often, investors who succumb to fear end up making terrible investment decisions, selling at the worst possible time.

Just as harmful is greed, which causes investors to hold on to questionable stocks that have risen to unsustainable levels. The greediest investors let winning stocks slip through their fingers, refusing to take any profits or, worse, waiting in vain until they squeeze the last eighth of a point out of a stock. Often, by the time these investors are ready to sell, the stock has made a roundtrip back to its starting price.

In addition, it's also common for investors to bring their emotional problems to the stock market. Dr. John Schott, a psychoanalyst and portfolio manager of Steinberg Global Asset, says, "Some people want to gamble and there it is everyday. You can do it with options or commodities or the most speculative stocks. You'll get the excitement but not the profits. For the people who want to lose, who are unconsciously guilty and want to be punished, all they have to do is buy the riskiest stocks and they will probably lose. Just about any psychological need you have can be gratified within the framework of the stock market."

Nevertheless, Dr. Schott says you can still do well in the market no matter what kind of personality you have. For example, narcissist investors might buy the hottest, flashiest stocks in the market and sell them at the first sign of weakness. It might not be the best strategy in the world but it still allows you to make money. He says you can make all kinds of neurotic errors in the market and still end up with a profit.

What can investors do to prevent emotions from ruining their investment portfolio? The first step, according to many experts, is to spend time analyzing your strengths and weaknesses. Dr. Schott agrees: "You have to begin with some degree of self-knowledge so you know what your weaknesses are." Unfortunately, self-analysis is not as easy as it sounds. Dr. Schott said that people naturally resist looking closely at their own personalities. It's always easier, he says, to see problems in the other guy rather than problems in yourself.

After self-analysis, the next step is to teach yourself to be emotionless. Gary Pilgrim, president of PBHG Fund, Inc., said he used to get emotional about the stock market but doesn't anymore. He learned over the years that it's not helpful. Although the pros aren't immune to emotional responses, many have learned to put their emotions aside when committing money to the market. They admit that they get into trouble when they rely on emotions to make investment decisions.

Even if you have difficulty separating your emotions from your money, there are a number of mechanisms you can use that might help. Dr. Schott says that putting a stop loss on a stock is very effective for some people. A stock with a stop loss is automatically sold when it drops to a predetermined price. This prevents a person who unconsciously wants to lose from losing too much money. A second method that works, says Dr. Schott, is *dollar cost averaging*, or investing a set amount of money at regular intervals. This method is ideal for many people because they win no matter what the stock does.

Dr. Schott also recommends that you keep accurate records of all your investments. Because people with trading difficulties often deny they are losing money, a detailed accounting of gains and losses will help them see the truth. Finally, if you are consistently losing money in the market, you could hire an investment advisor or invest in professionally managed mutual funds.

5. Learn from your mistakes

If this were a perfect world, we would never make mistakes. Because we know that is impossible, the best we can do is learn from the mistakes we do make. Groucho Marx said it best: "We should learn from the mistakes of others. We don't have time to make them all ourselves." Everyone, even the world's top traders, makes mistakes. When I asked financial experts if they make any mistakes, they usually laughed. "Every day," was a common reply. "Hundreds," another said. One fund manager sent me this comment: "I try to forget my mistakes and move on." Most professionals know that mistakes are a natural part of the investment process and the sooner they accept it, the more successful they will be.

Jack Schwager, author of *Market Wizards*, says that just because you lose money on an investment doesn't mean you actually made a mistake. "Even if you do everything right," he says, "a certain percentage of your decisions will end up being losing decisions. It doesn't mean you made a mistake. If you followed everything that is part of your game plan and you still lost, it is not a mistake, it is part of the probabilities. People equate winning or losing with correct or incorrect decisions. You can win on a bad trading decision and lose on a good trading decision." Schwager says if you consistently follow your criteria for picking a stock, even though you won't always win with every trade, in the long-term you should come out ahead.

The pros try not to take mistakes personally; instead, they treat them as useful learning experiences. William O'Neil, publisher of *Investor's Business Daily*, puts it this way: "I don't care if you are a professional or a brand-new investor, you are going to make mistakes. What are you going to do about that? Are you going to look the other way and pretend they will go away? Not in the market."

The pros say it is better if investors make small, manageable errors than one huge, devastating mistake that takes them out of the investment game. Professional traders say that as long as they can get back in to trade another day, there is always the chance they'll eventually succeed. That is why it is so important that you not risk all your money on one speculative trade. That is the kind of mistake you can't recover from.

It is also common for people to inadvertently compound a little mistake into a big mistake. For example, an investor might refuse to sell a stock that dropped in price. Instead of taking a small loss and admitting a mistake, this investor will buy even more shares, convinced that the stock will break even or rise in price. Unfortunately for some stocks, that day never comes.

The pros know that mistakes are inevitable. The trick is to make less of them. First, you don't want to repeatedly make the same mistakes. One of the ways to prevent this from happening is to keep a notebook of errors. Dan Leonard, portfolio manager of the INVESCO Strategic Technology portfolio, keeps a list of all his mistakes and what he learned. A number of pros do the same. They objectively review and analyze their mistakes and take steps to make sure they don't happen again. Keeping a notebook will also help you to identify trading problems.

To minimize errors, it is suggested that you have the discipline to stick to your strategy and follow your rules. According to several experts, errors are more likely to occur when investors veer away from their plan. Another option is to ask a knowledgeable friend to help analyze all of your stock transactions. It might help to have an objective third party look at your investments and see if mistakes are being made.

◆ Profile ◆

Ralph Wanger

President, Wanger Asset Management
Portfolio Manager, the Acorn Fund
Author, *A Zebra in Lion Country*

When Ralph Wanger started the Acorn Fund nearly 30 years ago, the country was in the middle of a dull and draggy bear market. Nothing was going on in the stock market and few people were buying. One of Wanger's analyst friends invited him to an afternoon meeting in Chicago with a company called Houston Oil and Mineral, who supposedly had a big story to tell. Wanger and a dozen other people reluctantly attended the meeting to hear the story. As it turned out, Houston Oil was a tiny company that had stumbled upon a substantial gas field in Texas. By the middle of the afternoon, Wanger's acquaintances had left the meeting to get some drinks at the bar, while Wanger stayed to hear the rest of the story. He ended up buying the stock. Over the next three to four years, the stock shot up, making 10 times Wanger's investment, and saving his fund. "I'm sure you could have found 50 little oil companies to invest in," Wanger said. "This just happened to be the right one."

Wanger says you have to be ready for those rare moments when a great opportunity appears. "Every once in a while something important happens that completely changes your life. You can't force these opportunities and they don't show up every day. You have to be alert when they happen," he adds. He says these defining moments come two or three times in a lifetime. "You have to listen, you have to pay attention, you have to follow your belief and act on it, and it has to come out right," Wanger says.

His decision to purchase Houston Oil was more than dumb luck. He realized that the price of energy was rising and would rise even more. Wanger thought it wiser to invest in energy producers than energy users. When Houston Oil appeared on his radar screen, he was prepared to act.

Wanger likes companies that hire aggressive, successful managers who are not afraid to make radical changes. "We have trained analysts who talk to the company and competitors and try to understand whether it is a good business or not. We continue to check every three months to make sure the story is still in place. Basically, we have to convince ourselves there is money to be made on the stock. If you buy it at a low enough price, if the story comes true, you'll make a good profit."

This approach has helped him select other big winners throughout the years, including Cray Research, which went up 1,333 percent between 1978 and 1985. "Seymour Cray was one of the great computer designers of the world," says Wanger. "Twenty years ago he left IBM to build a supercomputer. It was very unclear whether it could be done. IBM had tried and failed; Burroughs had tried and failed. But Cray thought he could do it. I finally decided that having the chance to invest with an engineer the caliber of Cray was like being offered the chance to invest with Thomas Edison. If the stock goes down, well, it's just a loss. But if you don't invest and the company succeeds, you'll kick yourself for the rest of your life."

Cray Research passed what Wanger calls the "Quit Test," which refers to companies so exciting that he'd quit running his mutual fund for the chance to manage the company himself. Wanger is always on the lookout for new investment opportunities. He specifically looks for small companies that could turn into big winners. He concentrates on companies that are reasonably priced but unique. The company might be going through an important change, like rapid growth, or developing a new product that could be a big success.

After purchasing a stock, Wanger and his associates monitor it at least weekly. They run screens on the stock to find which ones have higher or lower expected returns, and continually verify their conclusions. "The key is 'why do we own this stock?' " says Wanger. "There has to be a reason this particular stock was picked out of all the choices available. The analyst should write down in 12 words or less the reason the stock was bought. You must be able to convince yourself at least on that day. If the central reason you bought the stock in the first place is no longer valid or can't be articulated, it should be sold," he says.

Like most professionals, not all of Wanger's picks work out. He mentioned companies like Edison Brothers or House of Fabrics that were once strong and mighty but ended up bankrupt. They land in what Wanger calls the subworld of stocks. "You end up selling them for drill bit prices," he says. Wanger doesn't dwell on his mistakes. "Michael Jordan throws the ball at the basket. Sometimes it goes in, sometimes it doesn't. If you're going to be a great player, you can't worry incessantly about a missed shot. The question is, how did you do in the game?"

According to Wanger, the biggest mistake individuals have made for the last 40 years is being underinvested in stocks. Although it's not too late to get into the market, Wanger will not be surprised when it goes down. "It has been a liquidity-driven market and it goes until it stops. And when it stops, people will look around and ask 'How could anyone in their right mind pay that much for a stock?' "

Wanger says the key to minimizing risk is diversification. "If you buy Acorn, for example, you get 250 stocks in your portfolio. A single error is not going to destroy your return." For that reason, he feels the average individual is better off in mutual funds.

"Mutual funds have very valuable characteristics," says Wanger. "First is diversification. Second is single-line bookkeeping." If you make 50 trades during the year, he explains, your Schedule D will be a mess. "The third advantage," Wanger quips, "which is probably overrated, is professional management. The fourth, which is under-rated, is the ability to blame someone else. What's the biggest risk you have when doing something in the market? It's the risk of ap-pearing to be a fool to your loved ones. 'Sylvia, it's not my fault, it's that guy in Chicago who lost all our money.' The shift to the third party is very valuable. It frees you up to take more risk than you would otherwise."

Although Wanger suggests mutual funds are an excellent way for individual investors to get into the market, he admits that there is great satisfaction in picking your own stocks. "You can do it your-self," he suggests. "Security analysts don't have any magic system." Wanger emphasizes that you have to have a sensible reason for buy-ing a stock. Whatever your reason for investing in a stock, you must invest in companies you comprehend and understand. "That way you can get an advantage," he adds.

The most successful investors, according to Wanger, are patient, hold for a long period of time, and don't trade very often. When you overtrade, he says, transaction costs and taxes accumulate, depleting your profits. He also agrees that you should take advantage of every available tax-exempt vehicle, including 401(k)s and IRAs. Finally, Wanger says, "Have a sensible investment plan, one that won't change the first time something goes wrong."

6. Think independently

Many of the best investors are fiercely independent, refusing to be swayed by the opinions of others. In fact, the pros suggest that you focus less on what other people's opinion of the market is and more on facts and research. Because the market does not always perform logically, many pros say it is more important than ever to think independently if you want to find success on Wall Street.

Being independent means having the courage to invest in stocks that no one else wants. For example, it takes independence and courage to buy real estate during recessions or move to cash in the middle of a bull market. But if you're right, you will be richly rewarded.

Robert Rodriguez, chief investment officer of First Pacific Advisors, says it is easy to invest with the crowd but not very profitable. His greatest investment success was buying Nike at $1 a share by today's prices. At the time, no one on Wall Street supported his position. To make matters worse, every major financial magazine ran negative articles about the company. Although it wasn't easy, Rodriguez went against Wall Street and the media establishment and did what he thought was right. He was vindicated when Nike turned into his most successful stock, rising to nearly $45 a share. Because he was willing to think independently, he made a lot of money for his clients.

Many experts believe you should only do what you believe is right, even if it means doing the opposite of what everyone else is doing. If you are really right, the market should eventually come around to your way of thinking.

7. Prepare for the worst

It is a lot more interesting to dream of success than to analyze balance sheets or read annual reports. You enter the stock market with high hopes and great expectations of making a lot of money. However, realistic investors know that no matter how bad things get, they can always get worse.

Steven Romick, portfolio manager of UAM FPA Crescent Portfolio, put it this way: "Every individual investor should understand what he or she could potentially lose in an investment. It is as important as how much you could potentially make. Understanding risk is extremely important." Many individual investors like to focus on what could go right with an investment. Experts like Romick, on the other hand, pay more attention to what could go wrong.

Even if the overall market is rising in a strong bull market, your stock could sink. You may have patiently waited months or years for your stock to reach its all-time highest price when a whiff of bad news sends it reeling. There are many frightening examples of stocks that unexpectedly crash, leaving investors with millions of dollars in paper losses.

This is what happened at Oxford Health Plans, a well-known managed-care company. Oxford lost 62 percent of its value in one day, one of the largest single-day losses of market value in the past 10 years. The analysts rated it high, its earnings estimates were always on target, and revenue was increasing. Because of computer problems, however, Oxford wasn't keeping up with its bills. The company promised to solve the problem, but once the word got out, institutional investors starting selling, but it was too late for individual investors. On the news, the stock began falling, eventually going from $76 a share to $33 a share. A few months later, it was selling for less than $17 a share.

For the chance to make big money, some investors take huge risks without thinking of the consequences. When I was at a hardware store looking for tiles, I asked one of the employees for help. After directing me to the tile department, the man said he used to be an active options player who was caught by surprise in the 1987 market crash. At the time, he held extremely aggressive positions in call options. The only way he felt he could lose money was if the market dropped by more than 20 percent, an unlikely scenario at the time—or so he thought. When the market actually crashed on October 19, 1987, dropping by 22 percent in one day, he and thousands of other traders lost fortunes. In one day, his entire portfolio was wiped out. After declaring bankruptcy, he was forced to sell his business. Even though he was only a few years from retirement, to survive, he had to look for work. In one day, he changed from a financially secure businessperson to a salaried employee trying to make ends meet. His dream of a pleasant Florida retirement was destroyed.

This man made several mistakes. First, many pros say only the most knowledgeable and aggressive investors should dabble in call options. Further, once this man decided to buy options, he should have prepared for the worst possible scenario, a market crash. Because he was making so much money, it didn't cross his mind that this could happen. Although stock investors can ride out corrections or crashes, options players cannot.

Many pros believe that it is important for investors to think of the potential risk of any investment and to always imagine the worst. Robert Rodriguez, chief investment officer of First Pacific Advisors, says that investors should focus on the downside because the upside will take care of itself. If you hope for the best but prepare for the worst, you will take the necessary steps to avoid losing any or all of your money.

8. Be patient

According to most of the wizards of Wall Street, one characteristic of the most successful investors is patience. The patient investor waits for the perfect opportunity and the right circumstances to buy a stock. With patience, you ignore the day-to-day noise of the stock market and hold stocks for the long-term, waiting months or years for your stocks to compound and grow. For example, Warren Buffett, chairman of Berkshire Hathaway and financial guru, has been known to hold his stocks for years before he sells.

You also may have heard about Anne Scheiber, a New York woman who never bought a stock she wanted to sell. Beginning with an initial investment of $5,000 when she was 38 years old, Scheiber began buying stocks. At the time of her death at the age of 101, she ended up with an investment portfolio worth more than $22 million, a 17.5 percent return, which she bequeathed to Yeshiva University. What was her secret? In her job as an IRS auditor, she learned that one of the fastest ways to get rich in America was to invest in stocks. She bought only a few shares at a time and held them for decades. Because of the power of compounding interest, what Einstein called the eighth wonder of the world, Scheiber became fabulously wealthy. Unfortunately, she never liked to spend her money, either, but that's another story.

Unlike Scheiber, many people make the mistake of expecting instant returns on their investments. Some investors want to see 30-percent returns, not in a year, but in a week or month. Especially in a bull market, many people have unrealistic expectations of how their stocks will perform. It is the ability to patiently wait out short-term market fluctuations that separates the novice investor from the professional. Too many people look for immediate gratification and have difficulty waiting months or years for their investments to become profitable.

Unfortunately, it isn't easy to teach investors to be patient. One technique the pros use is to try and imagine how their stocks will perform in five or 10 years. This way, it is easier for them to ignore the short-term fluctuations in the market and concentrate on the bigger picture. As investors gain more experience, they learn that patience will ultimately lead to investment success.

9. Maintain a positive attitude

Many of the world's most successful people have tapped into the therapeutic power of a positive attitude. Thomas Edison spent 10 years and performed more than 50,000 experiments until he perfected his alkaline storage battery. He didn't listen to skeptics or give up at the first sign of problems. Like many successful people, he believed in what he was doing and nothing was going to stop him from realizing his dreams. Edison didn't wait for something to happen, he made it happen. Joel Barker, a futurist and public speaker, wrote, "Those who say it can't be done are usually interrupted by others doing it."

Some of the top traders and portfolio managers are not just positive about their work, but passionate. Erik Gustafson, portfolio manager of the Stein Roe Growth fund, explains the importance of passion: "All the successful investors I know have an undying passion for this business. It is the secret to success in everything, being absolutely passionate about whatever you do. The great investors have that passion for the markets and for this business. They are consumed by succeeding within that business and they love what they are doing."

Indeed, this passion was evident as I interviewed the professionals profiled in this book. They enjoy searching for undervalued or ignored stocks, talking to management, researching new companies, and taking apart balance sheets. For most managers, it is an incredibly challenging and stimulating job, and sometimes a lot of fun. I got the impression that they enjoy competing with other money managers for the best quarterly or yearly returns.

Although the pros are well-compensated for their efforts, it seems that many are motivated by more than money. It might be hard to understand if you don't work on Wall Street, but quite a few portfolio managers could retire tomorrow if they wanted to, but choose not to. To many Wall Street pros, money is just another way of keeping score. They stay because they enjoy managing other people's money.

Although you don't have to be passionate about investing to make money on Wall Street, it is an important characteristic. However, it is not always easy to remain positive when, as Jean-Marie Eveillard, president of SoGen funds admits, the market is hitting you over the head every day. Nevertheless, according to some pros, if you are negative, you are running against the tide. Generally, the economy grows, the world moves forward and profits go up. As one portfolio manager told me, "If you don't believe things will get better, you're increasing your chances of being wrong about the market."

Although most pros believe in the power of a positive attitude, they know it takes more than that to be successful in the investment business. They always back up their investments with research, analysis, and hard data. In other words, be positive, but never let down your guard. One pro calls this "cautious optimism."

◆ Profile ◆

John W. Rogers, Jr.

President, Ariel Capital Management
Portfolio manager, Ariel Growth Fund

It shouldn't be surprising that John Rogers, who chose a tortoise for his company logo, believes that patience is what wins in the investment business. His philosophy is based on the belief that wealth is created over the long-term. With that philosophy always in mind, Rogers constantly searches for companies he believes will have the capacity to grow within the next three to five years.

As a value investor, Roger also looks for companies whose stocks are undervalued. "It all revolves around valuation," says Rogers. "We are out kicking the tires, meeting management, doing our homework." He specializes in finding small-cap companies, primarily $1.5 billion in market capitalization or less, that are selling at relatively low prices compared with what he believes is their intrinsic value.

To determine a stock's intrinsic value, Rogers looks at P/E ratios and other quantitative data. Then, he tries to assess what the private value of the company is—that is, what a reasonable person might pay for the company if it were offered for sale. Rogers finds the private market value in two ways: "We look and see what price people are paying for similar businesses out in the marketplace. For example, if we own a drug store chain, we will study and see what prices big drug stores are paying when they go out and buy smaller ones." The second way Rogers finds the private market value is by analyzing the future cash flow of the company. He relies on the expertise of experienced security analysts to make these projections.

It is also critical to Rogers that these companies are temporarily out of favor on Wall Street, neglected or misunderstood in some way, so he can buy them at lower prices. Then he waits—patiently— for the market to realize their true worth.

According to Rogers, to be a successful investor, you must have the courage to "buy stocks that other people are selling, to delve into areas that people are shunning at the time and to be contrarian. The second thing is to stick to what you know, stick to industries you truly understand and have a feel for, to not pull too far afield from what Warren Buffett calls your 'circle of competence.' " Rogers calls Buffett's circle of competence message probably the best advice he's ever received. "You can't try to be all things to all people," he explains. "To be naturally contrarian, to be disciplined, you have to love the business, love reading about stocks, love meeting management, be extraordinarily competitive and have a fierce sense of independence."

He takes a number of steps to avoid risk. "We try to find companies that have the most consistent earnings streams, companies that are very predictable, companies that are in industries that lend themselves to predictability, that we believe can generate good, consistent profits in the future." He cites newspaper companies as one example of an industry that has been consistent over the years.

Although buying a company at a low price is important, Rogers is also concerned with the quality of the companies he includes in his portfolio. "We spend a lot of time, more than our competition, trying to determine the quality of the product and the quality of the people before we make an investment," says Rogers. "The objective," he says, "is to invest in superbly managed businesses that have the kind of quality products able to sustain a consistent 12- to 15-percent growth rate in the future." Rogers looks beyond the numbers to find managers who have competence and integrity. "When we invest in a company, we want people who will build their careers there, who care about the environment, community service, and are doing the right thing."

Like other fund managers, Rogers says he's learned from his mistakes. The biggest mistake he made, he says, was with Payless Cashways, a home do-it-yourself business. "We found out the business was more cyclical than we thought. It didn't have the ability to grow consistently the way we thought it did. We found out that the industry was much more competitive than we originally thought." According to Rogers, "We learned we must make sure any company we invest in has barriers to entry and also has the ability to generate consistent earnings, not just when their economic sector is doing well, but through all types of economic conditions."

Rogers will sell a stock when the company is no longer undervalued. "From a valuation standpoint," he explains, "if the company is overvalued, that is, selling at a high P/E ratio and selling at a high price relative to its private market value, we sell it immediately. Secondly, if the management is getting sleepy, if they don't have fire in the belly any longer, we'll sell." Roger is also concerned when there is a major change in senior management or when a company is acquiring businesses outside its area of expertise. "These things worry us," he admits.

One of the most common mistakes that individuals make, according to Rogers, is buying what worked yesterday. "They buy the hot stock that they read about on the cover of a magazine or newspaper. By the time it's widely known, most of the time, it's already too late. By the time everyone else sees the information and understands what a wonderful company it is, the money has already been made."

The advice Rogers has for the individual investor is simple: Look forward, not backward. "That's the key thing," he says. With the Internet and the easy availability of annual reports and research reports, Rogers thinks that individual investors can do their own research. "People buy a stock at $20 and it's gone down to $18 and they're unhappy and sad. There might have been an earnings disappointment that caused it, but they sell the stock because everyone else is down on it and all the analysts have put sell recommendations on it."

With the proper research, the patient investor will look forward a year or two to determine if the company will correct its problems and eventually get things back on track. "You've got to be able to get the short-term noise out of your system and look ahead." That is the key to success, says Rogers.

10. Take personal responsibility for all trades

It is important that you know exactly what is happening to your money at all times. No matter where you put your money, even in the hands of a trusted stockbroker, investment advisor, or money manager, the buck stops with you. Unless you are the victim of an investment scam, it won't help if you blame others for your losses. That is why it is so important to know exactly how your money is being handled.

If you leave your investment decisions to others, the pros suggest that you find out the background, philosophy, credentials, and record of the person managing your account. You should not be afraid to ask detailed questions about how your money is being invested.

Think of it this way: You are hiring this person to manage your money. Because you're the boss, you should expect honest, understandable answers to all of your questions. If you have any doubts, keep interviewing until you find someone you're comfortable with.

If you invest your money with a retail stockbroker, many experts recommend that you keep discretionary power over your account. If you give a stockbroker discretionary power, he or she can make unlimited trades on your behalf. Because brokers are compensated by the number of trades they make, an unethical broker could make meaningless trades on your behalf, just to generate more commissions. This practice, called churning, is not as uncommon as you might think. If your account is large and you don't have time to trade on your own, at a minimum, you should insist that your broker inform you of all transactions he or she makes on your behalf.

No matter how your investments are handled, the bottom line is that no one cares more about your money than you do. With that in mind, although you might allow other people to manage your money, never give up your right to be completely informed about your investments at all times.

11. Trade with confidence

Dr. John Schott, a psychoanalyst and portfolio manager of Steinberg Global Asset, conducted a study to determine the characteristics of the most successful investors. He discovered that the top traders he studied had one common trait: confidence. Dr.

Schott writes in his book, *Mind Over Money*, that these traders expected to do well and acted as if they would do well. And they did. Dr. Schott says that self-confidence is not just a good idea for stock market success, it is the major idea.

Some people confuse self-confidence with arrogance. When you are self-confident, you don't believe that your way is the only way. If anything, people with the most confidence are humble. They have nothing to prove. They believe in what they are doing and they know it works. It's what some people call quiet self-confidence.

According to a number of fund managers, Sir John Templeton, the legendary founder of the Templeton funds, has this characteristic. One of Sir John's associates remembered what happened when a couple of Sir John's stocks got decimated during a nasty market correction. While everyone else in the office was panicking, Sir John calmly assessed the situation and said he thought this was a wonderful development. He explained that it gave him an opportunity to buy more shares at a better price.

It is sometimes hard for people to trust themselves. It means having the courage to do what you think is right against incredible odds. This is not something they teach you in school. Rather, it takes experience, vision, and faith that everything is going to work out for the best when there is no evidence it will. If you have that kind of unwavering self-confidence, be thankful. It is a rare and valuable gift.

12. Be open to new ideas

Although one of the keys to investment success is discipline, successful investors willingly make adjustments to their strategies if they discover revolutionary ideas or new research. Sometimes, new ideas turn into unexpected opportunities.

To really understand the importance of accepting new ideas, you might want to study paradigms. Joel Barker, a futurist and author of *Future Edge*, says that a paradigm is a "set of rules and regulations that does two things: 1) It establishes or defines boundaries; and 2) it tells you how to behave inside the boundaries in order to be successful." Basically, it gives you the rules of the game. The idea, however, is to look for paradigm shifts. Barker says this means changing the game and the rules. Unfortunately, many people and organizations don't recognize that a paradigm shift is occurring until it is much too late.

An excellent example of a paradigm shift occurred with IBM during the 1980s. IBM was the undisputed market leader of the mainframe computer for half a century. For decades, American corporations generally didn't buy anything but computers with the IBM label. "No one ever got fired buying IBM," computer professionals liked to say at the time. IBM was, writes Paul Carroll, author of *Big Blues*, "the most profitable, the most admired, the best company in the world, maybe in the history of the world."

During the early 1980s, however, problems started surfacing. Carroll writes that IBM senior executives ignored the rest of the computer industry and focused too much on themselves. They talked a lot but didn't change the way they did business, and the business they knew best was the mainframe computer. It was inconceivable to senior management at IBM that anything could threaten their almighty company.

When a bunch of 20-year-olds from Microsoft began to develop their own software products for PCs, taking market share away from IBM, senior management held on to the paradigm that people only wanted mainframe computers. The idea that people would want a personal computer on their desk was inconceivable to IBM in the early 1980s. Even when they developed a highly successful personal computer to compete with the Apple, upper management at IBM refused to see the light.

According to Carroll, IBM's blunders in the 1980s and early 1990s cost IBM $75 billion in stock market value. Their stock fell from $175 a share to as low as $40. Among other mistakes, IBM kept pouring billions of dollars into losing projects yet failed to capitalize on what was actually working. Because of the corporate structure, IBM and thousands of companies like it were reluctant to adapt to the rapidly changing computer industry. While IBM was still operating in the "horse-and-buggy" days, the rest of the industry rewrote the rules, leaving IBM behind. Fortunately, the

IBM of today is a totally different company. It took IBM a long time to change its bureaucratic ways and adjust successfully to the future, but it did.

It's not easy for many people to change the way they invest. In fact, when new investment ideas are introduced, it is very common for some people to reply, "Why should we change? This is the way we've always done it." As IBM learned the hard way, sometimes the best time to make changes is when you appear to be the most successful.

Although it takes courage to change or improve on investment strategies or stock picks that aren't working, it is often the most profitable action you can take. If you detect that the strategy you're using is costing you money, you need to objectively analyze exactly what is going wrong and have the courage to make the necessary changes. No matter how much time and research it involves, if it will increase your future profits, it will be worth the effort.

13. Don't trade stocks when you're distracted

Many investors have learned that trading stocks involves complete and total concentration. If you are distracted by family problems, dreaming about your next vacation or feeling rushed, it is easy to make careless trading errors. Not only should you avoid trading when you can't concentrate, but you should also be careful about trading when you feel desperate to win back money you lost on other stocks.

Many people have trouble thinking clearly when they're under pressure. As a result, some stockbrokers or telemarketers will convince you to buy something by creating a false sense of urgency. Salespeople will use this technique to coerce people to buy cars, computers, or stocks. They will breathlessly whisper, "If you don't buy today, you will never get this opportunity again." Some salespeople are masters at pressuring you to buy. By the time they finish speaking, you feel like running to the bank and withdrawing all of your money. The fear of missing out on a once-in-a-lifetime moneymaking opportunity is one of the reasons many investors lose money in the stock market. More than likely, if you really do get a once-in-a-lifetime opportunity, it is unlikely to come from a stockbroker or telemarketer.

A number of times, I have mistakenly made trades when I was in a hurry. One day, a few minutes before I was leaving for a doctor's appointment, I decided to buy additional shares of Gateway. Although I had planned this purchase well in advance, it was the wrong time to execute the trade. I put in a buy order at the market price, then ran out the door. That night, after reviewing my order, I was shocked to discover I had mixed up the stock symbols. Instead of buying Gateway, a well-known computer hardware company, I had bought an unknown biotech company that was years away from earning a profit. By the time I corrected my careless error the next day, I had already lost several hundred dollars.

The best advice is to not trade stocks unless your mood is calm and your head is clear. If you feel you need a little more time before you make a trade, then wait until you are ready. If you find that trading stocks is causing you too much stress, you could switch to professionally managed mutual funds or hire an investment advisor. This way, you can pay the pro to make the stressful investment decisions.

14. Don't trade for entertainment

If you are looking for entertainment, the stock market has it all. Like a real-life game of Monopoly, there is excitement, competition, and prizes. When you win, you are rewarded for your efforts with real money. If you make mistakes or aren't careful, you can lose money or get kicked out of the game. The stock market is irresistible to people who have the money and want to play a very real and exciting game.

But there is a downside to using the stock market to play real-life games. First, it is a lot more expensive to play the market than to see a movie or go out to dinner. If you want the excitement of the stock market but are afraid to risk too much money, a better alternative is to join an investment club. For a minimal monthly fee, the investment club will give you a night of entertainment and an excellent education. In the long run, the club will probably save you a lot of money.

For the price of a cup of coffee, there are other alternatives. Almost every day, a dozen Florida retirees meet at the local Charles Schwab office to drink coffee, talk about stock prices, and catch up on investment news or gossip. Some gather around the computer terminals to check on stock quotes. A Charles Schwab representative says one particular group has been coming to the office for years. This scene is repeated at brokerage companies all over America. The stock market gives these people a reason to get together to share a common interest. It is a harmless way of getting entertainment without risking a lot of money. For many people, it makes more sense than sitting at home staring at a computer terminal.

Although the stock market can be entertaining, successful investing usually is not. Many of the most financially rewarding strategies are predictable and routine. Although many people believe the road to riches is only possible with rapid trading techniques and game-playing tactics, most people get rich slowly. It's not quite as entertaining, but it's a lot more profitable.

15. Don't panic

Panic is defined by the experts as a sudden, overwhelming fear. When it comes to investing in the stock market, panic causes you to think you will lose all your money and property. Physically, your stomach tightens, your heart beats faster and your head aches. You feel powerless and guilty. Feelings of panic are common during a market crash, correction, or bear market.

Dr. John Schott, psychoanalyst and portfolio manager of Steinberg Global Asset, says you can read all the books you want but panic is difficult to describe unless you've personally experienced it.

"You can look at a roller coaster and imagine what it's like, but until you ride one and go through those 360-degree hoops you don't really know what it feels like." But like the roller coaster, once you realize the market won't go to zero, you see bad market drops as buying opportunities. As Dr. Schott says, "Once you've done it, the excitement and thrill is there but a lot of the fear is diminished." The same is true of portfolio management, says Dr. Schott.

Because there haven't been a lot of market crashes, no one can predict with certainty how investors will react. Only a handful of current portfolio managers experienced the 1987 crash. In 1987, the entire market panicked, dropping by more than 22 percent, causing a selling frenzy. At today's prices, that would be a drop of approximately 1800 points. Although some claim this was far short of a true panic, it cost investors billions in losses. For a true panic to occur, say the experts, the world's economic systems would have to collapse.

During the next correction or crash, Dr. Schott predicts that professionals will remain calm. "A lot of mutual fund managers will be forced by the rules of the game to be 100-percent invested all the time and they are just going to have to weather the storm." He says it will be difficult for fund managers to raise cash because more individuals will be taking money out than putting money in. Managers who are able to raise cash will have a good buying opportunity, he adds.

Although mutual fund companies spend a lot of time educating customers on the benefits of staying invested through all the market cycles, no one can accurately predict how individuals will react during a correction or crash. A few investors are surprised to learn that mutual funds can actually lose money. "I didn't know it goes down," one woman told a fund manager after looking at her quarterly 401(k) statement.

Giving in to panic will cost you money. During an agonizingly painful bear market, when more investors are selling than buying, even the most experienced investors have a nagging feeling the financial world might end. For the individual investor, this feeling can be overwhelming. According to Dr. Schott in his book, *Mind*

Over Money, when you feel panic starting, short of contacting a psychiatrist, remember the following guidelines:

◊ Bear markets are a natural part of the business cycle.

◊ Every bear market in history has come to an end, usually within nine to 18 months, and then a bull market starts to build.

◊ Bull markets tend to last twice as long as bear markets, the reason why long-term investing is such a good way to get rich, particularly if you can take advantage of the buying opportunities that occur when the bear market starts to turn around.

According to the pros, you can ride out any bear market if you remain calm, think long-term and patiently wait until the market comes back to its senses. It took the market 18 months to completely recover from the crash of 1987. Remember that a bear market is a natural part of a business cycle, not a permanent condition, so the best advice from the pros is *don't panic.* Besides, says Dr. Schott, individuals who are in bonds or cash during these periods will have excellent buying opportunities.

◆ Profile ◆

Robert Rodriguez

Chief Investment Officer,
First Pacific Advisors (FPA)
Portfolio Manager of FPA Capital fund

Beginning with his first coin collection at the age of 6, Robert Rodriguez developed a lifelong interest in money. He recalls watching a movie about the stock market that showed a lot of people running around on the floor of the exchange yelling and shouting. To Rodriguez, a teenager at the time, it looked like the biggest casino in the world. He instinctively knew he had to work in the stock market if he wanted to make money. It's a decision he never regretted.

When Rodriguez studied investment theory in college, he admits that much of it didn't make sense. Nevertheless, he invested what little money he had in the stock market, relying on his theories to make him successful. However, he lost it all. "It was one of the most humiliating experiences of my life," he remembers. "My total assets were a 1960 Delta 88 Oldsmobile with 145,000 miles and $1.32 in my checking account."

Not long afterward, Rodriguez's life changed after he picked up a copy of *The Intelligent Investor* by Benjamin Graham. Graham's value investment strategies made perfect sense to Rodriguez. "I would say it was like finding religion. It was like being in the desert all these years and then coming out." It was then that he realized the importance of having an investment philosophy.

You must take the time to develop your own investment philosophy, Rodriguez says. "Developing a philosophy has to entail pain and suffering. People have to know what it is like to lose money and until you lose money, you really don't have a concept of what risk is." Rodriguez learned a lot about risk from his early investing experiences. In fact, when his associates bring him an investment idea, he says, "Don't tell me how much we're going to make. Tell me how much we could lose. Focus on the downside, because the upside will take care of itself." Rodriguez says you should never put yourself in a situation where you could lose all your money. "If you are out of the game," he warns, "you cannot make a comeback."

Once investors find an investment philosophy, they must have the discipline to stick with it, Rodriguez says. "If you have no philosophy, then you have no discipline. Some of the biggest investment failures I've seen over my career tend to be by people who weren't anchored to any investment philosophy. Maybe in one cycle they were a growth manager and in another cycle they tried to be a value manager. As a result, they were buffeted back and forth by these changes. I think you have to develop a very strong philosophical base and that is very hard to come up with. Generally, you don't pick it up very quickly. It evolves over a period of time."

Like many portfolio managers, Rodriguez believes investors need to be independent thinkers. "If you are going to run with the crowd, it is very comfortable but not terribly profitable. You have to be willing to stand alone," says Rodriguez. He claims that his greatest investment successes have been when he had no support from Wall Street.

For example, his contrarian beliefs were put to the test when he bought Nike several years ago. "During a six-week period, every major financial periodical wrote a negative article on the stock. At the time, Nike was trading at $1 based on today's price levels. It was very, very lonely out there," he recalls. He wondered what everyone else knew that he didn't know. It forced Rodriguez to think long and hard about his philosophy. "You've got to have a lot of patience to allow an investment time to work," he admits. Although it took a long time, Nike turned out to be one of his best investments. It went from $1 to almost $45 a share during the time he owned it.

Rodriguez is extremely picky about the stocks he buys, adding no more than five companies to his portfolio each year. "We look at a lot of good companies but buy very few," he says. He likes companies that are hated or ignored by Wall Street but are market leaders in their respective industries. "The greatest investments I've had over my career have been typically market leadership companies in industries that have been out of favor on relatively strong balance sheets and cash flows," says Rodriguez. "I rarely buy anything that has a P/E ratio greater than 15 times normalized earnings. I looked back at the stock market over the last 100 years and the average P/E ratio was between 14 and 15 times earnings. I've noticed that when it's above that, more negative things can happen to you, and when it's below that, more positive things can happen to you."

When you buy stocks that have high P/Es, he explains, you are betting on a number of positive outcomes. "In my experience, very few people have been able to forecast the future with any degree of accuracy or consistency."

He rarely invests in companies with new managers. "I like to see them in place for a couple of years. I like to have a period of time where I can look at what the new management is doing and see what their accumulative decision-making has been." Even though Rodriguez pays close attention to management, he has occasionally been fooled in the past. A case in point: He once bought stock in a bank that got caught up in the savings and loan scandal of the 1980s. He spent a lot of time interviewing the managers but didn't ask the one question he should have asked: Where are you investing your assets? As it turned out, the managers were investing in speculative real estate ventures that eventually collapsed. The stock went from $10 a share to 37 cents. "I thought I had my downside risk protected," says Rodriguez. "But management can still go off and do something stupid. Unless something is material, they don't have to disclose it."

Once a stock is added to his portfolio, Rodriguez likes to hold it a minimum of three to five years. "In the short run, you can either have good luck or bad luck. As you get over longer time frames, three years, five years, 10 years, the likelihood that it is bad luck is almost nil." He compares it to a long-distance running race. The idea is to stay as close as possible to the lead group, he suggests. "As long as you can stay with the lead group over a period of time, pretty soon you are going to be the lead group. It is a very long and tedious process and along the way there are many opportunities for you to make bonehead decisions about the market or individual stocks. It is very difficult to stay at the top."

The most common mistake he sees made by individual investors is a tendency to look for a quick payback. "There is so much focus on immediate gratification," he notes. "I think in terms of people. Our parents, for example, buy a house or apartment building, renovate it, work on it, raise the rent and over a period of 10 years, build value into the property. Pretty soon, they have an attractive return. But it took them 10 years to do it. People go from that style of thinking to: 'I bought the stock today, why isn't it up tomorrow?' "

When asked to reveal the secrets to being a successful investor, Rodriguez named three: First, develop an investment philosophy that makes sense to you and have the discipline to stick to it. Second, have the willingness to stand alone and think independently. And finally, have the patience to allow your investments time to work.

For those people who feel more comfortable in mutual funds, Rodriguez offers the following advice: Know the person who manages your money. "When I ask investors who manages their money, they tell me XYZ Corporation. That's not what I mean," insists

Rodriguez. "I mean, who is this person? What is his or her background and investment style?" No matter how big the operation, he says, there is one person who pulls the trigger and makes the investment decisions. "You need to know that person," suggests Rodriguez. "If this person has an investment philosophy and you can't say what it is, then you don't know what you own."

16. Don't fall in love with your stocks

Even the pros are guilty of this mistake. The company might have a great story, an innovative product, or a sexy idea. Once you buy the stock, you don't want to sell it, even when there is evidence that the company is not doing anything right. In extreme cases, you turn into a company cheerleader, convincing other unsuspecting investors to buy the stock at the worst possible moment.

As I mentioned in the introduction, I fell in love with the stock of a Texas cellular phone wholesale company. Because I had convinced myself that the stock was so great, I was blinded to the facts. I ignored any information that didn't support my partisan view. I refused to heed the warnings of knowledgeable people and newspaper articles that said otherwise. "But it already doubled once," I told myself. I secretly believed it would double again. When you fall in love with a stock, you lose all your objectivity. In the stock market, that will cost you money. I lost my shirt on that Texas cellular phone company.

Dr. Schott recommends that investors stand back and look at the facts. Pick up a copy of *Value Line* or *Standard & Poor's Research Reports* and objectively analyze the company. Try to be objective when listening to other people's opinions about the stock. Sometimes the most helpful advice is the opposite of what you want to hear. Nevertheless, if you want to avoid losing money, you might want to listen to all opinions, even if you don't agree. Finally, don't forget Warren Buffett's wise advice: A stock doesn't know you own it.

17. Don't make investing your whole life

Some people are so obsessed with the stock market they can't help but watch it all day long. They'll call their brokers, keep the television turned to *CNBC* or *CNNfn,* and check stock quotes every few minutes. Some carry beepers to keep up with breaking market news or dramatic price changes. A few try doing this while holding full-time jobs.

The danger of "marketitis," as one writer dubbed it, is that you feel compelled to do something with all the market information. It is so tempting to buy or sell when you are receiving a daily barrage of quotes and news. Unless you are extremely self-disciplined, your strategy could change from long-term buy and hold to short-term day trader. In this case, what you know *can* hurt you.

I know what it's like to be addicted to the stock market. Not long ago, while I was in Paris on vacation having a leisurely dinner with friends, all I could think about was the market. The six-hour time difference between countries was very distracting. Every half-hour, I excused myself to make a toll-free phone call to my discount broker. Instead of shopping, I searched the stores looking for a computer so I could log on to the Internet. The only time I could relax was when the market closed at 10 p.m. Paris time. When I finally returned home from my so-called vacation, I realized there was more to life than the stock market.

When it gets to the point where the market becomes your whole life, the experts recommend you step back and evaluate your priorities. As many workaholics know, you can pay a high price for success. You want to make money but not at the expense of your family, your health, or your future. A number of fund managers, some at the height of their careers, have simply walked away. For the individual investor, it means cutting back.

Sir John Templeton, the legendary fund manager who once ran the Templeton Growth fund, summarizes it best in an interview with *Mutual Funds* magazine. He says that money is as fleeting as human life. "What lasts is the spiritual."

18. Don't waste time thinking "If only..."

"If only..." The two most frustrating words in the English language. If only I hadn't sold Intel at $60 a share. If only I listened to my cousin who told me to buy the Internet stocks. If only I bought IBM when it was $40 a share. Many people seem to enjoy torturing themselves with "what if" scenarios. They obsessively dwell on how much money they could have made if this or that had happened.

Jack Schwager, author of *The New Market Wizards*, says it is not helpful to berate yourself for what you cannot change. He asked professional trader Robert Krausz if he agonized over past mistakes. Krausz said that one of the most damaging things an investor can do is worry about past mistakes. He compared it to a cartwheel going over the same tracks again and again. Krausz warned that you have to be careful of letting these negative messages get into your psyche.

Some people get mad at themselves for not making potentially profitable trades. In his book, *One Up on Wall Street*, Peter Lynch tells about traders who torment themselves everyday thinking about how much money they supposedly lost by not owning the 10 top winning stocks on the New York Stock Exchange. This kind of thinking can lead to total madness, says Lynch. The more winners you realize you missed, the more money you think you've lost. The worst part of this thinking, he adds, is that you try and play catch-up with the stocks you didn't buy. The end result is real losses.

One fund manager told me you shouldn't go through life looking through a rear view mirror. If you miss out on one great stock, there will always be another you can buy. It doesn't help to look back helplessly at all your previous mistakes. The "could-have, would-have, should-have" mode of thinking simply wastes valuable time and energy. It is more productive to learn from the past so you can make changes in the future.

19. Don't take excessive risks

Everyone interprets risk differently. On one extreme, you have people who are so risk-adverse they put everything in a savings account or CD. To these people, risk is a dirty word. They believe the stock market is way too dangerous for average people. Their main concern is to have enough cash to survive an economic collapse or depression. It's the only way they can sleep at night.

On the other extreme, you have people looking for a fast way to get rich. They are not concerned with risk. For these people, the stock market is a huge casino with slightly better odds. They think investing in the market is the same as placing a bet at the racetrack or buying a lottery ticket. For the chance to win big in the market, they will eagerly risk everything they own.

Dr. Schott calls these people market gamblers. They love the excitement of trading. He estimates that 10 percent of all investors fall into this category. They always think the next stock is going to be the winning one. And yet, Dr. Schott says, when you look closely at their investments, you find they have an unconscious need to be punished. They keep investing in the market until they lose. "It supplies them with an unconscious gratification of guilt," Dr. Schott says. Ironically, if you ask a market gambler how they're doing in the market, they often exaggerate their gains.

The media plays into the Las Vegas-like mood. As the opening bell of the New York Stock Exchange counts down, the television anchors talk faster, interrupting with news about individual companies. "This just in. Intel beat estimates by 7 cents a share. Analysts were expecting 72 cents a share but the company beat Wall Street expectations by a wide margin. Intel is already up $3 on the news."

Dr. Schott says that although everyone is born with a gambling instinct, successful investors have learned how to control their unconscious urges by investing more conservatively. They won't go on margin or invest more than they can afford. They minimize risk by diversifying among different securities, by avoiding speculative investments, and by buying only high-quality companies.

If you believe you are taking too many risks in the stock market, there are steps you can take to protect yourself. First, you should have a set of rules that tell you exactly when to buy or sell. Also, aim for a series of small successes rather than one big win. Dr. Schott recommends that you invest in so-called boring securities like insurance companies and banks. He also recommends that you find a trading buddy, someone who can talk you out of risky investments. Finally, if nothing else is working, he recommends you give up trading altogether.

◆ Profile ◆

William Berger

Former President and Portfolio Manager
Berger Funds

In 1994, William Berger retired from the money management business and sold the Berger funds to Kansas City Southern Industries. But that hasn't stopped him from investing. In paintings, that is. Since his retirement, Berger has bought more than 100 pieces of English artwork, dating from the late 14th century to the early 20th century. His collection can frequently be viewed at the Denver Art Museum.

Although Berger's reputation as the patron of the arts in Denver is just beginning to grow, he and his family have been a part of the city's history for more than a century. His family started Denver's first bank in the 1860s. As a young man, Berger worked in the family bank and in 1950 he was asked to manage the common stocks in the trust department. "At the time," Berger teases, "the Dow was under 200 and we all knew it couldn't go over 200, of course." He was an extremely successful investor, outperforming a number of large institutions.

Several years later, in 1959, Berger dreamed up the idea of a tax exchange fund, or mutual fund. It was called the Centennial Fund. To the surprise of many financial professionals, this new fund was wildly popular. Even Benjamin Graham, the father of value investing, was an early shareholder. Ironically, Berger had to leave the bank to start the fund because at the time, banks were not permitted to have any connections with the securities business. "Suddenly, I was competing with the biggest forces in the fund business," remembers Berger. "We got massive competition from Cabot and Fidelity in Boston and many others who picked up on my idea. But we succeeded in a small way, getting about 10 percent of the billion dollars that was being collected."

After the success of the Centennial Fund, Berger decided to start one of the first performance funds. "Detractors called them Go-Go funds," says Berger. It was the first time that investors could compare a manager's performance with the averages of other funds. The concept became extremely popular. "When I first came upon Sir John Templeton in 1964, our fund was number four in the country, his was number two. I gained and still have a great respect for him, although our styles are completely different."

That's why the investment business is so amazing, Berger adds. "There are few fund managers who have gone through both good and bad markets. I can think of a dozen funds that really showed their stuff through different kinds of markets. Every market has its stars, but their reigns are very brief. They are great in one market but you never hear of them again." Among the long-term managers, he claims, performance has been similar, although their investment styles were completely different.

The funds that he is most remembered for, or course, bear his name—the Berger Funds. When he was an active portfolio manager, Berger liked to buy the stocks of the most successful, profitable companies, stocks that would earn the most for shareholders. "I learned from Adrien Massy, one of my mentors," he explains, "that no corporate officer is going to know what they are going to earn the next quarter or the next year." That's why Berger says he looked for well-managed companies with good, demonstrable track records. "I didn't go just by the figures," he adds. "Coca-Cola, for example, showed how to bring a remarkable return on their retained earnings.

With our investments, we always ranked our companies by quality." Berger admits to being a bit conservative when he buys stocks. He says he once wore a button that read: "Don't confuse brains with a bull market."

When it comes to selling stocks, Berger doesn't believe in setting up target prices or sale points. "When something changed in the company that surprised us, we would sell, or if we found a better stock, we would sell something else so we could add it to our portfolio," says Berger. "When good companies come along, like Wal-Mart, for example, you have to own them, especially when they are bringing in high rates of return and putting it back into growth," he explains. "Wal-Mart was a good company. You let their managers do the work so the portfolio manager can sit back and enjoy. It's so simple and easy," he teases.

The biggest battle for investors is controlling their emotions, especially fear and greed, says Berger. "That's what the biggest risk is, how we handle fear and greed. If you don't understand what you're doing, you will build up too much risk in your investments." Berger says that many investors don't pay enough attention to risk. "Risk is like a bicycle," he says. "When you are young, you see someone on a bicycle, you can't believe they can do that. You get on one with training wheels and your parents hold you up and you're convinced it can never be done. And pretty soon, you are whipping around like the kids in New York City who call the pedestrians "pins" to see how many they can knock over. When you get to be my age, you look at the kids on the bicycles and wonder how the heck can they do that. Risk is in the eye of the beholder—it means different things to different people."

If there is a secret to being successful in the stock market, Berger believes a lot of it has to do with humility. "Investing is a very humbling experience," he says. "Those who run into trouble are those who think they are God. They let their egos get in the way. Eventually, they get their hat handed to them." He also says it is essential that investors keep an open mind about their investments. He says one of the biggest problems for individuals is not willing to admit their mistakes. "Many investors," he says, "often find they've been holding on to nothing stocks for years and years just to keep from taking a loss." Instead, he says, you must have the ability to admit your mistake and not make a second mistake to justify the first. Berger also recommends that people not invest in things they don't understand. "If it doesn't make sense, don't invest in it. If you don't understand the Internet, I suggest you not invest in the Internet."

In the near future, Berger sees public stock ownership reaching new levels. "There is nothing that bothers people more than seeing their neighbor making money when they aren't, so more people will be entering the market." He adds, "The market has steadily gone up over history. Individuals in general have been very successful because the economy has gone up and the market has gone up. The market cannot in the long run do any better than the underlying economy and the underlying economy cannot do any better than the social institutions that sustain it and encourage it. We happen to have a remarkable free enterprise system that other countries don't have. We have proven once again that we are able to outsmart, outcompete, outproduce and outperform the rest of the world."

While he concedes that stock valuations are sometimes ridiculously high, Berger says there is nothing to stop prices from getting even more ridiculous. "Charles MacKay, who wrote years ago on the delusions and madness of crowds, tells about the tulip panic in 17th-century Holland and the South Sea panic in 18th-century England. (See Lessons 91 and 94 for more on these panics.) Human nature has not changed much since then," he says. "Bull markets end not because somebody rings a bell, but because the last buyer has bought. There is no one left to buy the next tulip. I've watched this happen a couple of times in my lifetime." What happened in Japan could happen here, he warns. "It's going full circle. The question is, at what point will the last buyer have bought?"

During his years with the family bank, Berger remembers there was a tradition of recommending 50-percent bonds and 50-percent stocks. "I fought that tradition tooth and nail for many years, getting people to go up to 70 and 80 percent in common stocks. For the first time in years, however, Berger believes that it might be the time to think about the steady return of long-term government bonds. "Over the years, they have been a good value."

20. Don't be too conservative

One of the reasons investors are too conservative with their investments is they're afraid to lose money. When asked the secret of his success, Warren Buffett replied, "Rule Number 1: Don't lose money. Rule Number 2: Never forget Rule Number 1." Although no one wants to lose money, the fear of losing money causes some people to avoid the market altogether. However, many pros say that you are taking a bigger risk by staying out of the market than by staying in. Statistics have shown that the so-called safe investments—certificate of deposits, money-market funds, or Treasury securities—have given investors the worst returns over time. According to several studies, stocks have given the best returns over long periods of time. During any 20-year period, the returns of common stocks beat the returns of cash investments, primarily because of inflation, which can eat up as much as 60 percent of an investment.

Bill Miller, portfolio manager of Legg Mason Value Trust, put it this way: "A lot of times people don't realize that something which is conservative and low-risk in the short-term may be high-risk in the long-term. People tend to keep too much cash. In a short period of time, cash gives them confidence. Over a long period of time, cash is going to be a drag over their long-term results. In some cases, it can be quite risky to behave conservatively." He adds, however, that one of the basic rules of investing is that you shouldn't invest in anything you're not comfortable with. "If you're not psychologically comfortable with a course of action, you will not be able to stay the course."

So, risk is really in the eye of the beholder. Amy Domini, president of the Domini Social Equity funds, says the biggest risk for investors is time. She admits she has no idea what will happen to our economic systems over the next three years. "However, you can be pretty sure the economic systems over the next 60 years will grow." Domini says that because some investors are so conservative with their investments early in their lives, they don't have quite as much at the end. Like many pros, she agrees that it is important to be in stocks, especially when you are young.

21. Don't try and outsmart the market

Ralph Wanger, president of Wanger Asset Management, describes a disease he calls *aureodigititis*—the disease of the golden finger. He says it can strike anyone at anytime. You point your finger at a stock listed in the paper, you buy it, and then it goes up 30 percent. You point your finger at another stock and then it goes up 40 percent. Wanger says you begin to believe that whatever you point your magic finger at turns to gold. This is especially common during a bull market.

Although confidence is a key requirement of successful investors, arrogance, bragging, and highly aggressive trading are danger signals. Some of the most dramatic cases of investor self-destruction have occurred with people who are convinced they are brilliant. No one can be right all the time, especially when it involves the stock market. William Miller says, "One of the most common mistakes is that you believe you are not going to make a mistake."

Some pros suggest that it is wise for investors to be cautiously fearful of the markets. Martin Pring writes in *Investment Psychology Explained* that good investors and traders are "always running scared." He says they are constantly looking over their shoulder for anything that could threaten their trading position.

Jim O'Shaughnessy, CEO of O'Shaughnessy Capital Management, explained the futility of trying to outsmart the market by his retelling of a Taoist story: A younger man was walking near a powerful waterfall when he saw an older man being tossed around by the turbulent water. He rushed up to try and save him but the old man had already climbed out of the water and was walking safely along the bank. The younger man was astonished that the older man survived. He asked how he did it. The man replied: "I go down with the water and come up with the water. I follow it and forget myself. The only reason I survive is because I don't struggle against the water's superior power." O'Shaughnessy says the water is the market. If you struggle against it, it will overpower you. If you work with it, you will get a wonderful ride.

22. Don't be greedy

It is difficult but not impossible to control greed, according to Dr. Schott. The first step is to recognize the subtle signs that you are becoming greedy. He wrote about the nine most common warning signs, many of which are included with other lessons in this book. For example, you might discover that you are no longer satisfied with a 12-percent return; instead, you plan on doubling your money in six months or a year. Another sign is that you begin to favor overpriced stocks, ones you may have avoided in the past. Other signs include "diversification resistance," when you put all your money into only one stock.

Wall Street has long recognized that greed can strike any investor at any time. There is a wise and legendary Wall Street saying aimed at investors who aren't satisfied unless they sell their stocks at the absolute highest price: "Don't attempt to squeeze out the last eighth point from a trade." Some investors ignore this sound advice by refusing to sell until a pre-fabricated price target has been reached, even if they are short by an eighth or quarter of a point. Joseph Kennedy, father of President John F. Kennedy and an active trader, said, "Only a fool holds out for top dollar."

A co-worker of mine bought Intel at $70 a share and watched it rise to $99. He promised himself he'd sell it when it reached $100 a share. He watched it flirt with $100 all week but the stock always retreated before hitting the target price. Late in the week, after Intel's earnings were announced, he was shocked when the stock dropped sharply, eventually dropping back to $70. For the chance to squeeze out those last few dollars, he lost thousands in potential profits.

Most pros admit that it is difficult for people to resist greed. Dr. Schott says that you first must recognize that greed is a normal, universal emotion, one of the most basic human drives. However, he says that greed, when controlled, is the most valuable emotion an investor can have. He calls it "controlled greed," greed that can be directed to your advantage. Greed is valuable because it makes us hungry for profit, holds our attention and keeps us in the investing game. The answer, according to Dr. Schott, is to recognize that "greed is absolutely bottomless. Don't struggle to meet its demands; they cannot be met." Recognizing this truth should allow you to avoid the dangerous aspects of greed while taking advantage of the positive.

Other suggestions for controlling greed involve following your rules without exception. For example, once you have made a decision to sell a stock, sell it without hesitation. If a stock nears your price target, either raise the price target based on credible evidence or sell. The pros say it isn't worth the time or energy to try and guess the perfect target price, because it doesn't exist. If you are determined to sell the stock at a specific price, set up a stop or limit order. This frees you from worrying about eighth and quarter points. There's another old saying on Wall Street that's worth repeating: "Bulls make money, bears make money, pigs lose money."

PART 3

DOING YOUR HOMEWORK

23. Read everything you can about the market

Many successful investors have discovered that the most effective way to gain an edge over other investors is to read books. How to find the best stocks, the trading strategies of top investors, and other stock market secrets can be found at the public library or bookstore.

There are also dozens of magazines and newspapers to meet the needs of every type of investor. These periodicals give timely advice, include detailed interviews with top traders, and give you the information you need to find the best stocks. They also present a fascinating peek into how the stock market really works. *Investor's Business Daily* or *The Wall Street Journal* are required reading for financial professionals. *Barron's* is a must-read weekly periodical. *Money, Kiplinger's, Worth, Forbes, Business Week, Individual Investor, Smart Money, Bloomberg Personal Finance,* and

Morningstar's *Stock Investor* are all highly recommended monthly magazines. In time, you'll learn which periodicals are best for you.

Many investors rely on *Value Line*, a stock-research tool, or the *Standard & Poor's Stock Guide*. These publications are a bit expensive for individual investors but can be read for free at any public library. If you want specific guidance, there are hundreds of newsletters that do everything from predicting the direction of the market to advising you on which stocks to buy or sell. You can find the names of the most popular financial newsletters by logging on to the Internet. You can always get a sample copy of any newsletter for free. In addition to looking for newsletters, the Internet contains thousands of free resources for investors.

Of course, you don't have to wait until you have a lot of money or there is a bull market before you read about the stock market. Sometimes the best time to study the market is when no one else is interested. William O'Neil, publisher of *Investor's Business Daily*, read and studied for two years during an extremely slow market period. When the market finally turned around two years later, he was ready to apply what he learned. Keep in mind, however, that the best time to read and study is before you actually commit your money to the market.

24. Do your research before you buy

It is always amazing that people will buy a stock without taking the time to do the most basic research. The experts call it "doing your homework," which means finding out everything you can about a company before you buy its stock.

Most pros agree that people spend more time looking for a car than researching a stock. People will read all the car magazines, interview salespeople, visit showrooms, and look up *The Blue Book* prices. They will spend months comparing car prices and models. Yet these same people might buy a stock for the same amount of money based on questionable tips from unreliable sources.

There are two primary ways the pros conduct research. The first method is called *quantitative*. This involves looking at P/E ratios, earnings estimates, assets and liabilities, and other numerical data. The second research method is called *qualitative*. Using this method, the pros visit the company, meet with managers, observe how the company is being run, and speak with customers. Some pros call it "kicking the tires."

There are many ways for individual investors to do quantitative and qualitative research. For quantitative research, one of the best places to look is the Internet. With more than 8,000 financial sites, you can find out almost as much information as the pros. You will also see breaking news, delayed stock quotes, and proprietary research tools. In addition, many discount and full-service brokerages have company and industry reports, exclusive research, company conference calls, and analyst recommendations. A few of the more popular sites are listed in this book's appendix.

For qualitative research, the first call you should make is to the company's investors relations department for a current copy of the annual report. If you have the time, do what the pros do and visit company headquarters. You might not get to see the CEO, but the investor relations department can arrange tours of the facility. You can learn a lot by just observing. You'll get clues to employee attitudes, the cleanliness of the building, and company location. How does the company spend its money? Is this the kind of company you would want to own or work for?

If you are looking for socially responsible companies, you might look at employment practices, diversity, and product safety issues. Amy Domini, president of the Domini Social Equity funds, put it this way: "When you look at a company this way, when you do this kind of homework, you will learn a great deal about the corporate culture and the value system of top management. You will know your company a great deal better than people who only look at financial information."

There are also two dozen newspapers and magazines, two major cable stations, and hundreds of newsletters devoted to the stock market. *Investor's Business Daily, The Wall Street Journal, Barron's, Value Line Investment Survey,* and *Standard & Poor's Stock Guide* give detailed financial information on each stock. *Investor's Business Daily* provides additional details including stocks that have reached new highs or have attracted institutional interest. In addition, a number of discount brokerage firms provide third-party research reports to their account holders.

Another way to learn everything about a company is to assign yourself a written report. Write about the history of the company, its competitors, and its product. Also, if you belong to an investment club, volunteer to write a report for other members. By the time the report is finished, you will definitely know more about your next stock than your next car.

◆ Profile ◆

William J. O'Neil

Founder, Chairman, and Publisher,
Investor's Business Daily
Author, *How To Make Money in Stocks*

After William O'Neil joined the Air Force, he bought his first stock with $500, all the money he had at the time. Like many people, he tested and experimented with a number of different investment strategies, and at first didn't do particularly well. "It actually took me two-and-a-half years to figure out how to make money in the market," claims O'Neil. During that time, he read and studied everything he could about stocks. O'Neil says, "There was no one to get sound advice from. I had to do a lot of homework and a lot of studying. I had to dig it out through research and trial and error."

O'Neil admits that all his reading was worth it, especially books written by professional traders Gerald Loeb and Jesse Livermore. In fact, he attributes much of his success to the books he read because they helped him to develop the framework for many of his strategies.

"I bought all the market leaders and thought I was doing pretty well. By the end of the year, though, I determined that I'd actually only broken even. It was then that I made a major discovery: I knew how to buy stocks, but I had no idea when to sell them."

To address this problem, O'Neil developed a set of selling rules. His new rules told him to sell in 1962, just as the market fell on its face. O'Neil sold everything, even making money by selling a few stocks short. By the time the market turned around in 1963, he was ready to apply his buy and sell rules. Starting with only $3,000, O'Neil borrowed another $2,000, and pyramided his initial investment into a $200,000 windfall. He used his investment earnings to buy a seat on the New York Stock Exchange.

Most of the rules O'Neil developed are in his book, *How To Make Money in Stocks*. He developed a rule-based investing system called CANSLIM. Each letter stands for one of the common characteristics most winning stocks possessed before they made major price moves. The letter "C," for example, stands for current earnings. O'Neil will buy stocks with large increases in current earnings, usually 25 percent or more. The letter "L" stands for leading stocks, which suggests you look for leading companies in the strongest industries, with a relative price strength of 80 or more, found only in *Investor's Business Daily (IBD)*. "Every day, we show a proprietary relative strength ranking of each stock in *IBD*. I wouldn't buy anything that didn't have a relative strength ranking of 80 or higher," he says.

According to O'Neil, the rules in the CANSLIM system provide investors a formula for picking stocks because of what worked in the past. "These rules are based on historical precedents, not opinion," he explains. "If I say look for a return on equity of 20 percent, it's because I've studied all the successful stocks and found that the really great ones have a return of 20 percent or more. We are not guessing. We are just tracking what has worked best."

Stock charts are another of O'Neil's selection tools. "I would definitely suggest that people learn how to use a chart. You don't buy a stock just because the chart looks good. You buy it because you are buying a really great company with great earnings. You use the chart to confirm that it's the best time to buy. It's just one piece of the puzzle."

Not everyone believes in charts or has the time or skill to interpret them properly, although O'Neil thinks investors should take the time to study the patterns as well as subscribe to a chart service. "I think charts are an essential tool on top of having a set of rules that will let you buy really great companies with great earnings and great sales and profits."

Much of the information needed to make stock selection decisions can be found in *Investor's Business Daily*, says O'Neil. The Internet also allows investors access to more information than at any time in history. "But that is not enough to be successful," warns O'Neil. "An investor has to know which information is relevant. "It takes real knowledge and skill to know what information to use and what information not to use." For example, although any investor could look up the P/E ratio of a stock, O'Neil says it is what you do with the information that is important.

"I never look at P/Es," O'Neil says. "The market is an auction marketplace and stocks sell for what they're worth. You are not going to buy the best stock at the lowest P/E. The professionals in the market know which are the better stocks. They're going to run up the better stocks and these P/Es are not going to be 10 or 15."

When it comes to selling stocks, one of O'Neil's most basic rules is to cut losses quickly. Many people lose money in the market, he believes, because they refuse to cut their losses. O'Neil is willing to take a small loss *now* to prevent a major loss from occurring later. He will sell his stocks at the market price when they drop by 7 or 8 percent. "This is no place for your ego," warns O'Neil. "Even when you're good, you are not going to be right more than seven out of 10 times. What do you do when you're wrong? If you don't do anything, the loss can build and build and get so heavy you can't come back easily. That's why you start by cutting all your losses."

O'Neil does not like stop losses. He prefers to watch both the stock and the market carefully to see what happens. Knowing the overall condition of the market, says O'Neil, is as important as the stocks you pick. "Sometimes you can figure out if the market is not acting right before you get down to 8 percent. My average loss is 5 or 6 percent when I'm wrong."

In addition to limiting his losses, O'Neil is careful about how much he invests to minimize risk. "It's important to watch the quantities you buy," says O'Neil. "If I start to buy a stock, I will only buy half of what would be a normal position. If it goes up 2 or 3 percent, I might add a little bit to it, but not as much as the first time. After the second purchase, if it's up another 3 percent, I will probably add to it again, but less than the last time. Your objective is to make bigger money when you're right and the only way to do that is to make additional purchases."

According to O'Neil, the combination of getting out of a losing stock and adding shares to the winning one is what brings success to investors. "You could be right only half the time and make a bloody fortune," he says. "The big money is made when a stock goes up more than 30 percent and you have to hold it. That is a tricky decision for most people. "Let's say you buy five stocks. You don't know which one is going to be the winner." O'Neil says a stock often evolves into a winner over time.

O'Neil says one reason investors lose money is they buy low-priced stocks. "They listen to tips and rumors and get all excited about a stock rather than buying on facts. What is essential for individual investors, he says, is to have a strong set of rules to help make buy-and-sell decisions. "You can't go by how you feel or what your personal decision is. As Jesse Livermore said a long time ago, 'Personal opinions are frequently wrong; markets never are.' The market doesn't know you and doesn't care what your opinion is. The market is a tough taskmaster and it will make you face the music."

O'Neil says one investment strategy is not necessarily better than another, as long as you have a strategy and are disciplined about following it. He does, however, think individual investors are better off with a growth strategy rather than a value strategy. "Value investing is tougher and more complicated. Most people don't know how to take a balance sheet apart. I've never seen an individual investor do as well with a value method as they would with a growth approach."

O'Neil is very positive about the future. He says, "This country is the most successful in the world. We've got more than 500 new issues every year and some of them are phenomenal companies. If a person sat down and studied, there is no question they would do very well. Pick three or four of the best books written by people who have been successful and start to formulate your own sound principles." Then use the information available to you in sources like *Investor's Business Daily* and other publications, and get started.

◆ ◆ ◆

25. Use the Internet

The Internet is a powerful tool used by many individual investors to gain an edge in the stock market. In the old days, investors had to depend on word of mouth, stockbrokers, or corporate officials to get information about their stocks. Now, investors can use the Internet to conduct research, read analyst reports, check quotes, trade stocks, chat with other investors, and read minute-by-minute news on the market. Nearly every major company and brokerage has a Web site. In addition to providing investors extensive research and information, thanks to the popularity of online trading, the Internet forced many brokerage companies to lower trading fees.

At first, only a few companies had Web sites to help serious investors with investment decisions. Everything changed when David and Tom Gardner, "The Motley Fool," set up a Web site on America Online in the early 1990s to tell the world about the advantages of online trading and the power of the Internet. They told anyone who'd listen that online trading was cheaper, faster, and much more enjoyable than hiring a stockbroker. They set up a chat room devoted to investments and encouraged individuals to trade without listening to the voices on Wall Street. They strongly advocated a buy-and-hold philosophy.

Love them or hate them, after three books, a radio show, and numerous public appearances, The Motley Fool has a huge public following. When they buy and sell stocks, they let the world know before they make the transaction by posting it on their Web site. To the annoyance of many investment pros, they also keep daily track of their stocks' gains and losses. The Motley Fool has done exceedingly well with Lucent, Amazon.com, Iomega, and America Online. When they make mistakes, they analyze in excruciating detail what went wrong and exactly what they learned.

The traditional media didn't know exactly what to make of The Motley Fool. In the early days, the two received a lot of bad press for advocating low-priced stocks like Iomega and America Online. Everything that was wrong about Internet trading was blamed on The Motley Fool. To many on Wall Street, they were about as credible as a couple of monkeys picking stocks by throwing darts at a newspaper. But the "fools" fooled the experts. They were among the first to publicly announce buying America Online at $3 a share. This stock has returned an eye-popping 3,000 percent for The Motley Fool since they first bought it in 1994.

When it comes to investing, one of the more controversial aspects of the Internet are the chat rooms. On one hand, chat rooms are a good place to look if you want to check on breaking news or unsubstantiated rumors. As long as you don't buy any of the junk people recommend or give money to strangers, chat rooms can be informative, entertaining, and a good way to make new friends. The Motley Fool referred to them as a huge investment club. On the other hand, you can waste countless hours of your time chatting with anonymous people who generally have no idea what they are talking about. Some of the worst examples of hype and hysteria can be found in some chat rooms. For instance, a number of nearly worthless stocks are heavily promoted in some chat rooms.

Don Phillips, president and CEO of Morningstar, Inc., notices a difference in tone between stock chat rooms and mutual fund chat rooms: "I have found the mutual fund discussion groups to be very educational in tone and supportive. People are out there trying to help each other. It doesn't mean this doesn't happen in the stock chat rooms, but in equities there is always the sense that someone is a player trying to prop up the stock price. With funds, that simply doesn't happen." Phillips says that, for example, in the Morningstar chat room, participants give a tremendous amount of genuine counsel and advice. He says it is intriguing how the chat rooms and boards take on their own personalities.

Besides the chat rooms, Phillips says the Internet is erasing some of the advantages professionals have over individual investors. "The pros had access to more timely and higher quality information than individuals did," he explains. "That was largely an artificial barrier created by the high prices charged by people selling institutional data. Part of the reasons they could charge those prices was the exclusivity of it. The Internet is tearing down those barriers. It has made it more of a level playing field."

Newspapers and magazines have kept up with the Internet phenomenon by regularly publishing updated lists of the top financial Web sites (some of which are included in this book's appendix on page 247). You can also pay a monthly fee to access sites with proprietary research and analysis. Most of the fee-based sites allow you to use their services at no charge for a trial period.

No one expects the phenomenal growth of the Internet to stop. Instead of ignoring this new technology, it is recommended that you use it to your advantage. Start by buying a personal computer, then open an Internet account with online services such as America Online, Microsoft Network, or Prodigy. You can also sign on with an Internet service provider (ISP) such as Earthlink, MindSpring, or AT&T Worldnet. If you are new to computers, my advice is to start slowly. Eventually, you will find out why the Internet has become so popular with the investing public.

26. Learn everything you can about P/E ratios

Nearly every financial expert has an opinion about the P/E ratio, which indicates the relationship between the *price* of one share of stock and the *earnings* per share of the company. Quite simply, the P/E is calculated by dividing a stock's price by the company's 12-month earnings per share. Every stock has a forward P/E and a trailing P/E. The forward P/E uses next year's projected earnings. The trailing P/E uses earnings from the last 12 months. Whether you use current or anticipated earnings, many pros agree that P/E is an important indicator.

For some investors, it is a quick way to measure a stock's valuation. If you compare the P/E of a stock with the P/E of the entire market, you can get clues about the stock, such as whether it is overvalued, undervalued, or fairly valued. For example, let's say the P/E of the entire market is 20. (You can find this number in *Barron's, Investor's Business Daily* or *The Wall Street Journal.*) Then you look up the P/E of your stock and it's 10. Some people would say your stock is cheap compared to the market. It is selling at a discount and is undervalued. In fact, many investors seek out stocks that have low P/Es because they feel these stocks are less risky.

On the other hand, some pros, especially momentum investors, aren't concerned with excessively high P/E ratios, as long as the P/E is lower than the projected earnings growth. For example, you look up your favorite technology stock and the P/E is 50, which is pretty high compared to other industries. However, if the company is expected to grow by 60 percent a year, a stock with a P/E of 50 could be a bargain.

Paul McManus, senior vice president and portfolio manager of the John Hancock Independence Equity fund, says that high P/E stocks are not necessarily bad. "This means we could like a stock like Microsoft, which sells at what some people think is a lofty P/E." He does point out, however, that higher P/E stocks tend to have more volatility, which translates into more risk. To minimize risk, McManus would look at where Microsoft's P/E has sold in the past and how it compares to other software companies.

Some pros think investors put too much emphasis on the importance of the P/E ratio without really understanding how it should be used. Gary Pilgrim, president of PBHG Fund, Inc., says he hardly thinks about P/E ratios. He says that in high-growth companies, the P/E ratio is useless as a valuation tool. Some companies grow so fast or are expected to grow so fast that the P/E ratio looks excessively high.

In general, growth investors such as Pilgrim put more emphasis on earnings growth than on high P/E ratios. However, there are a lot of pros who avoid stocks with excessively high P/Es. Peter Lynch writes in *One Up On Wall Street* that a stock with a high P/E would need incredible earnings growth to justify the high price of the stock. He uses McDonald's as an example. At the time, the P/E of McDonald's was 50. Lynch says there was no way that McDonald's could live up to those high expectations. As it turned out, Lynch was right. McDonald's dropped from $75 a share to $25, returning the P/E back to 13.

It is obvious that serious investors should have a thorough understanding of P/E ratios. P/E is another piece of information that can help you decide whether to buy or sell a stock. You can find out more than you'll ever want to know about P/Es by visiting the local library. Most magazines and newspapers have regular articles on how to use P/E ratios to select stocks. At a minimum, you should be aware of the P/E ratio and learn how to compare it to the overall market, other stocks within an industry, and to the company's earnings growth.

27. Study stock charts

Stock charts are the tools of the technical analyst, who tries to predict the future direction of a stock by looking for predictable patterns. The technical analyst will look at many indicators besides charts, but will primarily use them to spot market trends, trading and price volume, or the relative strength of a stock. Technical analysts say that consulting stock charts for your investment decisions is similar to a surgeon looking at x-rays before operating on a patient. By studying stock charts, the technical analyst believes you can find clues as to how the market will behave in the future. In other words, when it comes to the stock market, the technical analyst believes that history does repeat itself.

William O'Neil, publisher of *Investor's Business Daily*, believes that investors can use stock charts to help with buy-and-sell decisions. He says many investors, even professionals, have difficulty using charts properly. Charts provide valuable information about individual stocks, he says. You shouldn't buy a stock just because a chart looks good. Instead, says O'Neil, you should consider it as another piece of information that will help you make a final decision.

O'Neil explained how a technical analyst might use charts to look for patterns in individual stocks. "You can determine if a pattern is sound or unsound. You can determine if it is under accumulation (buying) or under distribution (selling). There are such things as weak patterns, which are wide and loose. Another pattern will edge up against the lows and never really get a proper kind of correction. Some patterns have too much of their work done in the lower half, which is a weaker structure. There are patterns that break out where the relative price strength lags substantially and never goes into high ground. Those are risky. There are all sorts of patterns where a stock has a classic perfect pattern and is under accumulation, you see where the volume picks up a great deal more than normal and it rises on the pullback."

Donald Cassidy writes in his book, *It's When You Sell That Counts*, that stock price charts are a road map of price movement history. Cassidy says that even if you have no experience in reading charts, you can see if a stock is in a downtrend or whether the stock has reversed negative momentum. Cassidy suggests that investors take the time to analyze patterns to see how the stock performs.

There is a lot of controversy over stock charts. Some people jokingly refer to them as an advanced form of market voodoo. Burton Malkiel, author of *A Random Walk Down Wall Street*, is extremely skeptical of charting. Malkiel says there is no evidence to prove that charts can predict the future movement of stocks. He says the price has already been reflected in the chart. The market has no memory, says Malkiel and, therefore, stock charts can't possibly help.

Nevertheless, there are many ways an individual can successfully use charts. First, it's an unemotional way of scanning through hundreds of stocks at one time. It is easy to sort stocks according to specific patterns. You will eventually learn to pick out stocks that fit a recognizable pattern. Second, you can use charts to confirm a buy-or-sell decision. For example, if you notice a downtrend pattern on a stock you want to buy, you might want to avoid buying the stock until you see evidence of a reversal.

Almost every quote service, newspaper, and Internet stock site gives investors detailed chart information, including *Investor's Business Daily, The Wall Street Journal, Barron's, Value Line* and *Standard and Poor's Research Reports.* Two popular Internet sites for charting are www.bigcharts.com and www.decisionpoint.com. Although there are a number of books that will teach you how to interpret chart patterns, you may find these books rather technical. To become proficient with charting, it might take you a lot of time, yet it is not as difficult as you might think. In many ways, it will be like learning a new language.

28. Use fundamental analysis

In the previous lesson, you learned how technical analysts use charts to decide whether to buy or sell a stock. They look at a number of factors, including trading volume, historical price patterns, and volatility. Another method of evaluating a stock, used by a majority of professional investors, is fundamental analysis. Many pros tend to use both methods, however, when making investment decisions.

With fundamental analysis, investors use a variety of measurements to find out intrinsic facts about the company. William O'Neil, publisher of *Investor's Business Daily*, put it this way: "Fundamental analysis is the foundation you must have behind every stock you buy. This will determine the quality of the stock. It's how you separate the wheat from the chaff." O'Neil suggests that you use fundamental analysis to get information about the internal strength of the company and technical analysis to find out how the company is actually performing in the marketplace.

Although the pros don't always agree on what fundamental information is most important, here are some of the financial measurements they look for:

◊ Return on equity (ROE).

◊ Earnings per share (EPS).

◊ Price/sales ratio

◊ Price/book ratio.

◊ Net profit margin.

◊ Debt/equity ratio.

◊ Price/earnings ratio (P/E).

◊ Dividend yield.

◊ Cash flow per share.

Although all of the fundamental factors are important, the pros are especially interested in sales and earnings. Whether the company will continue to be profitable is really the bottom line to fundamental analysis. That's why the earnings per share (a company's after-tax profit divided by number of shares outstanding) and return on equity (shareholder's equity divided by net income) are often considered the two most important indicators.

The lesson for individual investors is to use the best tools available to determine whether the price of a stock reflects the value of its underlying business. Using both technical and fundamental measurements will help confirm whether the stock you are interested in buying is a good value. When the pros suggest you do your homework, they are generally talking about technical and fundamental analysis. As you can see, analyzing stocks can be a lot more time-consuming than many people think. However, anyone with a newspaper, calculator, or computer can evaluate stocks using fundamental analysis. It will take some time and practice, but it will help you decide what stocks to buy or sell.

29. Learn how to value a business

According to value investors, you must determine what a company is worth before you invest in it. Only when you know how much a business is worth can you decide whether its stock is selling at a fair price. To learn how to value a business, pick up a copy of *Security Analysis* by Benjamin Graham and David Dodd, the bible for value investors. This book, first published in 1934, is difficult to read and filled with complex mathematical formulas. Graham's second book, *The Intelligent Investor*, is easier to understand and discusses the reasons why value investing is so important. A number of successful investors, including Warren Buffett, saw the light after reading *The Intelligent Investor*. Buffett, however, made a number of successful modifications to Graham's original strategies.

Although the pros say you don't need to be a rocket scientist to understand how to value businesses, this exercise is not for everyone. Buffett has said it's part art and part science. There is no formula, but it does take a unique ability to understand and analyze businesses. Buffett uses the stock's book value, P/E, and dividend yield, among other objective measurements, to calculate a company's fair value.

To value a business correctly, it helps if you can read a balance sheet, determine the company's assets and liabilities, and calculate how much the company would be worth if it was liquidated. Mason Hawkins, co-manager of Longleaf Partners' family of funds, says that only a few people in the world can independently value businesses without being influenced by emotion or price momentum.

Many value investors look for companies whose stocks are selling at 60 percent of their appraisal value, i.e. what they think the companies are worth. The difference between the appraisal price and the price of the stock is what Graham calls the margin of safety. Value investors are always looking for the margin of safety, or stocks that are selling at a discount to their value.

For example, during the second quarter of 1998, America Online was trading at $75 per share. Bill Miller, portfolio manager of Legg Mason Value Trust, told me he thought the fair value of America Online was actually $120. Within months of our conversation, America Online shot past $120 barreling towards $130 a share. Miller and his analysts spent weeks determining what America Online was worth. It involved careful analysis and research. However, because of his calculations, Miller determined that America Online was a bargain at $75 a share—and as it turned out, he was right.

Nevertheless, it is not possible to value all companies. Warren Buffett once asked the audience at a Berkshire Hathaway shareholder meeting if they could tell him the value of the Internet stocks. No one raised a hand. Buffett said that is exactly why he won't invest in the Internet companies—because they are impossible to value. Like Buffett, many value investors avoid companies with little or no current earnings and sky-high P/E ratios.

Individual investors who want to learn how to value businesses should start with the Benjamin Graham books. If you find these books too dry, you might want to pick up a copy of *Value Investing Made Easy* by Janet Lowe. This book does a good job of explaining value investing so the average investor can understand it. You can also get help by using the Internet. For example, *Money* magazine has a calculator on its Web site that will help investors determine the fair value of a stock. If you don't want to do the calculations on your own, you can always subscribe to research services such as *Value Line Investment Survey* or *Standard & Poor's Research Reports*. Keep in mind that these publications are available in the reference department of most public libraries.

◆ Profile ◆

Mason Hawkins

Chairman,
Southeastern Asset Management of Memphis
Co-manager, Longleaf Partners' family of funds

Mason Hawkins distinctly remembers the first time he became interested in the stock market. When he was a senior in high school, his father gave him a copy of *The Intelligent Investor*, written by Benjamin Graham, the father of value investing. Not only did young Hawkins find the book fascinating, it has helped guide him for the past 20-plus years of investing.

The most important idea put forth in Graham's book is that you must determine what a company is worth before you invest in it, a theory that Hawkins adheres to and willingly accepts. "It's not a secret," he says. "To be successful, you need to take the time to value businesses so you can stand against the crowd. First of all, you need to intellectually understand a business. Second, you have to have the tools to value it." Unless you have determined a company's true economic value, Hawkins says it is impossible to know if its common stock is mispriced.

The foundation of Hawkins' investment philosophy revolves around appraising a company's intrinsic value, or what private buyers would pay for the company if they were bidding for it in a free auction. Hawkins' firm and steadfast rule is this: He will not pay more than 60 percent of appraisal and prefers to pay even less. Hawkins describes the difference between the value of a stock and its price as the margin of safety. "When you start off with a 60-percent-of-value relationship," he explains, "you have a significant margin of safety.

Buy a dollar for 50 cents and the dollar can decline quite dramatically in value before it affects what you've invested. That's your reason for having a large margin of safety of value over price when you go in." If you're a long-term investor, he adds, you're not going to lose capital if you build in a margin of safety at the outset."

To determine the value of a company, Hawkins and his associates examine it three different ways. "One way is determining what the value of a business would be if the company were liquidated and the proceeds distributed to the shareholders," says Hawkins. Another way is to determine what the free-cash-flow generation potential of a company is. Because Hawkins likes to keep stocks for at least five years, he believes it's important to accurately estimate how much free cash flow the company can produce in the future. "Free cash flow is the cash that is available from operations after maintenance capital expenditure and working capital needs," he explains.

The third way to value a business, according to Hawkins, is to look at what comparable companies have sold for. To this end, he and his colleagues maintain an extensive database, which contains comparable sales transactions for the industries they follow. In addition, Hawkins and his analysts strongly believe in doing all their own research and analysis. "The seven financial analysts that we have are the foundation of our company," he stresses.

Besides looking for undervalued stocks, Hawkins says it's important to learn as much as possible about the company and its management. "Companies should have good economics," he says, "and should have the potential to earn an above-average return on capital. We're interested in companies run by people we think are competent, not only to maximize cash flow production from the company, but also to make the right choices about how to reinvest the free cash flow that's produced by the business. Management, therefore, needs to have operational skill," Hawkins explains, "as well as capital allocation talent." To assess the management's capabilities, Hawkins and his associates spend tons of time discussing two issues: "1) What is their business plan and how do they expect to execute it, and 2) What criteria do they use to make capital allocation decisions?" Says Hawkins, "We always interview management and discuss these two very important issues before we invest."

To minimize business risk, Hawkins says it's important to make sure the company he buys is a dominant one, has significant market share, and can withstand threats from competitors, what he calls barriers to entry. Companies subject to regulatory risk should be avoided, says Hawkins, because there is a risk that inflation will drive up cost faster than the company can raise prices. "We want companies that have enough pricing power in their product line to be able to price the product at a point where, if the cost structure rises, they can maintain their operating margin." The only way to avoid market risk, he claims, is to buy a business for significantly less than it is worth.

When the value of the business grows, however, and the gap between a company's value and price closes, he thinks about selling. Hawkins admits he always sells his stocks at the appraisal price. "For example, let's say we purchase a company that's worth $40 for $20. The business value rises to $50 in three years and the stock rises to reflect our appraisal at $50. We would sell at $50 because at $50 we no longer have a margin of safety."

If people lose money in the market, Hawkins believes it's because they don't have the tools to value a business. "Most people focus on price and not on the economics of the company or the value of the business," he explains. "The price tells you nothing about the company and the underlying value. Price is only the last opinion of the market, and many times that's off by a wide margin. The free cash flow production of a business determines its intrinsic value. And in the absence of free cash flow, the net asset value determines the intrinsic worth."

According to Hawkins, there are four things that determine an investor's outcome: 1) the price one pays in relationship to value; 2) the growth of the underlying corporate value; 3) the closing of the gap between price and value; and 4) the bonus or penalty one gets from corporate management's capital allocation decision-making.

The price of a stock, Hawkins adds, is meaningless unless you relate it back to its value or earning power. For aspiring value investors who want to learn how to value a business, Hawkins suggests reading Graham's book, *Security Analysis*. "When you learn how to appraise businesses, you'll be able to think independently and act with conviction," he recommends. "And try to properly assess your management partners. You want good partners, you want good businesses, and you don't want to pay too much for the two."

◆ ◆ ◆

30. Watch economic conditions and world events

Although most experts suggest that individual investors not change their investing habits because of world events or economic conditions, it is recommended that investors be knowledgeable about anything that could affect their investments. This includes watching interest rates, inflation, and leading economic indicators.

Wall Street pays particularly close attention to interest rates and inflation. When there is a strong economy, things cost more, causing inflation. Inflation or anything that causes inflation is bad for stocks or bonds. When there is news that points to inflation, the Federal Reserve Board will react by raising interest rates, causing stock and bond prices to fall. That is why so many people listen when the Fed Chairman speaks. A signal by the Fed that interest rates will be raised could send stocks reeling. The opposite is also true. The stock market tends to rise sharply on news that interest rates will be lowered or kept the same. However, experienced pros have learned that you can't always depend on the schizophrenic market to follow the prescribed script.

Unexpected economic or world news can also cause the market to react. Wall Street doesn't like surprises. For example, the market will probably respond sharply to employment reports that contradict the economic forecasts. If the unemployment rate shows an unexpected decrease, many pros start selling, because a stronger economy could lead to inflation, causing the Fed to raise interest rates. To many investors, this is a perfect example of how Wall Street rewards bad news and penalizes for good news.

Sometimes the market acts unexpectedly. For example, when war broke out between the United States and Iraq in January 1991, most people expected the market to plummet. Martin Pring writes in his book, *Investment Psychology Explained*, that people were looking for a 100- to 150-point drop in the market and a chance to buy stocks at bargain prices. To the surprise of many, the market opened the next day in a buying frenzy, driven by European investors who were looking for a safe place to store their money. Analysts came up with all kinds of reasons for the unexpected market surge. Some even said it was Wall Street's way of predicting that the United States would win the war. Nevertheless, it was the beginning of one of the most powerful and lengthy bull markets in history.

Elaine Garzarelli, president of Garzarelli Capital Management, studies economic conditions very closely. She believes that it is essential for individual investors to watch and understand the economy. When interest rates go down, she invests in interest-sensitive groups like banks, insurance companies and brokerages. When interest rates go up slightly, during the early stages of an economic recovery, she invests in cyclicals, for example, housing, auto, and construction. If there were a recession, Garzarelli would move into soaps, foods, electric utilities, and natural gas, the sectors that do best in a down market.

Even though economic information is useful, it is still difficult for the individual investor to profit from it. Usually, by the time you've heard about it, the market has already factored the news into the price of the stock.

Generally, the pros suggest you pay attention to economic conditions that could directly influence your investments, especially to business cycles, which lead us from recession to recovery to economic expansion. Nevertheless, they suggest you not let short-term economic conditions or world events interfere with a well-planned, long-term investment strategy.

31. Attend shareholder meetings

When you buy a company's stock, you become a shareholder. Because you own shares, you have certain rights and privileges, including the right to vote on company proposals. One of the most interesting ways to exercise your right to vote and learn more about the company is to attend the annual shareholders' meeting. It will also give you the chance to meet with other shareholders to discuss concerns, complaints, and the company's plans for the future. You can attend the meetings no matter how many shares of stock you hold.

Charles Carlson, author of *Free Lunch on Wall Street*, writes that although most shareholder meetings are peaceful, a few have become tense affairs between disgruntled shareholders and upper management. Most of the time, however, shareholder meetings include guest speakers, free food, gifts, and a question-and-answer period. Some are quite popular. For example, the three-day Berkshire Hathaway annual meeting attracts thousands of Warren Buffett followers.

In fact, many shareholders attend the meetings just to receive the free gifts. Lots of companies offer attendees a variety of free or discounted products and services. Carlson mentions a few companies that offer freebies. National Penn Bancshares provides a family-style dinner to shareholders. V. F. Corporation, maker of Lee Jeans, and Vanity Fair, the magazine, put on a fashion show. Usually, you have to attend the meeting to receive the gifts. Sometimes, you can get discount coupons by writing to the company directly.

Although it might be difficult for some shareholders to attend the annual meetings, many companies move them around the country to allow more shareholders to participate. To learn the date and location of the next shareholder's meeting, call the company's investor relation department. Carlson suggests you might even be able to write off some of the expenses of attending the meeting from your taxes.

32. Read the annual report

If you are interested in investing in the stock of a particular company, many of the pros recommend that you become as familiar with the company as possible. To do business, any publicly held company must file documents with the Securities and Exchange

Commission (SEC). The SEC was founded in 1933 to provide safeguards to protect investors in the American stock market from deceptive practices like those that caused the crash of 1929. Regulations for publicly held companies are based on the notion of full disclosure—including any negative information—of a company's business and financial status.

Among other forms, public companies are required to file the following reports with the SEC:

◊ 10-K: an extensive annual report, including audited year-end financial statements.

◊ 10-Q: a quarterly version of an annual report.

◊ 8-K: a time-sensitive document reporting significant corporate events.

◊ Proxy statement: a report to shareholders prior to a proxy vote.

According to professional investors, a tremendous amount of information can be gleaned from these filings—information that can help you make more informed investment decisions.

A fast, cost-effective way to find out what a company does and whether you would like to invest in it is to review the annual report (10-K). If you already own a company's stock, you are a shareholder and should receive a copy of the annual report every year. The annual report can be used to find out information about the company, such as:

◊ Is the company making money?

◊ How has it done over the past five years?

◊ What are the annual sales?

◊ Are sales growing and, if so, by how much?

◊ Who's on the board of directors?

You can also review previous years' annual reports to determine how the company performed year to year.

Surprisingly, much of this information is readily accessible, thanks to the SEC's EDGAR (Electronic Data Gathering Analysis and Retrieval) system. The SEC created the EDGAR database in 1984 so that the investing public could efficiently and inexpensively obtain the information it needed. Since May 1996, all U.S. public companies are required to file electronically with the SEC. Once a document is filed, the information is immediately available to anyone who has a computer that can talk to the EDGAR database. Individuals with Internet access can take advantage of EDGAR Online. A variety of free and paid subscriber services are available. There's even a new service called EDGAR Online People, which allows users to search the SEC filings by an executive's name. With EDGAR Online People, you can see an executive's corporate board memberships, their stock ownership, and compensation arrangements. You can access EDGAR Online People by visiting their Web site at people.edgar-online.com/people.

Another source of online financial information for individual investors is Disclosure Global Access, a powerful research tool that can give you access to critical company information. Disclosure can be used to assess corporate finances, monitor corporate activity, and identify investment opportunities. Corporate Financial Online is a system set up to help companies disseminate their annual reports to the media, shareholders, and other interested parties. Although there aren't a large number of companies online at this time, the system does list some well-known names, including IBM, AT&T, Dell, Compaq, Eastman Kodak, Ericsson, Coca-Cola, Boeing, Intel, and Hewlett-Packard, among many others. This Web site is located at www.lib.utulsa.edu/database.dge.htm.

33. Be an expert on a few stocks or industries

The experts say that some people own way too many stocks. Like kids in a candy store, they find nearly all stocks irresistible, especially during a raging bull market. These people always have a reason to add another stock to their portfolio.

However, the pros say it makes more sense to have a more concentrated portfolio of stocks and mutual funds. William O'Neil, publisher of *Investor's Business Daily*, recommends four or five carefully chosen stocks, depending on how much you have to invest. He says that even someone with a million dollars doesn't need more than six or seven well-selected securities. In O'Neil's opinion, if your portfolio is less than $20,000 you should limit it to three stocks. O'Neil writes that the idea is to have one or two big winners rather than a bunch of little winners.

When you own fewer stocks, it is also easier to keep track of your investments. The more securities you have in your portfolio, the more buy-and-sell decisions you have to make. Unless investing is your full-time job, it makes more sense to know everything about a few stocks than very little about a lot of stocks. I followed this advice by learning everything I could about a company called Vitesse Semiconductor. When the market overreacted, causing Vitesse to drop in price, I bought more shares. When it reached my target price, I sold. Because I spent the time to thoroughly research this company, I felt I had a good idea of what the stock should sell for. This allowed me to take advantage of the temporary price dips that often occur with volatile semiconductor companies.

You don't have to concentrate on just one stock to make money in the market. Some of the most successful investors became experts on only one segment of the market. Don Phillips, president and CEO of Morningstar, Inc., explains, "I am convinced that for managers to be great investors they have to develop an expertise the market as a whole doesn't have. John Neff focused on income distribution when most people focused on capital appreciation. And Warren Buffett spent a career determining the subtle differences between what is truly a great business and what a good one is. They had an area that was their turf and they knew it better than the competition. It didn't mean it was the only thing they ever did, but it was some area they had a legitimate chance of knowing something the market as a whole didn't know."

By concentrating on a few stocks or industries, you could have a significant advantage over investors who try to master the entire market. Read and study everything you can about a stock or industry, then wait for the right opportunity to apply what you have learned.

34. Consider an account with a discount broker

In the last couple of years, discount brokers have increased at an astonishing rate, thanks in large part to the popularity of the Internet. Because of the Internet, millions of people have turned to discount brokers such as Charles Schwab & Co., Fidelity Investments, Quick & Reilly, and Jack White & Co. to trade stocks. Discount brokers are ideal for people who don't need the professional advice of a full-service broker and who want to save money on commissions and fees. You can place your trade through the Internet, a touch-tone phone, or by calling a service representative.

Discount brokers keep costs down because they don't employ commissioned stockbrokers. For one-third the price, the discount broker offers many of the same services as a full-service brokerage including proprietary research, analysis, and real-time quotes. Basically, their service representatives are order-takers. They will not give you advice, make stock recommendations, or in any way try to influence your investment decisions.

To save even more money, you could do business with a deep-discount brokerage such as E*Trade, Ameritrade, or Accutrade. Although their prices are the lowest, many deep discounters don't provide detailed research reports, 24-hour assistance, or a full range of investment options. For example, you might not be able to trade options or use more sophisticated trading techniques with a deep discounter. However, this depends on the brokerage.

I prefer using an online account with a discount broker. I especially like having 24-hour control of my account. The combination of low commissions, excellent online research, real-time quotes, and helpful customer service representatives convinced me to use a discount broker several years ago.

But there are a few disadvantages to using a discount broker. First, if there are problems with your broker's computer system, you won't be able to trade until the problem is fixed. If your discount broker has telephone representatives, this is nothing more than a small inconvenience. On occasion, during buying or selling frenzies, you might have trouble reaching your discount broker's service reps because of busy telephone lines. Fortunately, this is quite rare, although it does show what happens when millions of people try to place online trades at the same time. If there were a major correction or crash, even the regular phone lines would jam, blocking you from calling the telephone representatives.

You should spend as much time looking for a discount broker as you would a full-service broker. Most of the 60 or more online brokers are reputable, but you shouldn't open an account until you have thoroughly checked the company. Some run full-page ads suggesting that a press of a button is the only thing keeping you from making money in the market. As you should know from reading this book, investing in the stock market takes a lot more work than that.

To find the best discount brokers, start by looking in financial magazines. At least once a year, the magazines rate all the discount brokers for price, customer service, and ease of use. You can also ask friends who use discount brokers for advice or ask people who belong to an investment club.

It is relatively easy to set up an account with a discount broker. After you fill out the application and send a check, the brokerage will provide you with an online account number and a secret password. After that, you are on your own.

35. Consider an account with a full-service broker

After you open an account with a full-service stock brokerage company, a stockbroker will be assigned to work with you. The stockbroker might have other titles, such as account executive or financial consultant, but the purpose of a retail stockbroker is to advise you on the buying and selling of individual securities.

There are a lot of reasons why you would want to hire a full-service stockbroker. First, you get detailed reports and proprietary in-house research on every listed stock, the kind of information most people can't afford, even with an Internet account. In addition, every major brokerage company has a sophisticated in-house research staff that can provide customers with the latest news and information on individual stocks. Also, a stockbroker recommends stocks to buy or sell and serves as a sounding board for stocks you are considering.

A good stockbroker will patiently guide you through the buying and selling process, offering objective advice and ideas. In addition, the broker will call you with timely recommendations and be available to execute your orders promptly. The best stockbrokers have the same characteristics as the best money managers—they are patient, disciplined, and competitive. You want a stockbroker that finds stocks that fit your investment strategy. For example, if you are only a few years away from retirement, you don't want to be talked into speculative stocks. When you have a good broker, the higher commission charges are meaningless compared to the returns the broker may generate for your account.

If you have a large portfolio—$100,000 or more—the brokerage might assign you an in-house investment advisor. These professionals will look at your entire portfolio and plan investments that meet your financial needs. The higher commission charges pay for their advice. However, some brokerage companies have wrap accounts that include a flat fee of 2 to 3 percent of assets.

The biggest complaint against brokers is the system under which they operate. It doesn't matter if you make money or lose money in the market, the broker is paid a commission for each transaction. The more you trade, the more he or she gets paid. This system puts pressure on brokers to encourage you to buy and sell frequently.

There are other disadvantages to hiring a broker. First, many retail stockbrokers are experts at selling but have little knowledge about financial planning. They can tell you to buy a stock, but have no clue as to whether it's the right stock for your needs. If you're a new customer, you might be assigned a new broker, someone with little experience but hungry to generate a lot of business for the firm. This combination could put your portfolio at risk.

The decision to hire a stockbroker really depends on the size of your portfolio, your personality, and whether you have the time or patience to manage your own account. To keep up with the discount brokers, brokerage companies will likely reduce fees and increase services. In the end, this can only benefit the individual investor.

36. Know who is managing your money

Financial experts suggest that you spend as much time as you need to check the background and references of the people who will be managing your money. You must look beyond an impressive title and find out exactly what kind of company you are dealing with and the name of the person who will be handling your account. It is amazing how many people will hand over money to strangers without asking about their years of experience, commission structures, credentials, or past performance. Remember that it is legal for people without a degree or training to call themselves financial experts. The pros say you should not commit your money until you are absolutely convinced the person is competent and experienced.

You should spend as much time checking out the references of your stockbroker as you would a lawyer or accountant. A good place to start is with professional recommendations from other financial experts. You can also get ideas by reading the local newspaper or financial periodicals. The national magazines regularly rate full-service and discount brokerages for service and price. You can also use the Internet to look for news articles, biographical information and interviews. It shouldn't be too difficult to check out the references and credentials of stockbrokers in well-known, established brokerages. Although the larger brokerages usually have strict procedures to control unethical brokers, you should still do your own research.

Some of the worst abuses in the securities industries occur with retail stockbrokers in small, unknown brokerage companies. A few years ago, a friend of mine unwittingly opened an account with a brokerage with organized crime connections. Every week, the broker called my friend to promote another low-priced speculative stock. The broker had a dozen reasons why the recommended stock of the week did so badly, always promising that the next stock would be better. With every losing trade, the brokerage sent my friend duplicate confirmation slips with numerous changes and adjustments. By the time the SEC caught up with the New York-based brokerage and shut it down, my friend's account was almost wiped out. If he had thoroughly checked references, he would have learned the brokerage had a reputation for ripping off customers. He also would have found out the stockbroker was in business less than six months, only recently receiving his Series 7 license.

You don't have to hire a private detective, but a phone call to the SEC, the NASD (National Association of Securities Dealers), and NASAA (North American Securities Administrators Association) should flush out blatantly unethical stockbrokers. These agencies can verify whether the broker has been cited with any security or criminal violations or if there are impending lawsuits against the brokerage. You can also use the information to verify that the broker is being truthful about his or her record. The NASD also has a Web site that allows consumers to check relevant information.

Just because these governmental agencies have no information about the broker or brokerage doesn't mean your money is in good hands. Current complaints may not be listed and sometimes the information is incomplete. It is your responsibility as a customer to make sure you are dealing with reputable, ethical companies. At the very least, you should avoid doing business with people who solicit your business at parties or on the telephone. With a little research, you will eventually find a reputable stockbroker or discount broker.

37. Save on commissions and fees

Many people don't take into account the high cost of brokerage commissions and fees. Every time you buy or sell a stock, the broker charges you a commission. These commissions can range from as little as a few dollars a trade to hundreds of dollars, depending on the brokerage company. The absolute cheapest commissions are charged by no-frills deep-discount brokers such as E*Trade, Ameritrade, and Accutrade, followed by discount brokers such as Charles

Schwab & Co., Fidelity Investments, Jack White & Co., Quick & Reilly, and Waterhouse Securities. The discount brokers usually have one set price for all customers.

In general, full-service stockbrokers charge the highest commissions and fees, depending on the size of your account. Many investors would be shocked if they added up a year's worth of commissions. Because brokers make money when they buy and sell on your behalf, the more trades you make, the more money they make. You are also paying more for a live broker to make the trade.

It all relates to service. If you are paying hundreds of dollars in commissions and fees to a brokerage company, you should receive better and faster service. This includes access to up-to-date research, the expertise of a full-service stockbroker, and financial planning assistance.

Keep in mind that many full-service brokers have flexible commission structures geared to the size of your account. In other words, customers with larger portfolios will pay less in fees and commissions, including special discounts for certain trades. In addition, customers who trade a lot might qualify for lower commissions and favorable treatment.

You should feel comfortable discussing commissions, fees, and investment costs with your stockbroker or brokerage company. Keep asking questions until you completely understand the fee and commission schedule. You don't want any unpleasant surprises. Also, the broker should tell you in advance if there will be extra fees for special mailings or for registering the stock in your name.

The lesson for the individual investor is to always pay close attention to commissions and fees. If you think you are paying too much for trading, ask for a reduction. Sometimes that is all it takes to get lower commissions. If that doesn't work, you could always ask your broker's boss. Although this is not an ideal solution, it often works. If you are still not satisfied with your commission schedule, call other companies and shop around for the best price. When it comes to brokerage companies, you don't always get what you pay for. In the end, you are the only one who can decide if the price you pay the brokerage is worth the returns you are getting.

◆ Profile ◆

Jean-Marie Eveillard

President and Portfolio Manager, the SoGen funds
President,
Societe Generale Asset Management Corporation

Jean-Marie Eveillard, born and raised in France, first got interested in managing money in his last year of business school, when he had to spend six weeks as an intern writing for a French financial magazine. At the time, he knew little about investing, except for a few courses he'd taken at school. After graduation, Societe Generale Bank offered him a job doing securities analysis, and so began his investment career.

Although he calls himself a value investor, Eveillard recognizes the ambiguity between value and growth investing. "I am aware they are joined at the hip," he states. "As Warren Buffett says, 'I have never heard a value investor say he only wanted to buy a security that stagnated forever. And I have never heard a growth investor say that he only wanted to buy securities that provided absolutely no value.'" Each investor, Eveillard explains, must make adjustments to their strategies. "We try to be flexible," he says.

Eveillard says he doesn't select investments based on fixed criteria like, "I would not buy anything that is more than two-and-a-half times book value or more than 14 times earnings." Instead, Eveillard and his analysts try to find the discrepancy between what the company is worth and the price they have to pay for it.

"Because we are value investors," says Eveillard, "we are extremely reluctant to make rosy forecasts. We are looking at how profitable and stable the business is, if it generates cash, our assessment of the business today, and the price we have to pay for the security. We also take a long-term view. We hold securities an average of five years."

Like most professional money managers, Eveillard does extensive research before buying a stock. However, he prefers to do his own research rather than depend on outside brokerage firms and banks, which are often geared to the institutional investor. Because his firm invests in both U.S. and foreign corporations, Eveillard and his team of analysts pore over dozens of reports sent every day from around the world.

He doesn't usually find it helpful to meet with company managers. "I used to meet often with management and I came to the conclusion that management either tells you nothing, misleads you, or tells you things they shouldn't in the first place because it's inside information. In all three cases, I feel we are wasting our time." He does, however, insist on meeting managers of smaller, foreign corporations. "With foreign corporations, we want to make sure we're not missing something major."

Eveillard has learned to be extremely careful when investing outside the United States. One mistake he made was with an English television broadcast station. Although the stock did well for a few years, when the Prime Minister decided not to renew its license, the stock plummeted overnight. "Don't assume that the characteristics of a foreign business are identical to the same businesses in the United States," he warns. "You have to do more extensive research when investing in overseas companies."

According to Eveillard, the easy part of investing is determining whether the price of a security is reasonable. "The difficulty never lies in identifying what a good business is today. The true difficulty is finding what will be a good business five or 10 years down the road. In a competitive world, things change. All you have to do is point to IBM, which over a few decades was an extraordinarily good company, and then struggled quite badly for a couple of years. So things change."

Although Eveillard constantly evaluates the stocks he owns, it is sometimes difficult for him to know when to sell. "If a stock is overvalued or even fair value then maybe we will sell. We have to ask ourselves the question, 'Is this corporation a better business than when we bought it?' If we bought the stock at 30 and we thought a fair price is 50, if it is up to 45, we start selling. If we reassess and we think a fair price is 70, and it is at 45, we will hold onto it." The difficult part, Eveillard says, is determining the fair value of a stock.

Another reason Eveillard might sell is if he misunderstood the company or didn't assess it properly. This can be difficult to determine, Eveillard admits. "There is a difference between what Marty Whitman calls the permanent impairment of value and what he says is an unrealized temporary loss." If Eveillard thinks he owns a stock with a temporary unrealized loss, he will hold on, maybe even buy more. If there is a permanent impairment of value, he will admit the mistake and sell, usually at a loss.

Eveillard believes the two biggest obstacles to success in the market relate to self-perception. "If you think you are a genius, that you have the magic touch, Mr. Market will teach you a lesson fairly soon. No matter how smart you are," he says, "it is difficult to be successful in the market. One reason that people who are extremely smart do not take to the investment business is, psychologically it is very humiliating. Every day Mr. Market hits you over the head. Either you don't own enough of the stock that went up that day or you own too much of the stuff that went down. There is no day that is truly satisfactorily. And if you think you are an idiot because nothing is going well, then you will be paralyzed. What you learn over time is not to take it personally."

According to Eveillard, successful investors exhibit extraordinary judgment and self-confidence, although hard work and luck play a part. "Anybody can have one or two good years," he suggests, "but what matters is how one does over a long period of time. It's not a sprint, it's a long-distance race." He claims the technical side of investing, securities analysis and portfolio management, can be mastered in a few years. But good judgment and luck cannot be taught. As an example, he cited Warren Buffet's superior record. "Buffett is extraordinary," he admits, "because of his character and his ability to act according to his judgment. Sometimes in the investment business, people have bright investment ideas, but they don't have the self-confidence or strength of character to act on them."

Eveillard says the best advice anyone ever gave him was to think independently, or *penser librement* in French. "To think independently shows a willingness to swim upstream, to go against the grain, to be contrarian. The market is not always right."

The biggest mistake that individuals make, according to Eveillard, is buying stocks high and hoping to sell even higher. "Unless the individual has the skill, the interest, the time, and the emotional disposition to do it himself, he is much better off with an advisor." He explains that many individuals lost money in the 1920s because they bought stocks on margin. They lost money in the late 1960s because they bought IPOs and limited partnerships. "They didn't just lose a little bit of their money, which is what happens to professionals," he remembers, "they were wiped out." Because so many individuals are in mutual funds, Eveillard says, during the next bear market, they will lose money, but at least they won't lose all of it.

◆ ◆ ◆

38. Invest in businesses you understand

At a Berkshire Hathaway shareholder meeting a few years ago, Warren Buffett reportedly said he wouldn't invest in a computer networking company. Why? Because he didn't understand networking well enough to make a comfortable investment. He said he might buy a few shares out of curiosity, especially if someone like Bill Gates was involved, but he would never make a substantial investment unless he understood the company and its product.

It is amazing how many people ignore Buffett's advice by getting talked into gold, silver, initial public offerings (IPOs), limited partnerships, and other questionable investments. Some people believe the only way to make money is to invest in complicated deals with hidden clauses and complex language. High-pressure salespeople will call you to tell you about a sure-fire way to triple your money. Sometimes too-good-to-be-true advertisements appear in the newspaper or arrive in the mail. All you have to do is write a check and sign a 15-page contract with 14 pages of small type. Not surprisingly, this is usually a recipe for financial disaster.

You don't need a Ph.D. in business to make money in the stock market. Sometimes the most lucrative investments are the simplest. For many people, it makes more sense to stick with understandable investments like stocks, mutual funds, real estate, or fixed-income products. There is nothing wrong with admitting that you don't understand every product or every business on Wall Street. In fact, one of the reasons for Buffett's success is that he concentrates on the segments of the market he knows best.

As you become more knowledgeable about investing, you can always diversify into other investments. At first, it is wise to invest slowly. If an investment doesn't make sense, or if you have doubts about what you're getting into, you shouldn't do it.

39. Don't believe everything you read

It has been said that company news involves 90-percent public relations and 10-percent substance. And yet every day people make trading decisions based on what they read in the financial press. There is nothing wrong with reading everything you can about the stock market. After all, it is one of the best ways to become a successful investor. The trick is recognizing the difference between important financial information and marketing hype.

There are many examples of media misinformation. At the height of a bull market or during a short-term correction, articles will appear with titles such as *Sell Stocks Immediately* or *Buy These 10 Stocks Today*. Louis Navellier, CEO of Navellier & Associates, reminds us that publishers sell a ton of newsletters hyping greed or fear. He says that fear sells especially well. Unfortunately, those who follow the advice of the doomsayers sometimes miss out on great buying opportunities.

One well-known example was Joseph Granville, a popular forecaster and newsletter-writer of the 1970s and 80s. According to Burton Malkiel in *A Random Walk Down Wall Street*, Granville notified his 3,000 subscribers on January 6, 1981, to sell everything they could. The next morning, brokerage houses were overwhelmed with sell orders, causing the Dow to plunge, ending the day with more than $40 billion in paper losses. During this period, Malkiel says that Granville was as popular as a rock star. When

Granville talked, investors listened. He continued to warn investors of impending doom. Unfortunately for Granville's reputation, the Dow responded to his predictions by reaching spectacular new highs throughout the 1980s and well into the 1990s.

Some of the worst examples of media misinformation involve books and magazines that tell you which stocks or mutual funds to buy. If all you had to do was pick up a book or magazine to find out what stocks to buy, investing in the stock market would be incredibly easy. Sometimes, by the time these books appear in print, the recommended stocks of the year are old news. Usually, the market has already discounted the information. In other words, when you finally read about it in the newspaper or a book, it is too late to profit from the news.

Many pros, however, ignore the day-to-day news of the market or economy and focus on individual companies. "I pay no attention to the news," one fund manager told me. He ignores the economy, the Federal Reserve, Washington politics, and world events. Although his position is a bit extreme and is not advocated by most experts, he is able to concentrate on his stocks without distractions from the outside world.

Some top fund managers have said that the best thing they can do for their clients is to go on vacation. Don Phillips, president and CEO of Morningstar, Inc., explains: "What this means is that if they stay in their offices all day long and stare at computer screens, they will see tiny bits of information and try to extrapolate big trends out of it. In some cases, this causes you to miss the forest for the trees."

Although Phillips says it is wonderful that individuals have access to so much investing information, there is a downside. "You now have the professional's dilemma of figuring out what to do with all this information. You have to make sure you are focusing on the big picture where you can add value rather than drowning in all this minutia. That's how the game has changed. When we first started this company, the challenge facing investors was how do I get a hold of good, reliable information in order to make a decision. Today, if anything, it's how do I make sense of this overload of information."

There is no doubt that information is one of the key ingredients of successful investing, especially for professional traders. The ones who get the most reliable information fastest gain an edge over other investors. For individual investors, however, the quality of what you read is more important than the quantity.

40. Don't blindly follow the advice of experts

With so much conflicting advice and a constantly changing market, it is sometimes difficult for individual investors to know exactly who to believe. In the past few years, stock experts have regularly shown up on television, radio, the Internet, and in newsletters. The media continually searches for gurus to put a human angle on a story or to make a dramatic prediction. There is no shortage of experts who will declare the market is going to break all records or drop by thousands of points. Sometimes their predictions come back to haunt them. Every month, *Smart Money* has an amusing column listing expert predictions that turned out to be wrong.

Many pros wisely avoid making predictions in public. Newspaper and television reporters constantly ask them the following two questions: "Where is the market headed?" and "What stocks do you recommend?" If the pros are correct, their status as a market guru continues for another quarter. If wrong, their answers could show up in a future magazine column. Most pros prefer not to answer the first question and reluctantly answer the second.

According to a number of pros, you must be especially careful about believing the predictions of retail stockbrokers. Some stockbrokers are more comfortable selling their services than learning how to make money in the market. These brokers spend their time finding new customers or convincing current customers to keep buying or selling so they can increase their own commissions. The pros say to be cautious about what stockbrokers tell you, especially brokers who specialize in hot-tip or speculative stocks.

Nevertheless, many individuals have done exceptionally well by following the advice of successful experts, many of whom are profiled in this book. However, the stock experts I spoke with stress the importance of thinking independently, doing your own research, and selecting your own investments. They agree that you should be careful about blindly following the advice of any professional. The bottom line: If you're going to listen to the experts, the trick is to pick the right ones. You can start by reading the profiles and comments of the three-dozen experts featured in this book. Search for additional information by logging onto the Internet or reading books about the most successful investors.

Finally, if you're still not sure who to believe, you can always follow the tongue-in-cheek advice of economist Peter Bernstein, which some have claimed is the true secret of investing. His advice: "Keep your ears shut."

41. Be aware of overly optimistic corporate officials

It's quite clear that professional money managers have contradictory opinions about corporate officials. On one hand, they need to establish a close relationship with the top people so they can find out how the company is being run. On the other hand, overly optimistic corporate officials have been known to exaggerate the truth.

Richard Johnson, portfolio manager of the Columbia Small Cap Fund, says this about management: "Managers hope more than investors. They always look on the bright side. They are smart and entrepreneurial. One of the big dangers is that you want to believe them but you have to keep this cynical, questioning, jaundiced eye open. They are not going to tell you things have gone to hell until they have already gone to hell." Many money managers agree. Martin Whitman, chief operating officer of Third Avenue Funds, says he learned that he should never play tennis with the CEO. And Gary Pilgrim, president of PBHG Fund, Inc., prefers to look at financial statements rather than speak to managers.

Although it is unlikely that you will personally meet with the CEOs or upper management of major companies, you can still see them on television, at shareholder meetings, or read about them in the newspaper. The pros say you should try to be objective and rational about how they are running the company.

You can learn a lot about upper management by watching television. On CNBC *Squawk Box*, for example, the financial anchors routinely drill the CEOs on promises made but not kept. The anchors know how to ask the right questions to get to the truth. By watching them, you will get an idea of the kind of questions you should want answers to before investing in a company.

Keep in mind that corporate officials are not in the business of trying to deceive their shareholders. If anything, most are honest, competent, hardworking people who are extremely proud of what they have done for their company. The biggest problem is that many tend to be overly optimistic. Nevertheless, smart investors are cautious investors, making sure that every claim is backed up with objective research and hard facts.

PART 4

BUILDING A DIVERSIFIED PORTFOLIO

42. Diversify, diversify, diversify

According to many experts, one of the best ways to reduce investment risk is to have a diversified portfolio. When the pros talk about diversification, they mean to split your money among a number of different types of investments or asset classes—for example, stocks, bonds, and cash. Among these investments, you can diversify even further, into large and small or domestic and international companies. In the old days, financial experts used a simple formula to help people with their investments. If you were older, they recommended that you buy bonds. If younger, you should buy stocks. As you can probably guess, it's not that simple anymore.

Many experts now recommend that people design their portfolio based not only on their age but on their risk-tolerance and performance expectations. The portfolio will likely include stocks and bonds as well as mutual funds and cash.

Robert Levitt, an investment advisor and partner at Evensky, Brown, Katz & Levitt, explains how he helps his clients diversify: "You could say our philosophy is based on the concept of diversification. We are open to everything. If you invest it all in one philosophy like value stocks, what happens is you have a volatile portfolio." Levitt explains that by adding value and growth stocks to your portfolio, you reduce volatility. "You can't predict what will be in favor tomorrow," he says. "By diversifying among growth and value or investment processes like quantitative or behavioral, you have a smoother portfolio. This means that you can put more money into stocks, which will give you a higher return with the same level of risk." In many cases, he also recommends a passive investment like an index fund.

Harvey Hirschhorn, portfolio manager of the Stein Roe Balanced fund, agrees: "One of the key things is not to put all your money into one asset or specific type of asset. For example, if you put 100 percent of your money into Asia a couple of years ago you wouldn't be thinking that the 1990s was one of the greatest bull markets of all time."

However, some very successful investors have made bets on a handful of stocks and won. They say it is less risky than you think to have a concentrated portfolio. J. Morton Davis, author of *From Hard Knocks to Hot Stocks*, quotes Mark Twain: "Put all your eggs in one basket, but watch that basket." Davis writes that if you are going to be in the stock market, you must be willing to embrace the risk. He says that if you want to outperform the market averages, you should be very aggressive with 30 percent of your portfolio. Otherwise, he suggests, you might as well buy mutual funds.

Nearly every pro agrees that some degree of diversification is required. If you take the time, you could learn how to design your own diversified portfolio. There are computer software programs that will help. If you need additional assistance, you could also hire an investment advisor or financial planner. No matter what you decide, most pros say you should have a diversified portfolio. Although it won't completely eliminate risk, it is one of the best ways to protect yourself during market corrections or crashes.

The bottom line: diversification. When you diversify, it prevents one poor investment from ruining your entire portfolio. According to many pros, one of the most effective ways to diversify is to invest in mutual funds, especially if you don't have enough money to buy a lot of individual stocks.

43. Pay attention to asset allocation

If you think diversification is a good idea, you'll love asset allocation. After you make the decision to diversify, your next step is to determine what percentage of your portfolio should be allocated to each investment. According to many studies, most of your portfolio's return is determined by how you allocate your assets among different types of investments. These studies show that asset allocation is the most critical factor in determining your portfolio's long-term performance.

The advice on asset allocation has changed over the years. Several years ago, investors were told to put 50 percent in stocks and 50 percent in bonds. Others recommended 60 percent in stocks, 30 percent in bonds, and 10 percent in cash. Then the financial experts said to subtract your age from 100 and invest the percentage into stocks. For example, if you are 35 years old, you subtract 35 from 100 and you end up with 65 percent into stocks and 35 percent into bonds. Although some people still use this simple calculation to determine how to divide their investments, many experts recommend that you not use age in the calculation. The new strategy is to base your asset allocation on two factors: the amount of risk you are willing to take and your time horizon. In addition, many experts advise that a portion of your money be invested in stocks, no matter what your age.

Harvey Hirschhorn believes that individuals don't always give enough thought to asset allocation. "If you get the asset allocation right and you have X percent in stocks and Y percent in fixed income, that can go a long way to provide you the kind of returns you need over the long-term versus a lot of shifting in and out."

Elaine Garzarelli, president of Garzarelli Capital Management, agrees. She says that many individuals make the mistake of being too conservative by allocating too much into cash. She says if you are younger, you might want to have 70 percent or more in stocks; if you're older, you might want to put in less. Garzarelli says no matter what your age, it's a good idea to have bonds in your portfolio. She suggests that individuals seek out an investment advisor to help them with asset allocation. Garzarelli confirms the correct allocation depends on a variety of factors, including your age, risk tolerance, and your time horizon.

No matter what your age, you should spend a lot of time thinking about asset allocation. Most brokerage companies are willing to help. If you feel you need a more thorough analysis, you can always hire an investment advisor or financial planner who can design a portfolio that meets your specific financial needs.

44. Invest in mutual funds

The growth of mutual funds over the last few years has been astonishing. The popularity of 401(k) plans and intense media interest has fueled the growth of the highly regulated mutual fund industry. There are now more than 8,000 funds with more than $4 trillion in assets. Mutual funds are ideal for people who want to participate in the stock market but don't have the time or patience to trade individual stocks.

Basically, when you buy a mutual fund, you are combining your money along with thousands of other investors. All this money is pooled together into a professionally managed fund with specific objectives. Investors own shares, which represent ownership of many individual kinds of securities. There is a fund for every type of investment strategy: There are also sector funds that specialize in one industry, or international funds that invest primarily in overseas companies.

There are two types of mutual funds: load and no-load. A *load* is actually the same as a commission. When you buy a load fund, it means you are charged a commission as well as management fees. Some load funds charge as much as 8.5 percent, although loads average around 4 percent. No-load funds charge only a management fee, usually no more than 1.5 percent of assets. Not surprisingly, many pros recommend no-load funds because their expenses are lower.

Morty Schaja, chief operating officer of Baron Funds, makes a strong case for professionally managed mutual funds. "If you got hurt or sick, you wouldn't go to a library and pick up a book about medicine and treat yourself. But the average investor does that with his or her own finances. We spend all day long researching companies and meeting with management. We are professionals trying to do the best job we can. The average person on the street is at a real disadvantage when he spends five minutes in his spare time doing something we do all day long."

There are other advantages to buying mutual funds besides professional management. You also get instant diversification. Because mutual funds contain hundreds of individual stocks in different industries, a substantial loss in one stock will barely affect the total performance of the fund. Other advantages include telephone switching between funds, 24-hour access to your account, and, depending on the fund, check-writing services.

Some financial experts, however, point out the disadvantages of mutual funds. David and Tom Gardner, co-founders of The Motley Fool and authors of *The Motley Fool Investment Guide,* claim that each year, more than 91 percent of all actively managed mutual funds underperform the market. The Motley Fool believes that individuals should avoid mutual funds because it is difficult to evaluate a fund's holdings or strategy. Index funds are a better choice, they say, but they believe you can do better investing in individual stocks.

Don Phillips, president and CEO of Morningstar, Inc., which is in the business of researching and rating mutual funds, agrees that the last 10 years have not been flattering to many portfolio managers. However, he says part of the reason is that you are not making apples-to-apples comparisons. "The average fund manager running a U.S. equity fund has a lot of options with what he or she can do with the money," he says. "Fund managers can deviate from the S&P in a number of ways. They can hold bonds, they can hold cash, they can hold small cap stocks or international stocks. Whichever way you deviated in the last 10 years, you soured your returns. Because of that, the managers don't compare very favorably over this last 10-year period. That said, there are other 10-year periods where deviating from the largest United States-based companies have given sensational returns." He mentions the late 1970s and early 80s when actively managed funds ran circles around the S&P 500. "As early as 1993, 75 percent of the funds beat the S&P 500," he adds. Phillips says that without the fees, he expects half the fund managers to do better than the S&P 500, and half to do worse.

No matter what the statistics, there is no denying that millions of people are investing in the stock market by way of mutual funds. If you want to invest in mutual funds, begin by thoroughly doing your homework. The experts say you should spend as much time researching a mutual fund as you do a stock. All the major financial magazines, *Money, Kiplinger's, Business Week, Worth, Smart Money, Forbes, Your Money, Bloomberg Personal Finance,* and *Mutual Funds* magazine publish interviews with fund managers and include numerous articles on the top-rated mutual funds. In addition, they routinely rate the mutual fund companies for service, price, and rate of return.

Another excellent source is Morningstar. Using its proprietary star rating service, Morningstar is dedicated to helping individual investors find mutual funds that meet their financial needs. Morningstar's Web site, www.morningstar.net, will give you plenty of additional information.

If you decide to invest in a mutual fund, call the fund's toll-free number. The trained representatives will send you a prospectus, application forms, and an annual report. When you need to buy additional shares, you simply send a check to the mutual fund company. If you want to sell or redeem shares, call the service representative at the toll-free number. A check for the full amount will be sent within five days. You will get a statement detailing your transactions monthly or quarterly.

◆ Profile ◆

Don Phillips

President and CEO,
Morningstar, Inc.

When Don Phillips was in junior high school, his father bought him 100 shares of the Templeton Growth fund to teach him about the importance of investing. "He sat me down and explained what a mutual fund was and how I owned a piece of every company in the fund," recalls Phillips. Little did his father know that this exposure to mutual funds helped determine his son's choice of careers.

After earning a master's degree, Phillips contemplated a career as a college professor, planning to actively invest on the side. However, in 1986, before enrolling in the doctorate program, his passion for investing led him to answer an employment ad for a small firm named Morningstar, Inc. At the time, mutual funds were gaining in popularity, but there was little information about them available to the public. Morningstar's mission, as perceived by founder Joe Mansueto, was to provide unbiased data about mutual funds to individual investors. Phillips liked the idea so much he became Morningstar's first analyst.

During the last 12 years, Morningstar has become one of the leading providers of research and information. "The company has always been about helping investors make better investing decisions," says Phillips. In fact, it has been so effective its "star" rating system has become one of the most recognized measures of mutual fund performance by both individual and institutional investors. Today, Morningstar includes information on individual stocks and variable annuities as well as mutual funds. "We started off largely in print, then to software, and now it's shifted to the Internet."

Phillips has emerged as a very vocal supporter of the rights of investors to receive timely, accurate, and unbiased information. "We try to simplify things," he says. "We try to take the overload of information that is out there and put it in a format where people can use it to make good, solid, informed investment decisions. Our real passion is not to make a call on the market or say which managers are right or wrong, but rather to describe the different mutual funds or equities we are covering as accurately as possible." The ultimate goal, he adds, is to help the right investor get into the right investment for the right reason.

According to Phillips, individual investors can use Morningstar to get accurate, timely information on funds or stocks and find out how they're performing. "You can get apples-to-apples comparisons among all the funds in the universe to see how well they're doing," says Phillips. Nearly all of Morningstar's data comes from the mutual fund company, insurance company, or, in the case of stocks, from company documents such as 10Qs, 10Ks, or annual reports.

Having this research and being able to understand and evaluate your own investments is the first step to becoming a more successful investor, says Phillips. "We try to look at investments from a lot of different angles, not just performance, but also risk and cost, which are important considerations. Morningstar also provides written textual analysis to make it easier for people who understand stories better than numbers to manage their investments."

On a personal level, Phillips believes that mutual funds give you a way to gain access to great portfolio managers. "My initial experience with Templeton led to that belief. Sir John Templeton was unique because he went global before anyone else did," claims Phillips. "Templeton was making comparisons not just within industries but across geographic borders long before the vast majority of fund managers were, and I think that gave him a great strategic position in which to operate. He went international in the 50s. He was trained as a classic value investor, but this gave him a greater pool of companies to choose from than his peers." Phillips says that portfolio managers who do best tend to focus on microeconomic issues rather than where the Dow is headed in six months. "What Peter Lynch did was visit company management and talk with them to find small bits of information, small insights—such as if a new product was coming out or if there was a problem with competitors." What made Lynch a superior investor, Phillips adds, was the ability to see things that other investors didn't see.

When you are shopping for mutual funds, Phillips says a common mistake is to buy last year's leader's list. This practice can provide a false sense of diversification, he warns. "People will buy a number of funds that had good performance during the same time period and assemble their portfolio all at once. The top funds and the bottom funds at any given moment in time are going to have a lot of shared characteristics." He says that people mistakenly assume that because the funds have different names or are managed by different companies they are getting diversification. "The reason many funds appear on the leader's list at the same time is because they were doing the same things that happened to pay off during that time period. People think they are diversified, when in reality they have a portfolio made up of different shadings of the same investment style. Thinking you've got a 10-percent weighting in emerging markets when you've got a 40-percent weighting is a recipe for disaster."

Phillips believes that you can prevent diversification problems by doing more intensive research, an area in which Morningstar can help. In addition to providing research, Morningstar offers a tool on the Internet called Portfolio X-ray, which can help investors understand how their assets are being positioned. "Portfolio X-ray allows you to put in any combination of funds or stocks you might own and it will show you in the aggregate what your portfolio looks like. You can see what you have in stocks versus bonds and calculate your overall asset allocation—a calculation most investors get wrong, especially using mutual funds," adds Phillips.

Doing more research can also help individual investors make more informed stock-buying decisions. He explains, "People don't do their research. They don't look under the hood. They have some superficial understanding of the market, they see what stock prices have done, and they jump in. Doing detailed research on equities is not easy. It is time-consuming. It means poring through accounting statements. But I think it's very important. People don't understand the companies as well as they should, so they tend not to buy or sell at the appropriate time."

Even Phillips has been burned by not doing his homework. Using Peter Lynch's idea of buying what you know, Phillips purchased stock in a theater located in his Chicago neighborhood. He observed how the company fixed up the theaters in an effort to attract more patrons. Even though Phillips diligently studied the company's financial statements, it turned out they were grossly overstating earnings. In the footnotes of the statements, the company made extremely aggressive assumptions about the number of future patrons. "I took their earnings at face value. What I learned is that you really need to dig into the financial statements and do your homework. Management can distort the picture. Not everyone who owns a company embraces the most conservative accounting standards," he warns.

The best advice Phillips says he received came from Julian Lerner, former portfolio manager of AIM Charter fund. In his last year, Lerner said there are two things in the business that continues to astonish him. "First, how much a stock going up can keep going up, and second, how much a stock going down can keep going down. If it's a growth company, there may be lots and lots of growth left. Likewise, if you get a company whose stock is dropping in price, it can really go to zero."

◆ ◆ ◆

45. Invest in index funds

An alternative to investing in actively managed mutual funds is to buy a computer-driven, passively managed index fund. The purpose of buying an index is not to outperform the market but to match it. When you buy an index, you are basically buying all the stocks that make up the S&P 500, the Dow, the Russell 500, or dozens of other stock indexes. Because most people cannot afford to buy all the stocks in a specific index, many pros believe the most efficient way to invest is to buy a low-cost index mutual fund.

Indexing proponents like to remind you that most pros have difficulty beating the S&P 500 each year. If the pros can't beat the market, say indexing proponents, individuals don't have a chance.

They claim that investors would be better off just matching the market with an index fund.

One of the most vocal supporters of index funds is John Bogle, senior chairman of The Vanguard Group. He calls index funds the most underrated investment for individuals who pay taxes. The combination of low management fees, lower capital gains taxes, and broad diversification make index funds a very convenient alternative to an actively managed mutual fund.

Don Phillips points out that it's not just any index that has done so well, but primarily the S&P 500. He says that Morningstar tracked more than 100 different indexes and only three or four had a better return than the S&P 500 over the last 10 years. "What this really says is that large U.S. companies have been the place to be for the last decade and the strategies that most people associate with indexing happen to be a spectacularly good way of accessing these companies."

It is essential that the mutual fund industry, says Phillips, deal with the challenge of indexing strategies. He says the mutual fund industry should make a stronger case as to why investors will be better off in an actively managed mutual fund rather than an index fund. He says the industry has been slow in doing that. "My feeling is that too many funds take credit for giving investors broad-based exposure to the market, saying that 'we give you a diversified portfolio of stocks, and therefore, we should be richly compensated and highly praised.' Yet, if what you want is broad-based exposure to the market, you can get that for pennies from an index fund. If you are going to pay nickels and dimes for active management, they have to present a pretty good case of how they are going to give you something better."

As long as fees are kept low and taxes held to a minimum, many pros agree that index funds have a place in the portfolios of many individual investors. However, as Don Phillips points out, dozens of indexes have trailed the S&P 500 during the last 10 years. Therefore, if you do decide to invest in an index fund, it is essential that you learn what stocks are included before you part with your money.

46. Consider cash

To some investors, cash is a four-letter word. Some like to remind you of an old Wall Street saying, "cash is trash." In fact, some people don't consider cash, money-market funds, CDs, Treasury securities, or a bank savings account, to name a few, as investments at all, but a place to store your money until you figure out where to put it. These people believe that you should be 100-percent invested in stocks or bonds at all times. However, most financial experts encourage investors to keep at least a portion of their portfolio in cash. In fact, many say a cash reserve is the first and most basic goal of financial planning.

The main advantage of cash is its safety. No matter how the stock market is doing on a day-to-day basis, you always know your cash will be there the next day. At a minimum, you should have an emergency fund for protection against job loss, a prolonged sickness, or unanticipated emergencies. Although there is some disagreement on how much cash you need for protection, many experts say you should hold enough cash to cover from three to six months of living expenses.

Cash is considered the safest investment during market corrections or crashes. While other investors are calculating their losses, you get to go shopping for new stocks. Even the pros move to cash sometimes. Robert Rodriguez, chief investment officer of First Pacific Advisors, temporarily moved 30 percent of his funds to short-term securities when the Dow shot past 9,000 during the summer of 1998. As it turned out, Rodriguez transferred out of the stock market at the perfect time, although the pros say it's risky for individual investors to try and time the market.

However, there are definite disadvantages to holding cash. Statistics have shown that the biggest threat to your wealth over time is not the stock market, but inflation. If you hold cash for a long period of time, you may not only miss out on the spectacular returns of the stock market, you may actually lose money to inflation. Some experts suggest that if you're going to park a large amount of cash, make sure it is a brief visit.

Another strategy is to open a cash account with your brokerage. When you sell a stock, the surplus cash is automatically transferred to a money-market account. You can buy stocks or write checks from the account while earning interest on the money. Even if you don't open a cash account with a brokerage, it is extremely easy to open up a money market account with other financial institutions. They also offer the same privileges. Many experts say that when it comes to cash, invest in the highest-yielding money fund you can find in an institution that offers the best services.

47. Contribute to a tax-sheltered retirement plan

If time is your greatest ally, taxes can be one of your greatest enemies. As you well know, taxes can take a huge bite out of your savings. The longer you shelter your assets from taxes and keep them compounding on a tax-free basis, the sooner you can meet your financial goals.

Millions of people have discovered one of the best ways to invest in the stock market and defer taxes is through an employer-sponsored retirement plan like a 401(k) or 403(b) savings plan. These tax-favored plans have become very popular, and most financial experts strongly recommend them.

So does Ted Benna, president of the 401(k) Association and nationally recognized as the father of the 401(k). According to Benna, there are many advantages to participating in a 401(k), including:

◊ You make contributions through convenient payroll deductions. By contributing, you reduce your current income for tax purposes.

◊ Although not legally required, many employers match your contributions. This can translate into free money for you.

◊ Participants can usually choose to invest in a variety of professionally managed mutual funds.

◊ Your contributions and any earnings accumulate on a tax-deferred basis until you withdraw the money or retire.

According to Benna, thanks to the power of compounding and tax-deferred contributions over many years, 401(k)s have converted thousands of people into successful savers. When asked how he came up with the idea for the 401(k), he explains: "The myth is that I was sitting around reading the IRS code and discovered a paragraph no one knew about. It sounds nice but it's not true." What actually happened, says Benna, is that he was designing a retirement plan for a bank when he realized the 401(k) provision permitted him to include matching contributions and payroll deduction. Although this was not the original intent of the 401(k), Benna's interpretation of this section of the code allowed employees to make contributions directly from their paycheck and employers to match those contributions.

Even if you work for yourself or your employer doesn't offer a retirement plan, you have other options. For example, you may be eligible for a traditional IRA or a Roth IRA, or perhaps a plan designed for sole proprietors, like SEPs or Keoghs. With an IRA, you can stash up to $2,000 a year away and allow it to build tax-free. Depending on your circumstances and your current income, traditional IRA contributions may be tax-deductible, too. Although contributions to a Roth IRA are not deductible, you can earn tax-free income after age 59½ if you keep the money a minimum of five years. Remember, too, that if you leave your employer before retiring, you can roll over your retirement savings to an IRA or another qualified plan. Rollovers allow you to continue to defer taxes until you finally withdraw the money.

Of course, your tax-deferred retirement savings will be subject to income tax when you begin receiving withdrawals at retirement. But even taking this into account, your retirement savings could be substantially greater with a tax-deferred plan than through taxable investments. The power of compounding, tax-free contributions over many years has allowed a number of people to retire as millionaires. "Get in early, contribute as much as you can, leave it in there for retirement and pay attention to how you invest," Benna says.

The first step is to get a plan prospectus from the human re-sources or benefits department of your employer. Although it is a bit complicated, the prospectus contains detailed information on all the charges and expenses. Then choose among the investment al-ternatives that best meet your financial needs.

48. Rebalance your portfolio

Rebalancing your portfolio simply means periodically bringing your asset allocation back to its original target mix. The most im-portant reason for rebalancing is to maintain a consistent portfolio allocation. Without rebalancing, your asset allocation will fluctuate along with the market, creating additional risk.

When you initially select a plan for asset allocation, you must decide what level of risk and return you are willing to accept. For example, suppose you originally felt comfortable with a 60/40 stock/bond mix for your asset allocation. Following a strong period of stock performance, you now find that you have 80 percent of your savings in stocks and only 20 percent in bonds. Because your stock holdings are above your original allocation, your risk expo-sure increases. Conversely, if your stocks fall below their target level, your future earnings may be diminished. When you rebalance, you have to decide if you want to return to your original asset allocation plan or change it.

Jim O'Shaughnessy, CEO of O'Shaughnessy Capital Manage-ment, rebalances his fund's portfolio every six or 12 months, de-pending on the strategy of the fund. If it is an aggressive portfolio, he might rebalance in six months—a value portfolio, in one year. Most important to O'Shaughnessy, he rebalances according to the calendar, not to outside events. "We have no idea what is going to happen to the market tomorrow—up, down, or sideways—but we have good information about what is going to happen over the long-term. Therefore, we are going to use that information to rebalance annually."

There's another reason for rebalancing your portfolio: The portfolio you choose at age 35 may no longer be adequate when you reach 55. If your investments are in taxable accounts, of course, taxes should be a consideration. Instead of selling shares of well-performing stocks, which would result in capital gains, some pros suggest you contribute more to lagging investments until you bring the allocation back into balance. Of course, at some time, you might have to sell an investment if it no longer fits your strategy or is performing poorly.

Most financial experts suggest you rebalance your portfolio on an annual basis. The start of the new year is always a good time to take a fresh look at your portfolio, review your portfolio's risk exposure, and determine if your asset allocation needs changing.

49. Don't forget about bonds

During the last few years, bonds have not received as much respect as stocks. Because of an extended equity bull market and mediocre bond returns, a number of investors have reduced or eliminated bonds from their portfolios. The reason for this is simple: The average diversified stock mutual fund has earned approximately 30 percent annually in the last three years. During the same period, government bond funds have earned less than 8 percent.

When you buy a stock, you are buying a part of a business. It represents ownership in a company. However, when you buy a bond, you are lending money to the corporation or government. A bond is considered a debt instrument; in other words, an IOU. A bond is a fixed-return investment, meaning it will pay a fixed-rate of interest for the life of the bond. Conservative investors prefer bonds because they provide a steady and predictable investment return.

There are many types of bonds, including tax-free municipal bonds issued by state or local governments, corporate bonds, and money market instruments. When the bond matures, or comes due, the money the bond investor loaned to the corporation or government must be repaid. The longer the term of the bond, the more volatile it is. In addition, there is always the risk the bond will be downgraded by the credit-rating agencies. Bonds with the lowest ratings are called high-yield, so-called junk bonds. Basically, for the opportunity to receive a higher yield, you take on more risk.

So, do bonds have a place in the portfolio of individual investors? Gary Goodenough, Loomis Sayles Fixed Income portfolio manager, says there are several advantages to having bonds in your portfolio. "They generate substantial steady income. A lot of investors, especially middle-aged and the elderly, rely on this income as do foundations and endowments. They rely on the cash flow to pay benefits to their retirees. So cash flow guarantee is very important. Secondly, people don't realize there are significant diversification benefits to adding bonds to a portfolio of stocks. If you have a portfolio of stocks and high-grade corporate bonds or Treasuries, and you add high-yield to that portfolio mix, you actually reduce the overall risk or volatility of returns of the portfolio. So high-yield bonds should be included in an optimal portfolio mix."

Goodenough says there are other advantages to high-yield bonds. "They would lower the long-term expected portfolio return because stocks over time have returned more than bonds, but they also lower the risk. What you are looking for as an investor is a portfolio of assets that generate high return but generate them as independently of each other as possible," says Goodenough. "If you knew you could make 13 percent a year for the next 10 years, that wouldn't be so bad, would it?"

However, most experts believe it is dangerous for individuals to buy high-yield bonds on their own. If you want to add bonds to your portfolio, it is smarter and safer, they say, to invest in a professionally managed high-yield mutual fund. The reason for this is simple: Most people do not have the time or expertise to check out the credit-worthiness of a company, an important prerequisite when buying bonds.

Nevertheless, bonds are not for everyone. "You shouldn't buy them for your new granddaughter that was just born," Goodenough says. "She should have stocks. There are different points in your life when bonds make sense."

The experts recommend that you take the time to understand how bonds work before you invest in them. It can take quite a bit of knowledge to fully understand and appreciate the bond market. If you are interested in a bond mutual fund, call the 800 number of any mutual fund company and ask for information on fixed-income securities. For additional information, read the financial magazines and newspapers. They regularly run articles on how you can use bonds to meet the needs of your portfolio.

◆ Profile ◆

Elaine Garzarelli

President,
Garzarelli Capital Management

Elaine Garzarelli became famous on Wall Street for accurately predicting the 1987 stock market crash and subsequently moving her clients' money out of stocks into cash. The day the market went down by 22 percent, her fund went up by 6 percent. Ever since, she's been asked repeatedly by the media to predict the future direction of the market.

Like a number of money managers, Garzarelli comes from a financial family. She followed the stock market even as a young girl. Although she majored in chemistry, after graduating, Garzarelli became an assistant to the chief economist at Drexel Harriman Ripley, moving up quickly in the investment ranks.

Before Garzarelli buys a stock, she looks primarily at earnings growth. "I find that if the earnings growth for a company or an industry outperforms the earnings growth of the overall S&P 500, there is a 90-percent chance the stock or the group will outperform the market. The other thing I look at is valuation," she explains. Although Garzarelli feels that valuation is important, she emphasizes that earnings growth is even more important. "You can have a stock that is very cheap," says Garzarelli, "but if it doesn't have earnings growth beating the S&P, it can stay cheap for five years. What gets a stock going is the earnings performance." If you look at earnings growth and valuation at the same time, she says, you can outperform on a quarterly basis.

Garzarelli relies heavily on computer models to determine which sectors of the market are undervalued or which sectors will outperform the market. These models help her determine what makes the stock market go up or down. She not only looks at corporate earnings, but also at economic indicators, interest rates, and inflation. "We use econometric models to project earnings for all industries in the S&P 500, like automobiles, retailers, and food companies. We have found throughout the years that 70 to 75 percent of a stock's performance is due to the performance of the industry."

According to Garzarelli, the economy is critical in determining how an industry will do. "If the economy performs well—for example, if interest rates go down—car sales will be stimulated because of easier loans and less interest expense for the consumer. If the Fed tightens and interest rates rise, people will cut back on auto spending." Garzarelli tries to find those industries and sectors that will benefit from the economic setting.

"The key to everything," she suggests, "is knowing the economic setting. When the economy is growing and interest rates are coming down, you want to be in sensitive groups like banks, insurance companies, brokerage firms, and housing-related stocks that benefit from lower mortgage interest rates. It's all based on inflation, because that's what determines interest rates. If we go into a recession, the market will probably go down 20 or 30 percent. Then you go into the four sectors that do well in a down market, which are only soaps, foods, electric utilities, and natural gas. Everything else pretty much goes down."

Garzarelli says she consistently follows her computer models. "If my model on the overall market is bullish, I stay invested until it becomes overvalued and then we sell it. I don't worry about short-term fluctuations in the market because in any bull market you can have a 4- to 7-percent correction at anytime. You just live through them."

The biggest mistake Garzarelli made was not following her own advice quickly enough. "Shortly after the crash of 1987," she explains, "our indicators turned bullish. The market rallied so much I wanted to buy on weakness. I didn't buy fast enough because I waited for a correction. You can't do that. If you get a bullish reading and the market is up 200 points that day, get in anyway and don't wait for a pullback. When you are running a fund, cash is the worst thing you can have in a rising market. You will just underperform."

The mistake taught her to stick closely to her strategy. "When your indicators go from bearish to bullish, don't try to be cute and wait for a pullback to get in, just get in immediately because the market may not pull back for six months."

To minimize risk, Garzarelli won't put more than 5 percent of any one stock in her portfolio. She stays fully invested if her indicators are bullish. If her indicators are bearish, Garzarelli will raise cash or sell if a sector is overvalued.

One of the secrets to being a successful investor, says Garzarelli, is to not get scared and sell too quickly. "I know a lot of individual investors who get scared if the market drops 200 points in one day. They sell right at the bottom. Don't be scared by short-term market swings or other short-term factors. Keep focused on the underlying fundamentals—the inflation rate and long-term interest rates. If you can forecast these two things and earnings, you've got it made."

Garzarelli says that most of the time, the stock market does badly when we go into a recession. "The Fed raises interest rates so a recession develops. They engineer it because there is high inflation and that is a way to get inflation down. If inflation is okay, the Fed won't have to raise interest rates and cause a recession." A bear market is unlikely, she predicts, unless inflation goes up, but there will be many signs of that before it begins to happen.

Advises Garzarelli: The Fed will let the markets know in advance if interest rates are going to be raised. "Watch the Fed chairman make comments before he raises interest rates. He doesn't want to shock anyone or cause a crash. If they are going to raise interest rates and cause a recession, the market will go down. Then more people will choose bonds over stocks because you can get higher yields."

Garzarelli believes that people generally lose money in the stock market because they don't know what they're buying. "Too many people buy stocks they hear about on television or read about in magazines," she says. "I meet so many people who are going to lose their shirts. It is really sad. They start out making money the first couple of days. They get really hooked on it."

Instead, Garzarelli recommends that individual investors do more research on the stocks they buy. "Know the fundamentals of the economy, the industry, and where we are in the economic cycle." In addition, individual investors should minimize risk by diversifying. "Don't put all your eggs in one basket," she suggests. "Don't put more than 5 to 10 percent of your assets in any one stock. Have real estate, stocks, bonds, and a little bit of cash."

If you're not sure how much of your assets to allocate among these different investment classes, Garzarelli suggests you find a good investment advisor. An advisor, she says, can help you develop an asset allocation plan that meets your personal financial needs.

◆ ◆ ◆

PART 5

MANAGING YOUR MONEY

50. Start early

Most of the books you read about getting rich are true. If you start early and invest often, investing $50 or $100 a month into the stock market, you really can become a millionaire in your lifetime. What is the secret? It's something called compound interest, what Albert Einstein called the eighth wonder of the world.

Here's how compounding works: Let's say you can afford to invest $200 a month in the stock market. For the sake of discussion, we will estimate an average annual return of 11 percent with compounding. So every month, you invest $200. Here's the magical part: After 10 years, your investment will be worth $42,000. After 20 years, it's worth $160,000. After 30 years, it's worth $500,000.

The power of compounding cannot be underestimated. Many financial advisors like to refer to the Rule of 72. The formula behind the Rule of 72 works like this: You take the fixed annual rate of return from your investment and divide that number into 72. The result is the number of years it will take you to double your money. For example, an investment with a 12 percent rate of return would take only six years to double. If you invested $5,000 into the market and the fixed annual return was 12 percent, in six years, you would have $10,000.

David Dreman, chief investment officer of Dreman Value Management, proves the power of compounding with statistics from Jeremy J. Siegel's book, *Stocks for the Long Run.* He shows that stocks outperformed every other type of investment for the last 200 years. According to Siegel, "A dollar invested in stocks over the life of the study [1802 to 1996] became $512,232" after inflation and with reinvested dividends. Before inflation, you would have $6,770,887. If you invested in bonds and Treasury bills, you would have $721 over the same period. After inflation, you would have $262. If you invested in gold, after 195 years, you'd have $1.12.

After two centuries, Dreman says that stocks have returned 7 percent after inflation. The statistics show that you can double your money in stocks every 10 years and 6 months. After 21 years, your real capital increases fourfold. After 42 years, Dreman says it increases 16 times.

Although the statistics show that compounding can bring you untold wealth, when you are dealing with the stock market you must keep in mind that there are no guarantees. Some people mistakenly assume it is all but certain they will make 15 percent or more a year in the stock market. The experts warn that just because the market has posted average returns of 11 percent since 1926 doesn't mean it will continue in the future. No one has a clue what the market will do in a year, 10 years, or 30 years. In fact, even if the entire market goes up by 30 percent one year, it does not mean *your* stocks will. It is just as easy for individuals to lose 15 percent in the market as it is to gain 15 percent. Richard Johnson, portfolio manager of the Columbia Small Cap Fund, put it this way: "Don't count on 20-percent returns. You have to count on 7 or 8 percent. To count on anything more than that is foolish. Anyone who has to crank more than 8 percent into their calculations in order to hit their retirement goals is putting themselves high on the risk curve."

As long as you realize there are no guarantees, the pros say the stock market is the best place to put your money over a long period of time. You can start at any time, and they suggest you do. Because of the magic of compounding, the earlier you start investing, the better. By starting early, nothing should stop you from using the stock market as a valuable vehicle to meet most of your financial goals.

51. Use dollar cost averaging

The pros agree that one of the most effective ways to maximize returns and minimize risk is to use dollar cost averaging—investing equal amounts of money at set intervals. For example, you could invest $50 or $100 a month into the stock market or mutual fund without worrying about the economy, market conditions, or stock prices. Many people utilize dollar cost averaging by automatically investing a set amount from their paychecks into company 401(k) plans, IRAs, and mutual funds.

Studies have shown that dollar cost averaging is extremely effective if used consistently over long periods of time. The combination of a tax-free investment and a lengthy bull market has helped millions of people become wealthy by the time they retire.

Don Phillips, Morningstar president and CEO, strongly believes in dollar cost averaging. "It removes all emotion from the picture," Phillips says. "I do all my investing through an automatic investment program. The 401(k) is the easiest because it comes right out of my paycheck." Phillips says that the biggest advantage of having a set amount taken out of your paycheck is you won't be inclined to double the amount when your stocks are up or reduce the amount when your stocks are down.

Even Burton Malkiel, author of *A Random Walk Down Wall Street*, approves of dollar cost averaging. Although Malkiel has been critical of many of Wall Street's investment strategies, he writes that dollar cost averaging will substantially reduce the risks of investing in the stock market. However, Malkiel points out a drawback to dollar cost averaging: If you buy stocks using dollar cost averaging, you will pay a potentially high brokerage commission on each purchase. On the other hand, writes Malkiel, this problem is eliminated if you invest in no-load mutual funds.

Another way of buying stocks using dollar cost averaging is to participate in a dividend reinvestment program (DRIP). DRIPs allow investors who already own shares of stock in a company, even one share, to make additional purchases without paying commissions. Instead of going through a brokerage, you send your check directly to the company.

Although hundreds of companies have no-fee DRIPs, it's been reported that some companies add extra fees to discourage small investors from participating in the program. Nevertheless, this shouldn't stop you from taking a close look at DRIPs to see if they will fit into your portfolio.

I was discussing the benefits of dollar cost averaging with a frustrated officer of an insurance company at a conference a few years ago. Even though the Dow Jones Industrial Average had just passed 6,000, he was upset because he had transferred all his 401(k) money out of the stock market into cash a few years before, right after the Dow passed 4,000. He couldn't believe the market could go so high. For years, he continued to stay in cash, waiting for the Dow to plunge so he could buy back at bargain prices. As far as I know, he is still waiting. While his co-workers doubled and redoubled their money using dollar cost averaging, he angrily waited with cash on the sidelines as the market passed him by.

There are a couple of things to remember about the stock market: First, the pros say it is extremely difficult to successfully time the market. Even they don't get it right most of the time. That is why dollar cost averaging is so effective. Second, research has convincingly shown that if you invest in the stock market or a successful mutual fund on a consistent basis over a long period of time, it is possible for you to beat the market.

52. Invest only what you can afford to lose

Mark Twain summed it up quite well when he wrote, "There are two times in a man's life when he should not speculate: when he can't afford it, and when he can." Although Twain was probably joking, many pros agree that one of the biggest mistakes people make is to invest in the stock market when they cannot afford it. It is risky to buy stocks with money that might be needed for rent, mortgage, or bills. When you are in the market with money you cannot afford to lose, you are vulnerable to short-term corrections or crashes.

There are people so anxious to invest they'll do anything to get money. Some people even borrow from their 401(k) plan, take cash advances on their credit cards, or take a second mortgage on their house. "That is really scary," says Ted Benna, father of the 401(k).

It's hard to trade successfully when you're afraid you'll lose all your money. Jack Schwager, author of *The New Market Wizards*, writes that if you can't afford to be in the stock market, you will probably make errors. He says you will be so worried about losing money you will miss out on the best trading opportunities. Because you can't afford to lose, you could be overly cautious. He calls it trading with "scared money." Schwager says it could cloud your decisions and virtually guarantee failure.

Trading with money you can't afford to lose, adds Schwager, stacks the emotional deck against you. "Trading is emotional enough, but if you need the money to pay the next mortgage payment or send your kids to college, if that is the money you're risking, then the emotional challenges of fear and greed are magnified. The question you have to ask yourself is this: Would my life materially change or would it make a difference if I lost the money I'm trading with? If it would, the bottom line is if you can't afford to be trading with that amount of money."

If you'll need the money back in a year or less, the pros recommend you invest in a CD, Treasury securities, or a money market account. Will Rogers once joked he was more concerned about the return *of* his money than the return *on* his money. He was a perfect candidate for a money-market account.

If you cannot afford to invest directly in the stock market, you might consider a mutual fund, especially if you have a longer time frame. Although there are no guarantees, you will likely get a better return than a money market account. This depends, however, on the mutual fund you buy. One of my friends wanted to buy a house within a year so he invested his money in a highly aggressive Russian sector fund. Because of the uncertain Russian economy, the fund fell by more than 80 percent a few months after he bought it. My friend might break even or make a profit someday, but he'll definitely have to wait longer than a year.

You shouldn't worry if you can't afford to buy stocks immediately. It is more important, say the experts, that you first have enough cash to cover three to six months of unexpected living expenses or emergencies. Once you have enough cash to take care of emergencies, if stocks fit in with your long-range financial goals, then invest whatever you can afford.

◆ Profile ◆

Robert Sanborn

Portfolio Manager,
Oakmark Fund

Robert Sanborn says he stumbled into the investment business when trying to decide on a career. He was looking into becoming a university professor, but eventually concluded that school politics weren't for him. Money management, he discovered, provided the intellectual challenge and competitiveness that appealed to his personality. He gravitated toward the value-oriented investment philosophy of Warren Buffett, reading every shareholder letter he wrote. "I looked more and more at the theories and concluded that I was a value investor," says Sanborn. "Oakmark has a value-oriented philosophy that matches mine, and that's how I got here."

Sanborn approaches the investment process as if buying a piece of a business for the long-term rather than a piece of paper for the short-term. "We have five guidelines we adhere to," says Sanborn. The first is to buy at a market price that is at a significant discount to underlying value. "Underlying value," explains Sanborn, "is what a buyer with perfect knowledge would pay for the entire business to own it forever. We like to buy at 60 percent of that value."

The second guideline is to invest in owner-oriented management. For Sanborn, this means two things: First, he wants to know exactly what a company does with its free cash flow. And second, he wants to know the company's strategy of redeploying its free cash flow—for example, repurchasing shares and making acquisitions.

He believes that most American managers do a pretty good job of running their companies. "There are very few grievously bad managers," Sanborn suggests. "Only once or twice in the fund's history have I concluded that management was not capable of running the business." Despite that opinion, he spends a lot of time with top management, asking a lot of long-term structural questions. "We try to ask things that get us to the point that allow us to decide whether or not this management team is driven to maximize per-share value in the long-run."

"Our third guideline is concentration," says Sanborn. "We have very concentrated portfolios at Oakmark. Today, the top 20 holdings are 72 percent of assets, the top five holdings, 30 percent. We have no utility, no energy, and no technology holdings, and we don't care about being different from the S&P 500." He suggests that many fund managers are afraid to get too far away from the S&P. According to Sanborn, "There is so much of the S&P in their portfolio that the odds of them outperforming it in the long-run are minimal to zero, especially given the typical fee structure."

Sanborn's fourth guideline is to have a long-term strategy. "Our turnover is low," he says, "about 20 percent per year, one-fifth or one-sixth of the average fund." Sanborn says he isn't interested in how a company will do in the next quarter, but rather, what it will do in the next 10 years.

Lastly, doing his own research is of paramount importance to Sanborn. "Extensive research is the hallmark of our firm," he says. "We do our own research. I believe Oakmark is the largest equity fund in Chicago, and I haven't met with a Wall Street salesman or analyst in at least five years. We don't do any macroeconomic forecasts, and we don't do any market predicting or market timing or any technical analysis whatsoever. We just focus on buying companies that we think are priced attractively." By finding out everything he can about a company, Sanborn believes he minimizes risks for his fund shareholders.

In addition, Sanborn likes to invest in stable, simple businesses that he could personally run. "Warren Buffett likes to invest in businesses where the major strategic decisions are easy. Buffett said that as a member of the board of Coca-Cola he never had to make a tough decision. I feel the same way. I like to invest in businesses that can be run by the average guy, businesses that tend not to change that much. If you invest in a business that is structurally superior," says Sanborn, "it will likely remain so for the long-term and you will do well."

Sanborn is as disciplined about the stocks he sells as the stocks he buys. "We like to buy at 60 percent of value and sell at 90 percent of value. Let's take a simple case of a company that is worth $100. We buy it at $60 and we sell it at $90 if the value hasn't changed. There are many investors who, at $90, will say, 'I think it is going to run up some more.' We don't do that. We adhere to our discipline at all times."

Not following their strategy is a mistake that people frequently make, observes Sanborn. In fact, he believes that having a discipline that makes sense and sticking to it is essential if you want to be a successful investor. "You have to develop a philosophy," explains Sanborn, "and then adhere to it."

Sanborn suggests that investors not pay too much attention to short-term market noise. He mentions a popular financial television program. "They are jubilant on the up days and so sad on the down days. One has to avoid the day-to-day schizophrenia." With the proliferation of financial networks and news, he says, it seems to be getting worse and worse. "It tends to instill a mindless, short-term mentality."

The answer, Sanborn says, is to have a long-term plan. "It's really important to have a game plan because there are going to be times when you're not doing so well. A game plan will help you get through this period. You need to understand why you are investing in certain assets or securities. Don't let short-term movements dominate your strategy."

Finally, he believes that investors should take a close look at the mutual funds they own. According to Sanborn, the average large cap fund is overdiversified, meaning that it has a substantial portion of the S&P 500 imbedded in it. He says that if investors aren't careful, they might inadvertently own too many funds that are similar. If this happens, Sanborn says, you should do one of two things: "First, get rid of all these funds and buy an index fund because by owning all these funds you are effectively owning a high-cost index fund. Number two, if you are comfortable being more focused, own a couple of funds in the asset categories you believe in."

◆ ◆ ◆

53. Think about your time horizon

The number of years until you retire or need to use the money you have saved is called your *investment time horizon*. Before you begin investing, you may want to consider how much time you have until you need the money. Generally speaking, the experts say the more years you have until you need the money, the greater risk you can accept. Because you'll have a longer time to hold your investments, you can weather the ups and downs of the stock market to take advantage of its long-term growth potential.

Studies have shown that the longer an asset is held, the less chance it will experience a loss. According to Ibbotson and Associates, from 1926 to 1993, the S&P 500 shows there were 57 "up" five-year holding periods and only seven "down" periods. As you extend the length of time of your holding from 10 to 15 years, for example, the down periods disappear. However, when you invest for less than five years, the statistics show you have a greater chance to experience a period of negative performance.

While statistics indicate that stocks are volatile in the short-run, the experts agree that the passage of time tends to smooth out the day-to-day fluctuations of stock market prices. For this reason, they agree that stocks should definitely be viewed as long-term investments, and your investment time horizon should influence your investment strategy.

If you need money for a specific purpose, for example, the down payment on a house you want to buy in three to five years, then investing in stocks might not be the best place. Instead, you might consider a CD, a money market account, or a Treasury bill, since this would provide you with the principal when you need it.

When you're investing for retirement, however, your time horizon might be 15 or more years. Anyone with this much time, say the pros, should consider placing at least some money in higher-risk investments to maximize their potential return. And thanks to medical advances and increases in life expectancy, keep in mind that your time horizon might extend 15 to 20 years after retirement as well. In fact, many people underestimate the amount of money they will need to live on. Robert Levitt agrees: "Time horizon is for the rest of your lives, not retirement. You definitely need to focus on the five-years-or-less issue. In other words, if I needed the money five years from now, I should be getting out of equities now, not investing because I have five years." The pros say when you have some idea of your time horizon, it will be easier to decide where to allocate your money.

54. Assess your risk tolerance

As you might guess, risk means different things to different people. In the financial world, risk can be defined as the chance the actual return in an investment will be different from the expected return. In other words, risk is the chance you could lose some or all of your money in an investment. Unfortunately, there is no such thing as a risk-free investment.

In stocks, there is a risk that a company's stock will decline. In bonds, there is the risk that prices will fall due to a company's bad credit rating or higher interest rates. With CDs, money market funds, and U.S. Treasuries, there is a risk that investors will lose money to inflation. Many pros say investors might as well accept the fact that no matter where they put their money, they are taking a risk. Too many investors, say the pros, spend time avoiding the wrong risks. They are so fearful of losing their money in a stock market crash they avoid stocks altogether, limiting themselves to savings accounts and CDs where they think their investments are safe.

With all this conflicting advice, what is an investor to do? On one hand, you might be afraid to lose money to the stock market, and on the other hand, you're concerned you won't have enough for retirement. The answer, say many pros, is to determine how much risk you are willing to take and at what level before it starts making you uncomfortable. This is known as your risk tolerance.

Unfortunately, even the pros agree that determining risk tolerance is difficult. Robert Levitt, investment advisor and partner at Evensky, Brown, Katz & Levitt, explains, "If you don't have experience with a variety of economic environments, you aren't going to have any idea how you are going to react during a severe market correction." Levitt says it is easy to complete a questionnaire indicating that you are willing to lose 20 percent in the market. However, when it actually happens—that you've lost 20 percent and could possibly lose a lot more—you might have a different reaction.

To help give you an idea how you might react, the pros suggest you think about risk when you develop your investment strategy. For example, you might feel better investing only in high-quality, low-P/E stocks paying high dividends rather than high-P/E stocks paying no dividends.

There are various questionnaires and calculators on the Internet that will help determine your personal risk tolerance. These calculators will let you know if you're a conservative or aggressive investor based on how much risk you are willing to take, how much time you have to invest, and other variables. In addition, a number of financial magazines regularly publish risk-tolerance question-naires. If you want professional risk analysis, you can always go to a financial planner or advisor. Remember, in the end, you are the only one who can decide how much risk you're willing to accept before you start losing sleep over your investments.

55. Monitor your investments closely

Although mutual fund and stock brokerage companies send regular statements that show how many trades you've made and your current holdings, it is still a good idea to keep your own records. If you are an active trader who often buys and sells stocks, it is essential that you know how many shares you own, the price you paid, and the stock's current price. Even if you hold a stock for several years, you should still be aware of what and how much you own, and what you originally paid for it.

The goal is to be in control of your own investments. As you probably guessed, the best tool in the world for keeping track of investments is the personal computer. Although you don't want to spend your whole life in front of a computer, you might want to devote a minimum of once a week to looking at your investments.

When you track your own investments, taxes will be easier—especially when you sell. Computer software programs will help you determine the cost basis of your investments, which the IRS needs to determine a loss or profit. Your tax accountant will be pleased that you have already calculated the cost basis of every investment.

I used to work with a man who thought it was a waste of time to keep such close track of his investments. He rarely checked the status of his investments and as long as he had enough money in his checking account, he was happy. One day we were talking about the stock market when he admitted that everything in his 401(k) portfolio was in a money market account rather than in stocks. Several years ago, he had forgotten to transfer his money back into equities after temporarily parking it into cash. This meant he inadvertently missed out one of the greatest bull markets in stock market history because he had not paid attention to his account.

There are dozens of software programs that will help you monitor your investments. If you are serious about money management, you could learn how to create a spreadsheet using Microsoft Excel or Lotus 1-2-3. Spreadsheets not only allow you to control your investments, but to also keep track of income and expenses, inventory, and salaries. If you aren't interested in creating your own spreadsheets, it is even easier to purchase software programs like Quicken or Microsoft Money. These programs have everything you need for keeping close track of your investments. They also include charts and graphs that will give you a full-color view of how much your portfolio is worth, your cost basis and detailed information on asset allocation and diversification.

If you really want to get serious, you could purchase a sophisticated database like Microsoft Access. With a database, you can collect information about a company, such as the name of the CEO, the number of active employees, current earnings, or analyst comments. You can also keep track of stock tips and keep detailed notes on when you should buy or sell. Nearly every professional uses sophisticated databases to keep track of their stocks. The difference is they have the resources to hire dozens of computer programmers to enter, update, and interpret the data.

After you have chosen a program to track your investments, you should take time to evaluate your portfolio on a regular basis. At the very least, you should keep track of your portfolio's quarterly performance. According to numerous studies, many people think their investment returns are doing better than they really are. The only way you can know for sure is if you keep close tabs on your stocks.

56. Consider taxes when buying or selling

Whenever you sell a stock, you either make or lose money. If you sell a stock for more than you paid for it, you trigger a capital gain, which must be reported on your federal income taxes. Conversely, if you sell a stock for less than you paid for it, you can possibly claim a loss on your taxes. Because taxes can take a big chunk out of any earnings, the pros suggest that you consider the impact of taxes on your total investment return before you buy and sell.

There are a number of creative ways to make gains and losses work in your favor. For example, some investors routinely sell their stocks in December if they can take it as a loss on their income taxes. There are two advantages to this strategy: First, it forces investors to sell their losing stocks, one of the most difficult decisions investors have to make. Second, after taking the loss on their income taxes, investors can buy back the same stock in January. In fact, so many people were buying back their losing stocks in January, causing the stock market to rise, the pros dubbed it the January Effect.

However, sometimes people are hesitant to sell simply because they don't want to be hit with taxes. One financial planner told me about a client who refused to take a substantial gain on his stock because he didn't want to pay income taxes. While he hesitated, the stock fell dramatically. The client got exactly what he wished for—no taxes. Unfortunately, he lost a fortune on the investment.

If you want to limit taxes, one way is to purchase municipal bonds instead of stocks. These are exempt from federal and, in some cases, state and local income taxes. Depending on the yield of a tax-exempt security such as a municipal bond, you could receive a comparable yield to other investments whose income is taxable.

Another way to limit taxes is to buy stocks in companies that pay relatively low dividends. These companies reinvest in their own long-term growth rather than pay dividends to shareholders. You won't pay taxes on dividends, and if the stock prices rise significantly, your tax on the return is deferred until after the shares are sold.

If you want to avoid paying capital gains on some successful investments, many financial planning experts advise that you leave these stocks to children or others. When you bequeath stocks, the inheritor receives them at the price in effect at the time of inheritance. Say, for example, in 1990, you paid $20 a share for 100 shares of XYZ Company at a cost of $2,000. In 1998, the stock is valued at $150 a share. Now your investment is worth $15,000. If you were to sell the stock, you would have to pay a capital gains tax on the earnings, or $13,000. If you leave the stock to a child, however, the inheritor receives the stock at $150 a share. If he or she sells the stock at $150 a share after inheriting it, there is no gain, and therefore, no taxes.

◆ Profile ◆

John C. Bogle, Sr.

Senior Chairman and Founder,
The Vanguard Group
Author, *Bogle on Mutual Funds*

John Bogle remembers to the day when he first got interested in the mutual fund business. It was December 1949, and he needed a topic to write about for his senior thesis at Princeton University. He came across an article in *Fortune*, titled *Big Money in Boston*, which explained the mutual fund industry, then centered in Boston. "They described the industry as tiny, but contentious," he recalls. "Because I wanted to write about something no one else had written about before, I chose mutual funds." After writing his thesis, Bogle got hooked on mutual funds, ending up in 1951 at Wellington Management Company. "It all started with an article in a magazine when I was 20 years old," marvels Bogle.

His career has come a long way since then. In fact, Bogle has been called "Saint Jack" by many, primarily because of his willingness to side with shareholders against some overpriced, casino-driven mutual funds. This is an unusual attitude among fund managers.

Even the company, Vanguard, is unusual in the mutual fund business. Unlike other companies that manage mutual funds, Vanguard is owned entirely by the shareholders.

Bogle is reluctant to call himself a success. "I don't know how successful I am, honestly. But to the extent I have been successful, I think the secret has been holding myself to unsparingly high standards of trying to do things that are ethical and proper for shareholders." According to Bogle, this includes making sure investors receive not only the best possible investment returns and the highest level of service available, but also the lowest possible fund charges. He credits Vanguard's popularity to its low fees, which have led to higher fund returns.

Throughout his career, Bogle has promoted mutual fund investing over selecting individual stocks. He says that attempting to build an investment program around a handful of individual securities is, "for all but the exceptional investor, a fool's errand." Instead, Bogle believes individuals will fare better by choosing mutual funds.

Mutual funds give investors many advantages not available by investing in individual stocks, Bogle says. For example, they provide instant diversification. Because your money is pooled with thousands of other investors, you have access to a wider array of securities. "I believe fundamentally in diversification and balance," says Bogle. "Some stocks, some bonds, some cash—even though you could argue successfully that being in bonds during the last decade has sacrificed considerable return. But having bonds is the price you pay for the feeling of security. There is such a thing as holding stocks only in an amount that lets you sleep at night. You have to sell down to the sleeping point." This doesn't mean you should have a huge amount of bonds and cash reserves, just enough to be an "anchor to windward," he says, for a rainy day. "The idea is to set a reasonable target based on your needs, modify it—not when the market changes but only as time goes on, and stay the course. We say 'stay the course' a lot at Vanguard," says Bogle. "I think it may be the best investment advice ever given."

Not staying the course is one of the reasons people lose money in the stock market. According to Bogle, emotions destroy you in the market. "Time is your friend, impulse is your enemy. When are you most optimistic? When the market is at an all-time high. When are you most pessimistic? When the market is at an all-time low. When you are optimistic, you want to buy at the top. When you are pessimistic, right at the bottom. I think it is a good idea to put those emotions aside."

Bogle says that investors also make the mistake of thinking they are smarter than the market or buying the hot stocks that have already run up in price. On the other extreme, Bogle says that some people are too conservative in their investments. "A lot of 401(k) investors have been investing for years and years and are still largely invested in cash and stable value contracts. Not taking enough risk is almost as common as taking too much," he says.

Even Bogle admits he should have put more money in common stocks at the beginning of his career. He explains that stocks carry more risk than other types of investments, but the greatest risk is not keeping up with inflation. "It's easy to say that a Treasury bill has no risk. It has no risk in the short term because you know exactly what you are going to get and for how long you're going to get it. In the long-run, however, it carries a very large inflation risk. What people have to understand is if they don't invest in stocks, there is a risk they will lose real dollars to inflation."

For individual investors who want to minimize some of the risks of investing in the stock market, Bogle recommends investing in index funds. Simply put, an index fund attempts to mirror the performance of a particular index, for example, the S&P 500, which is made up of 500 stocks listed and traded in the U.S. stock market. There are literally hundreds of indexes.

Because index fund managers only try to match the performance of the index, not beat it, does this mean they are settling for mediocre results? Not at all, says Bogle. "Very few investors have been able to beat the market," he says. "There were only nine out of 272 mutual funds with 15-year records that beat the index by more than 1.5 percentage points. Those aren't good odds." With low-cost index funds, Bogle says, you can easily approximate the average return of the index year after year.

It appears that the public has caught on to the fact that during the last 10 years many mutual funds have underperformed the S&P Index. As a result, index funds such as the Vanguard Trust 500 have become quite popular. "If you are not a complete convert, at least choose index funds for the core portion of your portfolio," Bogle suggests. "Make sure you choose low-cost index funds, because in the long-run, the principal challenge of investing is to get the highest possible portion of the return in the market segment in which you are investing. High fund expense ratios, sales charges, and tax ineffi- ciencies prevent most actively managed mutual funds from giving you an adequate share of the market's return. Costs can destroy your investment program."

Bogle offers some last words of advice for people who want to make money in the market: First, put your money to work in an equity-oriented program. Then put every penny you can into tax- deferred vehicles such as a 401(k) or IRA. And finally, stay the course. "Investing is not witchcraft," Bogle suggests. "Successful in- vesting can be done through index funds without any investment management at all. There are so many things that you can do that are worse than having two-thirds of your money in a stock index fund and one-third in a bond index fund; or you can actually have both stocks and bonds in one fund, for example, a single balanced index fund. You can own the entire market and minimize costs. That's the secret to being a successful long-term investor."

◆ ◆ ◆

57. Don't treat account statements like junk mail

In the old days, monthly statements from mutual fund or bro- kerage companies were difficult to read. They contained too much jargon, too many mathematical calculations, and used vocabulary that was beyond the understanding of most investors. As a result, many people didn't read them.

Today, however, many mutual fund companies and brokerages are making an effort to improve their statements. According to contract experts, the monthly statements should include a person- alized rate of return for the period, the investor's cost basis, and the performance of each security. Statements should also include a beginning and ending account balance.

After you receive your statement, you should review it carefully. You need to check for mystery or duplicate trades, churning, or unnecessary commissions or fees. Sometimes there are legitimate mistakes. If you see an error, you should call the company immediately. Most errors can be corrected on the first phone call. Customer service representatives are experts at dealing with customer complaints and problems. The more documentation you have, the easier it is for the representative to help you. If you don't get an answer within two or three days, you should speak with a supervisor. Your last recourse is the Securities and Exchange Commission (SEC) or the National Association of Securities Dealers (NASD), but most reputable brokerages will try and solve the problem before it goes that far.

You should also double-check any orders you place with the broker. If you want to be methodical, you can write down the date of the order, the number of shares, the quoted price and any other pertinent information. Calls are usually recorded, and most brokers will verbally repeat your order over the phone. When you receive a confirmation of your transaction, verify it against your own records.

PART 6

Deciding
What to Buy

58. Buy stocks in companies you know and like

Peter Lynch, author and former portfolio manager, strongly advocates investing in companies you know or care about. He got many of his investment ideas by visiting the local shopping mall. Lynch would walk into a store and see whether it was filled with shoppers, how much merchandise was on display, and whether the store was properly managed. Some of his best ideas came from his children, who bought the products of the most popular companies. In his book, *Beating the Street*, he shares his rule: "If you like the store, chances are you'll love the stock." Lynch says the average person might get one of these ideas two or three times a year.

David and Tom Gardner of The Motley Fool also preach this philosophy. They devote a chapter in their book, *You Have More Than You Think*, to buying stocks based on who you are and what you do. If you are always running to the local grocery store to purchase Campbell's Soup, think about buying the stock. If you and your children love everything about Disney, you might want to buy its stock. The two also suggest that you pick up good stock ideas from your place of work. Think of how many employees of Home Depot or Wal-Mart invest in these very successful companies simply because they work there. Taking this one step further, when you invest in a company you work at, you will also have a better understanding of the industry. This will help you to make comparisons with other companies and to recognize the threat of competitive products. Keep in mind that most pros recommend that you study the industry and the competition whether or not you work at the company.

Although the strategy of getting ideas from the mall or workplace works well for many people, you should be cautious when following this advice too literally. The critics contend there is more to finding good stocks than visiting the local shopping mall. For example, you might like wearing Fila athletic shoes, but it does not mean you should run out and buy stock. Lynch counters that people have taken his advice to the extreme. In an interview published in *Money*, Lynch called this strategy a starting point, but a good starting point. Although Lynch gets stocks ideas from what he observes in the world, it is extremely unlikely he would buy a stock unless he or his analysts have conducted intensive research.

I learned the value of Lynch's advice when I visited friends in Sweden. I was amazed that so many people in Stockholm were carrying cellular phones. My friends told me about Ericsson, a Swedish telecommunications company and cellular phone manufacturer. At the time, few people in America had heard of Ericsson. After I returned home, I thoroughly researched the company, then bought 1,000 shares. It turned out to be one of my most successful stocks, returning more than 200 percent in less than a year.

59. Find out what the pros are buying

If you're like most people, it's hard to decide what stocks to buy. Some people look for ideas among the daily top 10 stock winners published in the newspaper. Others look at every listed stock in the NYSE or NASDAQ. Others follow Peter Lynch's strategy of looking for ideas at work or the shopping mall.

Bill Miller, portfolio manager of Legg Mason Value Trust, suggests that you limit your search to stocks owned by successful investors. He says this strategy could dramatically improve your chances for success. If an expert owns a stock, there is a good chance this person has done the necessary research and believes the stock will perform well. No expert is going to own something he or she thinks will underperform the market.

Ralph Wanger, president of Wanger Asset Management, says there is an entire school of investing that uses the "follow-the-guru" strategy. Wanger says the people who use this strategy mimic the trades of specific people. For example, when the media reports that Warren Buffett or George Soros is buying a particular stock, thousands of individual investors put in an order to buy the same stock. Even though this strategy has been successful for some people, Wanger lightheartedly adds, "Our analysts would be nervous about copying an idea like that." Some investors seek out local gurus. "If Murray told you to buy a stock and Murray has a terrific record as a stock picker, you will hold the stock as long as Murray likes it," Wanger quips. "Every three months, your job is to call Murray." The problem with this approach is that you don't always know when to sell. For example, the experts might sell their shares weeks before you find out about it.

There are several ways of learning what the pros are buying: You can discover some of their picks by reading financial newspapers and magazines, listening to television interviews or looking at annual reports. As required by regulations, at least twice a year every portfolio manager lists all the stocks in their fund. In addition, every week *Investor's Business Daily (IBD)* lists the names of stocks the top mutual fund companies are buying or selling. In addition, *IBD* lists the percentage of institutions that own the stock.

You can also get stock ideas by watching *CNBC, CNNfn, Louis Rukeyser's Wall Street Week*, or *Moneyline*. The featured guests are always asked to reveal the stocks they are buying and why. Although you should never blindly follow the advice of every guest, it is a good place to get ideas. Choose experienced professionals who have excellent long-term investment records, then select their most promising recommendations. Most pros agree that you should not buy a stock based on a recommendation until you have spent the time analyzing and researching the company on your own.

◆ Profile ◆

William H. Miller, III

Portfolio Manager, Legg Mason Value Trust and
Special Investment Trust

Bill Miller's interest in stocks began at the age of 9, when he noticed the typeface of the stock section was different from the other parts of the newspaper. His father explained that the smaller typeface was used to display all the stock prices. Pointing to a stock that had gone up a quarter of a point, his father said, "If you owned one share of that stock, you would have just made 25 cents." Young Bill asked what you had to do to make the stock go up. "You don't have to do anything," his father replied. "It just goes up by itself." It was precisely at that moment Miller decided he wanted to be in the stock business, where you could make money without doing any work.

Although Miller has outgrown his early misconceptions about the stock market, he still finds investing a fascinating experience. "Virtually anything in the world, any topic, any subject affects investing—either at the macro or micro level," he says.

In fact, Miller believes that the stock market functions as a "giant real-time information-processing machine" where most of the news and information about a stock has already been reflected in its price. In the short-term, Miller sees the market as random and unpredictable—what academicians call market efficiency. "When we look at investments, we really think of ourselves as investors and not speculators, meaning that we are not trying to guess stock prices or figure out which stocks are going up in price or predict the market. We don't make any forecasts of the economy or of stock prices. We just try to understand what is going on." In other words, Miller won't try to predict when the Fed is going to raise interest rates or predict what is happening with the Asian economy. He has no control over these events. Instead, Miller and his associates focus on trying to understand the businesses they buy and where a company might be in three to five years.

"If we are going to add value to our investors," he says, "we need to find a portfolio of names we have some reason to believe will outperform an unmanaged index." To find these stocks, Miller and his associates perform exhaustive quantitative and qualitative research.

"We start off with all the basic tools that happen to be at anyone's disposal," he says, "like computer databases that allow you to look at the historic P/E ratios, price-to-book ratios, price to cash flow, and other accounting-based data." He looks at how much the business would be worth if it were sold or liquidated, and other factors that might help determine the company's value. "If you get down to the one thing we look for in an investment, we look for the price of a stock that is radically less than what we calculate the value of the business to be. That is the key we are looking for and we use extensive valuation techniques to do that." He is quick to point out, however, that the quantitative data only provides him with landmarks, not roadblocks. "This data can give the investor a sense of what is going on, but there is no magical algorithmic answer to be found in this data," he admits. "If there were, someone would have already found it."

Once a group of stocks meets his quantitative criteria, Miller and his associates perform qualitative research. "We talk to management, suppliers, and competitors, look at the company's strategy and products and try to get a sense of what the business is going to do over the next few years," he explains.

Miller closely monitors any stocks that he buys. "We know that at any point in time, probably 30 percent of our portfolio is not going to outperform the market over some multi-year period. We just don't know which 30 percent it is." So Miller and his analysts spend a lot of time trying to figure out what in their portfolio is not going to work. "The way we go about this is we try and build a strong investment case to get something into the portfolio. As soon as it's in, we try to find the strongest reason to get it out." This requires an in-depth understanding of the companies in your portfolio. "If you buy a stock that underperforms for three months or six months, it doesn't mean it won't triple the next year. You have to understand what you own."

To avoid risk, Miller buys stocks that are trading at a discount to their business value. "Over long periods, as Ben Graham said, the market is a weighing machine, not a voting machine. Stocks will tend to bounce around somewhere near their fair value. Our risk-minimization strategy is to own things that trade at big discounts to fair value."

He will sell a stock for three reasons: First, when a company reaches what he thinks is fair value. Second, if a better bargain emerges. "If we uncover something that has a higher implied rate of return than something else we own, we sell the stock with the lower rate of return." And finally, Miller will sell when he thinks he may be wrong. "If the world changes in some fashion or other, we may conclude we shouldn't own the stock."

What is the secret to being a successful investor? "The secret is, there is no secret," Miller says. "Part of what we do is study other successful investors. We look at what these men and women are doing and try to figure out where they are finding value. I am surprised that many people try and pick their investments from a broad list of stocks. It would seem to me that you would improve your chances of investing dramatically if you only select your investments from among those owned by other successful investors. Because they've already done the research and have selected the 20 or 50 names of all the possible stocks they believe will do the best, you could take their collective stock universe as your universe." If an individual investor focuses on just these stocks, says Miller, you would probably do pretty well.

A common mistake occasionally made by Miller and many of his professional counterparts is to sell a stock too soon. Research shows, according to Miller, that the stocks people sell systematically outperform the ones they buy. "Most people, as Peter Lynch said, water their weeds and cut their flowers. And they should do the opposite, sell their losers and hold on to their winners. One of the reasons we have been successful is that we tend to have a lower turnover in our portfolio. We never sell something just because the price went up.

We only sell it because we expect that its future rate of return will be below the market."

Too many people focus on the price of a stock, says Miller, which leads them to speculation and overtrading, two other common mistakes. "People think that if a stock goes up, it must be good; if a price goes down, it must be bad. Price tells you nothing about value." Instead, Miller believes individual investors should develop a long-term investment policy. The best investors, says Miller, are not only dedicated and disciplined, but are totally focused on generating above-average results. "They have a process they believe in and they are constantly testing to see if it is the best process. Like any other profession," says Miller, "the more time and effort you devote to it, the better you should be able to do."

His advice for the individual investor: Adopt a patient, long-term attitude toward investing, stick to a strategy, and do not be swayed by day-to-day market fluctuations. He says, "There is nothing that will prevent individual investors from generating above-average investment returns with the appropriate strategy, discipline, and dedication."

◆ ◆ ◆

60. Buy stocks in the best companies

Why do so many investors ignore the stocks of well-managed, high-quality companies and buy speculative, low-priced junk? If you believe that the stock market is a huge casino driven by luck, it doesn't matter which stock you pick. You'll simply buy any stock that moves. One stock will do as well as the other depending on the roll of the Dow. However, if you believe that not all stocks are alike, you will seek out the stocks of the best companies at the best price you can get.

Warren Buffett once said he would rather buy a good business at a fair price than a fair business at a good price. The tricky part is figuring out which businesses are best. Peter Lynch prefers dull and simple companies. He wrote in *One Up On Wall Street,* "The perfect stock would be attached to the perfect company, and the perfect company has to be engaged in a perfectly simple business, and the perfectly simple business ought to have a perfectly boring name. The more boring it is, the better."

To find the best companies, the experts use a number of criteria. Depending on their investment strategy, they might consider some of the following:

◊ Superior earnings growth.

◊ Excellent management.

◊ Market leaders.

◊ Industry groups and companies that will outperform the market.

◊ Stocks selling at a discount to their underlying value.

◊ Companies that are currently out of favor.

Amy Domini, president of the Domini Social Equity funds, uses additional criteria to seek out the best companies. She is an advocate of socially responsible or value-based investing. To be added to the Domini 400 Social Index, a company must reply to more than 60 questions, such as: How many women do you have on the board? Does your company give to charity? The purpose of the survey is to give Domini a total picture of the company's corporate culture. She says, "I am not looking for the best companies. I am looking for the better half of companies."

The pros unanimously agree that you have to do your homework if you want to find the best companies. Although you can get ideas from shopping at the mall, listening to financial experts, or reading periodicals, nothing replaces good old-fashioned research. You can get ideas from your workplace or while traveling. You can do your research at the library, bookstore, or the Internet. Every year, the financial magazines publish a list of the top 100 companies in America. From this list, you would have found General Electric, Lucent, Cisco, Wal-Mart, and Home Depot, among dozens of others. The bottom line, according to the pros, is to find the best companies and invest in them.

61. Invest in companies with the best managers

With thousands of good-quality, well-run companies to choose from, it is always surprising why people buy stocks in poorly managed companies. Many pros believe that you need an extremely knowledgeable and experienced manager to run a company. That is why so many professional investors insist on meeting with upper management before they invest in the stock. At the same time, some pros question whether there is a connection between a well-run company and competent management. The most amusing quote on management has been attributed to Peter Lynch: "Buy shares of businesses that are so simple that even an idiot could run them—because one day one will."

Nevertheless, most pros believe it's a good idea to meet with upper management. They routinely talk with the CEO or other top managers to discuss how the corporation will be run, how fast the company is expected to grow, and the corporate official's expectations for the future. Others look for a business plan or strategy, whether the managers invest in their own company, and the number of women or minorities in top management. Obviously, everyone has a different definition for superior management.

Steven Romick, portfolio manager of UAM FPA Crescent Portfolio, will not buy a stock unless he understands management philosophy. "If you don't understand the manager," he says, "you're looking at a potential mistake." Romick looks for incentivized management, managers whose salaries are tied to their performance. Coca-Cola, for example, is a company with properly incentivized management. Not surprisingly, quite a number of portfolio managers mentioned Coca-Cola as one of the best-run companies in America.

When a company has a change of management, most money managers will interview the new team as soon as possible. "When you see new management coming in, it is interesting to find out their view of the company," says Oscar Schafer, a Barron's Roundtable member and partner of Cumberland Associates. "They could change things around and capitalize on the company's strengths while reducing the weaknesses. Individuals should watch for a change in management." Schafer is amazed at how much information you can get from top managers in the United States as compared to Europe. However, Schafer found that, because of recent shareholder pressure, European managers are becoming more open to visits, especially to U.S. money managers.

Fund managers use different techniques to evaluate and research managers. Morty Schaja, COO of Baron Funds, explained how Ron Baron, the Chairman and CIO, conducts interviews. "Ron is excellent at assessing the ethics and skills of a company's management team. He meets with management for hours, develops a relationship with the team to understand whether they are honest, ethical, and good at what they do." Schaja says they are not stock traders but investors alongside a company's management team. "We are investors in businesses and the people running these businesses are our partners."

If the pros don't get the right answers from management, they consider selling. "If I can't convince these guys to the correctness of our point of view," says Robert Sanborn, portfolio manager of the Oakmark Fund, "we will move on. I'm not going to risk our shareholder's assets to a below-average management team."

On the other hand, some experts don't even bother to meet with management, especially those *quants* who depend heavily on computer models. They prefer to depend on financial statements or other hard data. Most, however, aggressively interview managers and look for data that backs up manager's opinions.

Before you buy a stock, the pros say you should find out as much as you can about the people running the company. Although it could be difficult for individual investors to contact upper management directly, there are other ways to get information. "I bet if a person was sophisticated enough they could call the investor relations person and ask them about the business," says Schafer. In addition to calling investor relations, you could use the Internet to search for biographical information on the CEO or other top managers. If you visit the store or factory, you might get second-hand opinions from employees. It will also give you a first-hand look into how the company is being run.

62. Back up intuition with hard evidence

There is contradictory evidence on whether investors can use their instincts or gut feelings to make money in the stock market. Although many individual investors rely on their instincts when investing in the stock market, the experts do not agree on whether this is logical. Occasionally, it can lead to very successful trading opportunities. For example, if you work with computers, you might have a feeling that a certain software company you're doing business with will be successful. Even if the company has no earnings and few customers, because of your knowledge and experience, you buy the stock because you are convinced that one day the company will show a profit.

Richard Johnson, portfolio manager of the Columbia Small Cap Fund, put it this way, "Intuition doesn't exist in a vacuum. To me, it is judgment. It is knowing the history of the stock, knowing the management, and knowing all the quantitative and qualitative information, including psychological factors, that you can gather about that stock. It is a combination of all that information that creates good intuition."

Although your instincts can be used to assist in making trading decisions, you should proceed with caution. The experts say that people get into trouble because they confuse their instincts with what they wish would happen. If you buy a stock because you have a feeling it is going to go up, you are not relying on instincts, but hope. The instincts of a professional are based on years of experience and knowledge. For instance, when money managers walk into a company to talk to a CEO, they are relying on instincts and gut feelings to evaluate his or her performance.

A number of fund managers say they often get into trouble when they rely only on instincts, especially managers who use quantitative data. There can be a conflict between what the data shows and what their instincts tell them. The fund managers who rely primarily on quantitative information say that most of the time, the data is correct.

Jim O'Shaughnessy, CEO of O'Shaughnessy Capital Management, believes that investors who rely on instinct to pick stocks are destined for substandard returns. O'Shaughnessy writes in his book, *What Works On Wall Street*, that traditional, intuitive forecasting methods are highly unreliable and will wreak havoc with your returns. He backs it up with numerous statistical data and experiments. "We have a lot of bad instincts," he says. Instead of relying on intuition and gut feeling, use quantitative models based on statistical data.

Although there are conflicting opinions, there is no proof that investors who depend on intuition to buy stocks will do better than those who don't. Yet, many people still depend on intuition to pick stocks. If you feel compelled to buy a stock based on gut feelings, the experts recommend that you back it up with hard, objective evidence.

63. Invest in the future

It takes a lot more skill to anticipate future market trends than to play number guessing games with the Dow. The people who can accurately predict the industries or companies that will be successful in five or 10 years have a huge advantage over other investors. In fact, if you can accurately predict the future and invest in it, it is possible that you would be wealthy beyond your wildest dreams. Unfortunately, this is extremely difficult to do.

It involves more than making accurate predictions. You must also be willing to back up your predictions with hard-earned money. Many people believed in the power of the Internet, but pioneers like Bill Gates, Steve Case, and Michael Dell, among hundreds of others, invested time and money into their dreams. Only a couple of years ago, America Online was languishing at less than $10 a share while many experts declared that online communications was a passing fad. It takes insight, courage, and conviction to invest in the future. Not many people are successful at it.

Joel Barker, a futurist and author of *Future Edge*, questioned why intelligent people with good motives do such a poor job of anticipating the future. Barker says the people who will anticipate and ultimately improve the future are paradigm pioneers. The paradigm pioneer dispenses with the old rules and creates a new set of rules. Barker says it takes incredible courage and intuition to be a pioneer. Paradigm pioneers do more than observe; they act. They see the world differently and go on to create new paradigms.

Sometimes paradigm pioneers show up in the most unlikely places. Thomas Watson, the former chairman of IBM, encouraged the company to hire "wild ducks," or "highly intelligent, individualistic employees who ignore bureaucratic procedures, shun set schedules, and resist attempts to make them more efficient," according to an article written by Beverly Geber in *Training* magazine. Watson felt it was useless to try and tame the wild ducks. Instead, he wanted them to feel comfortable in a large organization like IBM. Watson felt that the highly creative wild ducks would help the company see things differently if allowed to flourish.

One way of using predictions to make money in the stock market is to think of all the industries that aren't going to make it in the future. Back in the early 1900s when steel and railroads were the dominant industries, few people accurately predicted the end of the industrial revolution and saw the coming of the technological revolution. Those who did, however, made enormous profits.

Even the experts have trouble predicting the future. Charles H. Duell, commissioner of the U.S. Office of Patents, in 1899 said, "Everything that can be invented has been invented." Other notable predictions that missed the mark include the following, pulled from the GEMS Web site:

"640k ought to be enough for anybody."

> —Bill Gates
> 1981

"There is no reason anyone would want a computer in their home."

> —Ken Olson, president and chairman
> Digital Equipment Corporation
> 1977

"We don't like their sound, and guitar music is on the way out."

—Decca Recording Company,
rejecting the Beatles

1962

"I have traveled the length and breadth of this country and talked with the best people, and I can assure you that data processing is a fad that won't last out the year."

—editor in charge of Prentice Hall
business books

1957

"Computers in the future may weigh no more than 1.5 tons."
—*Popular Mechanics*

1949

"I think there is a world market for maybe five computers."
—Thomas Watson, chairman of IBM

1943

"Stocks have reached what looks like a permanently high plateau."

—Irving Fisher, Professor of Economics,
Yale University

1929

64. Find out what the insiders are doing

One clever way of finding good stock ideas is to track the stock transactions of company insiders. Although corporate managers are prohibited by law from revealing inside information, their stock transactions are part of the public record. You can get an idea of whether the company has reached new highs or lows by watching if insiders are buying or selling. Erik Gustafson, portfolio manager of the Stein Roe Growth Fund, explains: "We love to see insiders coming in and putting their own capital into stock. We love to see that. Insiders have a pretty good view of the company's future, and they are usually pretty good at calling bottoms."

Gustafson says it is easy for individuals to watch insider trading. "There is software that is available. You can also track it by reading *The Wall Street Journal* or *Investor's Business Daily*. And there is a lot of charting software available both on a subscription basis or free over the Internet that will tell you when insiders are buying. There are also insider services available that will track it immediately via the Federal filings."

Bill Miller agrees that insider trading is another important tool for investors to use. "For us, we will look at patterns of insider buying to see if we should be doing additional research. But we would never buy or sell because insiders are buying or selling. The patterns are another piece of evidence to tell us that maybe we should do more research."

Although the pros use professional financial services such as Bloomberg's to track insider trading, individuals can get the information for free on the Internet, for example, at www.yahoo.com.

◆ Profile ◆

Erik Gustafson

Vice President, Stein Roe Mutual Funds
Portfolio Manager, Stein Roe Growth Fund and
Young Investor Fund

Erik Gustafson's first memory of the stock market was watching his father create point and figure charts of the stocks he owned. Young Erik was very curious about the charts his father was making and, as a result, his interest in the stock market grew. After graduating from college, Gustafson began his career with Stein Roe in Ft. Lauderdale, Florida, as a manager of institutional funds dealing with large foundations and endowments. In 1994, he was asked to switch to mutual funds and moved to the Chicago office to manage a number of individual funds.

He considers himself a growth investor and looks for high-quality, large cap stocks. "I am looking for a history of earnings achievement and earnings success. I need to have confidence that earnings growth will continue into the future, so I look for sustainable growth in earnings and high-quality financial characteristics."

Before Gustafson buys a stock, he makes sure it meets a number of qualitative and quantitative guidelines. "Quantitatively, a stock has to meet certain criteria," he explains. "A company has to have earnings per share growth of 15 percent; an ROE (return on equity) that is greater than 15 percent; an ROI (return on income) of greater than 10 percent; a P/E multiple of less than one-and-a-half times the three-year earnings growth rate; and a three-year expected minimum return of 50 percent."

On the qualitative side he looks for companies that have high sales growth, market dominance, protected market positions, and companies that create their own competitive advantage, among a number of qualitative characteristics. "We want to see not only outstanding managers, but also managers whose compensation is tied to the stock price performance. When managers are tied to the performance of the stock price," he suggests, "the stock price tends to go up."

When the quantitative or qualitative fundamentals change, however, Gustafson will sell without hesitation. "Changes in fundamentals typically drive us out of stocks," he explains. The fundamentals he refers to include a company losing its dominant market position, if the management team has been unable to manage effectively, or if management becomes too distracted when moving into new markets. "We'll put up with a couple of quarters of missed earnings if we have confidence the business will rebound. We know businesses go through problems. Sometimes we just don't have that confidence."

He will also trim back a holding if it becomes more than 5 percent of his portfolio. "It isn't an exercise in selling your winners," he explains, "it's an exercise in making sure that no one company becomes too dominant in your portfolio. We love to have that problem, by the way. We don't see it as a problem, it is a positive."

The biggest mistake Gustafson says he made was getting out of a good stock because analysts claimed it was overvalued. "I sold half of my Cisco Systems on an analyst's call, not our own analyst, but someone I had a lot of respect for who said that Cisco was going to have problems with certain product categories. We bought at a low price, around a dollar, and had owned it for a very long time. We sold it on a split-adjusted basis of 30."

However, the stock continued to go up. "Cisco was a great company with outstanding fundamentals," says Gustafson. When Gustafson realized his mistake, he bought Cisco back, where it went on to double. "Typically, analysts tend to be exceedingly valuation sensitive, which means they have a preconceived notion of what the proper value of the stock is based on their exhaustive analysis. They spend their whole lives focused on the industries and the stocks they cover. Sometimes they get so caught up in those issues they miss the larger picture."

Gustafson suggests that investors be cautious about following the recommendations of stock analysts. "The worst, most dangerous words out of an analyst's mouth are 'that is too cheap to sell.' When I hear these six words from an analyst, I run for the hills, because the stock is about to get cheaper." Gustafson says he listens to analysts for informational purposes but not for buy-and-sell decisions.

In addition, Gustafson says individuals should be careful about buying stocks on the recommendations of stockbrokers. "Retail brokers are typically great salesmen, but they are not great money managers. They're doing what the firm tells them to do. The large sell-side firms have much different agendas than do individual investors or institutional investors."

Instead, Gustafson says that individuals should take personal responsibility for investment decisions. "Go out and kick the tires," says Gustafson. "Peter Lynch says that you can do some of the best research on your own. Look at the products you consume. Look at the movies you watch." Even simple research can provide individuals with good investment ideas, he suggests.

According to Gustafson, the most common mistake that individuals make is to hold their losers and sell their winners. "Individual investors suffer from the malady of owning a stock, watching it go down, and then saying, 'Oh please, if it ever gets back to even I'll sell it.' That's a huge mistake, an absolute, unequivocal formula for failure. What it results in is a portfolio of losers. And they will sell their winners in order to realize gains too quickly."

Gustafson believes that investors should initiate a strict selling discipline. "Stocks that go down tend to keep going down and stocks that go up tend to keep going up. If a stock starts going down, it's for a reason and the market knows what it is, whether it is insiders selling it or whether the company is giving the news to institutional investors, there is some reason the stock is going down." He admits it is tough for many people to sell losing stocks. "If you can cut your losers early and let your winners run, you will be successful in investing in the stock market."

In addition, Gustafson feels individuals should hold stocks for the long-term. "Own a concentrated portfolio of seven to 10 great stocks," he suggests. "Add money to them on a rigorous, disciplined investment plan, namely, every quarter, do it for the long-term, and you'll win."

◆ ◆ ◆

65. Don't ignore your dreams

There are hundreds of examples of people solving problems, winning the lottery, or discovering the truth because it appeared in a dream. Although some people might dismiss dreams as unproven psychological hocus-pocus, there is enough evidence indicating that dreams can unlock many mysteries, including unconscious and repressed feelings. Sigmund Freud spent much of his life showing how you can use dreams to improve your life.

In *Market Wizards*, Jack Schwager interviewed Dr. Van K. Tharp, a research psychologist, about the influence of dreams on trading. Dr. Tharp said it is quite common for top traders to have dreams about the market. He said that some of these dreams are surprisingly accurate. Einstein, he says, dreamed the theory of relativity and Paul McCartney heard the song *Yesterday* in a dream. Because most people don't take the time to interpret their dreams, says Dr. Tharp, they miss the symbolic predictions.

Schwager says he doesn't think there is anything supernatural about trading on dreams. "When you are sleeping, your inhibitions are gone. You have a more open door to your subconscious. For whatever reason, it is not registering on a conscious level, but it comes out in a dream state." Schwager recalls trading the Canadian dollar and dreaming that the market would go much higher. When he looked at it on a conscious level, he felt the trade was too risky because the market had risen so much. However, his dream told him otherwise. As it turned out, Schwager's dream was correct. Fortunately, he successfully acted on the information he received from his dream, realizing a very profitable trade on the Canadian dollar. "The market did go higher just as I dreamed," he marveled.

Schwager also profiled a professional currency trader, Bill Lipshutz, who had a vivid dream about a report that could affect the price of the dollar. Lipschutz' assistant laughed when he heard about the dream. "The day you start trading on dreams is the day we might as well pack it up," the assistant said. Because Lipshutz felt uncomfortable about acting on a dream, he didn't make the trade. As it turned out, when the report was released the next day, the numbers were exactly the same as in the dream. Lipschutz says it was confusing and very odd. Ironically, he says if he didn't have the dream, he might have made the trade.

There isn't a lot of research on how you can use dreams to be successful in the stock market. None of the pros will publicly recommend that you buy stocks based on your dreams, yet few will tell you to dismiss them completely. Schwager summed it up by saying that although trading dreams happen infrequently, when they do, you should pay attention to them.

PART 7

TRADING

TACTICS

66. Have a selling strategy

According to many portfolio managers, selling stocks is one of the hardest parts of their jobs. That is why it is so important to the pros to have a strategy for selling stocks. It is a decision they take very seriously. Spiros Segalas, portfolio manager of the Harbor Capital Appreciation Fund, says you can always think of 15 reasons why you should buy a stock. When you buy, you are feeling confident and optimistic. You're thinking of how much money you could make if your stock does well. On the other hand, he says, selling makes many people uncomfortable.

There are a number of conflicting psychological forces at work. Donald Cassidy, author of *It's When You Sell That Counts*, writes that if you sell a stock for a loss, you are admitting you are wrong and made a mistake. It is extremely difficult for some people to admit they lost money. Even if you sell your stock for a gain, says

Cassidy, there is always the lingering doubt that you sold too early, that if you held on longer, you would have made even more money. Either way, selling causes problems for investors.

The pros say you should have specific and credible reasons to sell. It is not enough to sell when you make a profit. That is one of the main reasons investors consistently underperform the market. Jean-Marie Eveillard, president of the SoGen funds, remarks that there is a saying on Wall Street that no one gets hurt taking a profit. "We have repeatedly said this is idiocy," he says. "The mere fact that a stock has gone up is no reason to sell."

To avoid the psychological turmoil many investors go through when selling, the pros have strict selling rules based on their investment strategy and philosophy. For example, value investors might sell when they calculate a stock has reached fair value. A growth investor might sell if there is a change of management or lower corporate earnings. If you were a technical analyst, you might sell if a stock advanced rapidly on low volume. A less precise method is to follow the advice of a wise but old Wall Street saying: "Sell down to the sleeping point." In other words, keep selling your stocks until you can sleep at night without worrying.

There are other effective strategies for selling. As soon as Bill Miller, portfolio manager of Legg Mason Value Trust, buys a stock, he and his associates think of all the reasons why they should sell it. At any point in time, he says, approximately 30 percent of his portfolio will underperform the market. The problem is, he doesn't know which 30 percent it will be. As he puts it: "You've got to have the courage of your convictions to get rid of stocks that are not adding value to your portfolio. If a stock is acting poorly or not acting well in any short period of time, that may be a signal that you should get out of it. On the other hand, if a stock has gone down significantly after you bought it, either you should get out of it or you should buy more of it if you are convinced you are right." Miller and his associates are continually on the alert for stocks they shouldn't own. They think of all the reasons they should buy a stock, and after they buy it, think of all the reasons to sell it.

Steven Romick, portfolio manager of UAM FPA Crescent Portfolio, makes an interesting analogy. If the price of your home was published in the newspaper every day and you found out that the price of your house dropped, it is unlikely you would sell. You live in your house; you know what it is worth. The same should be true for your stocks. Even if the price of your stock falls a bit, if you know what the underlying business is really worth, you will be hesitant to sell. You will wait until the price of your stock rises to reflect the value of the business.

Overall, the pros believe you should spend as much time thinking about selling as you do about buying. Think of a strategy for selling stocks that fits your investment philosophy. Then develop a specific set of rules that will help you to decide when to sell. Finally, after you have a set of selling rules that makes sense to you, be sure to follow them. This could help you to avoid many of the most common mistakes made when selling stocks.

67. Buy low, sell high

When asked to reveal the secret to making money in the stock market, one legendary Wall Street trader replied, "Buy low, sell high." If you use this deceptively simple strategy, you are guaranteed to make money on Wall Street. Unfortunately, buying low and selling high is a lot more complicated than many people think.

Of course, everyone wants to buy low and sell high. In reality, what usually happens is that people do the opposite. Robert Sheard, author of *The Unemotional Investor*, says that buy low, sell high is hard because it goes against human nature. There are few investors who have the courage to buy the abandoned stocks that no one else wants. Also, few people will sell a quickly rising stock at the time everyone else wants to buy it.

According to Sheard, the most effective way to buy low and sell high is to use the *Dogs of the Dow* strategy. He says the results of this method have been proven in studies going back to the 1920s. Every year, you simply buy the 10 highest-yielding Dow stocks. The 10 stocks with the highest dividends can be found in any financial newspaper. At the end of the year, you readjust your portfolio by selling the stocks that no longer have the highest yields and replacing them with the ones that do. Sheard says this strategy will lower transaction costs, reduce taxes, and beat most professional fund managers. This strategy has only lost money twice in the last 26 years, he claims.

Another buy low, sell high method was introduced by Wade Cook, author of *Wall Street Money Machine*. Cook doesn't try to find the precise top or bottom of any stock. Instead, he looks for a dozen or so stocks that move up or down within a narrow trading range. He calls them rolling stocks. For example, a certain stock might roll back and forth between $10 and $15 a share over several years. Cook would probably buy it at $11 and sell it at $14. With the right stocks, you can make money using this method. However, it is not only riskier than the *Dogs of the Dow* strategy, it involves a lot more trading.

Although you should aim to buy low and sell high, you should not be obsessed with it. The pros suggest you buy the best stocks for the lowest price you can get. By looking at the stock's price history, you will learn how low the stock has gone in the past. Although difficult to achieve, few investors would dispute the logical strategy of buying low and selling high.

68. Buy high, sell higher

Although this advice contradicts the buy low, sell high strategy, a number of investors have been extremely successful buying stocks high and selling higher. These so-called momentum investors will buy stocks at higher prices with the anticipation that future earnings will drive the price even higher. The best examples of this phenomenon are the Internet stocks. These stocks shot up by huge percentages before the companies made a penny in earnings. Nevertheless, investors poured money into these stocks with the expectation of superb future earnings. Anyone who bought Amazon.com, Yahoo!, and America Online in the early days was richly rewarded for the effort.

J. Morton Davis, author of *From Hard Knocks to Hot Stocks*, writes that it seems counter-intuitive to buy a stock at its high.

Just like in physics, however, a stock on its way up tends to keep moving up. Davis provides numerous examples of stocks that have reached new highs on the major exchanges and continue to go even higher. The new high is a signal that something big might happen. Davis says institutional investors will jump on the bandwagon and push these stocks even higher. He says that when you find a winning stock, you should keep riding it until you see signs that it is no longer a winner—for example, if earnings aren't growing as fast as you expected. Although this strategy does not always work, Davis says you are following one of Wall Street's oldest sayings: "The trend is your friend." This is the mantra for the momentum investor, who buys the stocks that everyone else is buying.

I have a friend who has had excellent success with this strategy. He did well buying stocks while they were moving higher. At one point, he sold Yahoo! for a huge return, then bought it again when it didn't show signs of slowing down. This extremely aggressive strategy has been successful for him because he started off small, then added to his position as these stocks showed further strength. He didn't buy more shares immediately after his stocks went up. He waited until he was sure his stocks were winners.

To be fair, not everyone agrees with this strategy. Peter Lynch says the biggest fallacy of investing is the idea that if a stock goes up in price, it must be a good investment. Lynch says the only reason the stock is going up in price is because someone else is willing to pay more for it than you are. Some have sarcastically called it the "greater fool theory," meaning that you can always find another fool willing to pay more for it.

The bottom line from momentum investors: When you find a great stock, a winning stock, hold on to it, buy more shares, pyramid up. It is a simple strategy. If you buy a stock and it goes up in price, you buy more shares. Momentum investors claim that in an especially strong bull market, buying high and selling higher can reward aggressive investors. However, momentum investing can be risky, especially if a stock has been run up a lot. At the slightest hint of bad news, momentum investors will quickly abandon stocks, leaving some investors holding the bag. One expert compared this to a game of musical chairs.

Like any other strategy, you should not participate unless you have learned everything you can about it. When trying to find momentum stocks that are going up in price, look for stocks that have reached their 52-week highs. You can find many of these stocks by picking up a copy of *Investor's Business Daily*, *The Wall Street Journal*, or *Barron's*. In addition to the 52-week-high list, there are dozens of other technical indicators, such as trading and price volume, that will help you find momentum stocks.

◆ Profile ◆

Gary Pilgrim

Chief Investment Officer,
Pilgrim, Baxter & Associates
President, PBHG Fund, Inc.
Portfolio Manager, PBHG Growth Fund

By the time Gary Pilgrim graduated from college, he was convinced he wanted to be a money manager. While taking courses in security analysis and portfolio management, he found himself instinctively drawn to the growth strategy. "I am a growth stock investor by nature and design," Pilgrim says. "I look for companies that are growing rapidly and have the potential to continue that growth. As an investor, you have to figure out what you think makes stocks go up and what is the best investment strategy for you to pursue." For Pilgrim, it is earnings growth. "It has always been pretty straightforward to me that if a company increases in size and profits, it's inevitable that the company's stock will eventually be worth more."

Pilgrim is not impressed with P/E ratios and other valuation tools. "People speak very glibly about price/earnings ratios as a simplistic tool. I think it is particularly unproductive in smaller, high-growth, highly energetic, and dynamic companies. I learned early on that P/E is one of the least important things to think about, not the most important."

Instead, Pilgrim uses a stock ranking system he personally developed. "The most fundamental thing you look for is a group of companies that is clearly above average in what they are accomplishing in terms of growth," says Pilgrim. "We usually look at companies that are growing at least two to three times the market rate. Because most people think of the market as the S&P 500, we typically are interested in companies that are growing at 20, 30, or 40 percent better than the average rate."

Pilgrim looks at other factors beside growth to ensure that a company is not just a "flash in the pan." He uses earnings estimates from only the most credible analysts, and constantly monitors information coming from the company. "We pay very close attention to developments as they occur," says Pilgrim. "And we actively engage in the process of traditional fundamental research, which includes talking to people who are supposed to be experts on the company, getting updates, and seeing what's going on. This is how I spend my day."

Pilgrim says he is very sensitive to what he calls inflection points of both negative and positive change. "The only way you can be aware of these changes is if you continuously provide due diligence on how your companies are doing." It has nothing to do with the price of the stock, explains Pilgrim, but rather the perception of how a company is doing. "It has to do with maintaining the business momentum that keeps investors comfortable with the price that exists for the stock," he says. "If there are positive changes, people want to buy the stock. If there are negative changes that cause people to be apprehensive about the company's stock, we might look for an exit."

Unlike some growth investors, Pilgrim is resistant to meeting with company managers. "Some of the mistakes I made involved having too much confidence in what management said about the company's prospects in the face of evidence to the contrary," says Pilgrim. He mentions Chesapeake Energy as an example. "I basically didn't come to grips quickly enough with the idea that things were not unfolding as we had hoped. We continued to believe the manager's assertions that things were different than the marketplace said they were. I ended up taking the stock from $25 to $5." Now, he says he's learned to be skeptical about what management says and doesn't waste too much time with personal contact. "I am much more interested in financial statements and facts as I see them," he adds.

Pilgrim also took a wild ride with Citrix, a computer chip company, that went from $10 to $70 a share. "The largest holding in our fund was Citrix, and in the couple of years that we owned it, we probably made four or five times our money. The ride was bumpy because misconceptions have frequently arisen about the company's prospects, but all through the period the company's earnings have come through, and come through." Pilgrim held on because he focused almost exclusively on earnings growth.

Asked if it's difficult emotionally to handle these wild price swings, Pilgrim replies, "That is the growth stock world. I used to get emotional about stocks. I don't anymore. One of the things you learn over the years is that emotion is not very helpful. All of us have emotions and the quicker you learn to get them under control, the better."

If a company has unexpectedly bad earnings or if others begin lowering their growth rate targets, Pilgrim will sell without hesitation. "Even though sometimes the price penalty is pretty heavy, it is better to watch the company recover from the sidelines than to sit there and engage in wishful thinking. Investors make the mistake of trying to be opportunistic in the face of adverse news. That is pretty risky."

Pilgrim suggests that individual investors act quickly when a stock doesn't perform as expected. "Because of the law of averages, you are going to make mistakes," he says. "I think that when anyone makes the decision to buy something, it is difficult to admit along the way that you were wrong. It is difficult to take a loss. It is easy to rationalize. Most people like to buy things that are down and they don't like to sell things they lost money in. Those two characteristics are fraught with problems."

To be a successful investor, Pilgrim believes that you need a strong belief in the approach you use. Then, you have to practice it consistently through all market conditions. "The secret to many successful investors is an unwavering confidence in their particular approach to managing money, which comes from practice and a refinement of their techniques."

Unless they have the time to pick stocks on a full-time basis, Pilgrim believes that most individuals should invest their money in mutual funds. "Today information changes hands so quickly that somebody who is doing it part-time is at a severe disadvantage," he suggests. "You don't have access to information that the professional investor has; you don't have the staff and; you don't have the resources."

In fairness, Pilgrim points out that he is only talking about the growth stock or emerging-growth stock investor. "An individual who buys very high-quality, established companies that tend not to waver in their long-term trends is in a different ballgame. But for the investor who wants to participate in the small company growth part of the world, I think the risk of being out of the loop of information is substantial. You usually won't find out what's really wrong in the company until days later."

◆ ◆ ◆

69. Cut your losses

According to many professional investors, there is no trading rule more important than cutting your losses short. The pros say that selling stocks for a loss is one of the hardest decisions any investor has to make. When you take a loss, you are admitting defeat. It goes against every instinct in your body. That is why it is so common for investors to hold on to their losers, hoping their stocks will rebound. To make matters worse, while holding onto their losers, many investors sell their winners too soon. Peter Lynch calls this "watering your weeds and cutting your flowers." They sell their winning stocks for small profits but hold on to the losers, praying for a miracle.

To counteract the emotional difficulties of selling losing stocks, many pros decide in advance when they are going to cut their losses. William O'Neil, publisher of *Investor's Business Daily*, developed a loss-cutting plan. He will sell any stock that drops 7 or 8 percent below his purchase price. He says this is extremely difficult for investors, who will say things like, "I can't sell this stock. I just know it will turn around and go back up." O'Neil says a stock doesn't know you and doesn't care what you think, so don't be afraid to sell it. He suggests that after you sell a losing stock, you look for stocks with stronger potential.

O'Neil says that even the best investors aren't going to be right more than 7 out of 10 times, a figure confirmed by other stock experts. By cutting your losses at 8 percent, at worst, you'll have a bunch of small losses that won't adversely affect your portfolio. If you don't do anything about the loss, says O'Neil, it will build and build until it's so heavy you can't recover. In extreme cases, you end up with a portfolio of losing stocks. In fact, says O'Neil, "The secret to winning in the stock market is to lose the least amount possible when you're wrong. In other words, in order to win you've got to recognize when you may be wrong and sell without hesitation to cut short your loss."

When bad things happen to good companies, cutting your losses will prevent you from holding dead money. That's what happened when I owned Iomega, a Utah data storage product company. The stock, after reaching a high of $55 a share, slipped as low as $12.50 a share before splitting 2 for 1. A less than spectacular earnings report and a series of management mistakes led to its price decline. I personally believe that Iomega is a good company with an excellent product, the Zip drive. Because I didn't have any sell discipline at the time, I let the losses get away from me. It would have been smarter if I had sold Iomega when it began to decline in price, even for a small loss. Then I could have used that money to buy an even better stock.

There are a number of ways you can cut your losses short. One popular method is to arrange in advance with your brokerage to automatically sell your stock at a predetermined price. Other investors, uncomfortable with automated sell programs, prefer to play it by ear. It isn't important which method you use as long as your goal is to sell your stocks for small losses rather than hold out for bigger ones.

70. Set buy and sell price targets

Nearly every stock analyst or portfolio manager, after publicly recommending a stock, will set a six- to 12-month price sell target. The pros do not pick price targets out of the air. They do extensive research using complex valuation tools and other objective methods to determine an accurate target price. Many analysts purposely give conservative estimates. On occasion, the stock hits the target price within weeks of the prediction.

You can copy the pros by setting price targets for the stocks you buy or sell. There are two ways to do this. First, you can try to determine the fair price of a stock. If you do this on your own, it could take some work. There are a number of valuation calculators on the Internet, such as the one at the *Money* Web site, www.money.com. You can also pick up a copy of Graham's *The Intelligent Investor* or read other books on how to value a business.

If valuing a business sounds too complicated, you could set up price targets tied to how much the stock increases. For example, some people will sell when a stock rises by 30 or 40 percent. Although not recommended by all experts because it limits your gains, the advantage of this method is that it forces you to be disciplined. Other investors have a rule to sell half of their shares when their price target has been reached.

Dan Leonard, portfolio manager of the INVESCO Strategic Technology portfolio, revealed how price targets are useful to individual investors: "You might want to set up a target price. When it reaches that target, you have to reassess how things have changed: Are my earnings going up higher? Should I increase the target price? Should I take money off the table? Be aware of what you own and be willing to sell. I see so many people who let their stocks go round trip. The stock runs up and they don't do anything about it. Then things begin to change and the next thing you know, it's back to their cost."

After you set up a price target, you must take action when the stock hits the target. It helps if you write down the price on paper. For instance, if your stock hits the target price of $40 a share, you either sell the stock or reevaluate by raising the target price. Most important, the target price must be realistic and attainable. It cannot be based on hope.

71. Trade as little as possible

With the media interest in low-cost online trading accounts and a chance to make big bucks in the market, it seems that more individuals than ever are trading stocks. According to the pros, however, people are overtrading. Many pros believe that overtrading is costing investors a lot of money in the long-run, not only in taxes and transaction fees, but also in investment returns.

Gary Klott, a personal finance columnist, writes about a study at the University of California at Davis. Professors Terrance Odean and Brad Barber tracked 10,000 customer accounts at a discount brokerage firm. They concluded that "trading is hazardous to your wealth." The professors found that stocks people buy frequently underperform the stocks they sell. When you factor in commission charges and taxes, the results are even worse.

In his book, *Market Wizards*, Jack Schwager interviews Mark Weinstein, a professional trader. Weinstein says he doesn't lose much money on his trades because he waits for the right moment to take action. He illustrates his philosophy by using the following analogy: "Although the cheetah is the fastest animal in the world and can catch any animal on the plains, it will wait until it is absolutely sure it can catch its prey. It may hide in the bush for a week, waiting for just the right moment. It will wait for a baby antelope, and not just any baby antelope, but preferably one that is also sick or lame. Only then, when there is no chance it can lose its prey, does it attack. That, to me, is the epitome of professional trading."

Schwager says the most successful traders are extremely selective about the trades they make. "You should not trade all the time," he says. "You should only trade when the opportunity that you define actually exists." In some cases, this could even mean waiting months or a year before making a trade.

When I first got involved in the stock market, I was compelled to make as many trades as I could afford, sometimes dozens of trades a week. I convinced myself that I was investing but now I realize I was speculating. Sometimes, after losing money on one trade, I would immediately make another one to try and win back my money. This endless cycle lasted for months until I finally realized I was afflicted with what one writer called "marketitis." I realized the futility of overtrading when I looked at my one-year returns. Although I was trading all the time, by the end of the year, I barely broke even. That was all the evidence I needed to change my trading habits.

The research is quite clear that frequent trading does not necessarily lead to greater profits. If you recognize that you are overtrading, the pros suggest you adopt a more patient buy-and-hold philosophy. It will not only save you money in taxes and commissions, but also allow you time to study and research the best trading opportunities.

72. Start small

A quick way to lose all your money in the stock market is to risk everything you own on an all-or-nothing investment. However, the pros say you don't have to risk a lot of money to make money in the stock market. For example, William O'Neil, publisher of *Investor's Business Daily*, started with only $500 when he first got out of college, buying five shares of Procter & Gamble when he was 21. Even now, when O'Neil buys a new stock, he often begins with a small purchase. If the stock moves up a few points, he buys a little more. When he is right, he continues to make additional purchases.

When the pros talk about starting small, they think in terms of dollars, not shares. In fact, many recommend that you not worry about the number of shares you are buying. For example, if you have $5,000, you could invest half into the best company you can find. If the stock goes up a bit, you could buy more. If the stock turns out to be a winner, eventually you will have invested the entire $5,000. This is much safer than risking the entire amount on only one stock at one time.

It is possible to get rich slowly, say the pros, by buying more shares a little at a time. Using this method, you could make a lot of small purchases over a long period of time. You might be surprised at how quickly your money builds up and compounds over time.

◆ Profile ◆

Shelby Davis

Chief Executive Officer, Davis Selected Advisors
Director, Davis New York Venture Fund and
Selected American Shares

You could say that successful investing for Shelby Davis is a family tradition. Davis' passion for stocks was inherited from his late father, Shelby Cullom Davis, who started the family strategy of investing in bargain-based companies with steady earnings. Because Davis Sr. had an affinity for insurance stocks, young Shelby's first investing memories were visiting insurance companies with his dad during summer vacations.

In 1997, Davis continued the family tradition by turning over the day-to-day fund management to his son Chris. That doesn't mean Shelby Davis has retired, however. As the chief investment officer, he spends more time actively picking stocks and searching for new investment opportunities.

The Davis strategy has historically focused on finding fundamentally sound growth companies that appear to be undervalued but have the potential for long-term outperformance. Says Davis: "What we do is try and buy a growth company at a value price. In practice, we're not looking for the most extraordinarily growth-rate companies, called the emerging-growth universe; instead, we are looking for big companies that are temporarily out of favor, but have a good long-term franchise and a good long-term growth outlook. For one reason or another, these companies are out of favor when we buy them. That's how we get the value part. To get the growth part, we study the company's long-term record."

These companies tend to be industry leaders run by extraordinary managers. They are also companies that have stood the test of time and can adapt to change. That's one of the reasons he especially likes financial stocks. "The product they deal with is money," Davis says. "Money doesn't go out of style; it doesn't get obsolete. Making a spread on money, between what you paid for it and what you lend it out at, is the second oldest business in the world."

When Shelby Davis decides to buy a stock, he likes to think he is buying a fractional interest in the underlying business, not just a piece of paper. "You want to be able to buy a stock as if you were willing to own 100 percent of the company for several years. If you are going to lose faith in that business or that company, then you shouldn't own the stock." Lack of conviction can be a real problem, according to Davis. "The most costly mistake is to buy a stock too high, have it drop, then sell it too low because you don't have conviction in what you own." If you have faith in the company, you'll be less apt to panic and sell out when prices start to drop, claims Davis.

"Another big mistake is not paying attention to the balance sheet," he adds. "If things go wrong, the balance sheet is often your safety net. If it's a poor balance sheet, then you have no safety net. You will fall right off the cliff into bankruptcy or a big hole."

Before investing in any company, Davis performs rigorous research, routinely meeting face-to-face with management to ask tough questions. Davis looks for managers "who don't just want to receive a diploma, but want to get on the honor roll. At a minimum, we ask management to tell us their three-year goals. We ask what their objectives are and what they're trying to drive the company toward. We talk about accounting, competitors, cash flow, and in general try to size up the management." He wants to know not only how much the company will grow in a year, but how it is going to do it. Then he decides whether the management can deliver or not.

Even though he meets extensively with management, Davis admits that it is possible to misread the signals. "Sometimes," says Davis, "you find out that managers are bluffers, not doers, always making excuses for their numbers. If management resorts to creative accounting practices to bolster earnings, when the collapse inevitably comes, it can be devastating," he explains. When Davis loses confidence in management or detects unusual accounting practices, he will sell the stock. He'll also sell if he feels a stock has become overvalued or when he sees deterioration in the company's growth prospects.

According to Davis, people lose money in the stock market because they act on hunches rather than spending the time to research the stocks they want to buy. He agrees with Peter Lynch, who says that people spend more time researching a microwave or automobile than a stock. "People will read all the car magazines, buy *The Blue Book*, know everything about the various models and go in and buy it. That's a $20,000 purchase that's guaranteed to go down in value over 10 years. If they had spent the same amount of time researching the companies they want to own, they are almost guaranteed over 10 or 20 years to make money."

Davis says that if there is a secret to investment success, it is the ability to think long-term. "We think beyond three hours, three days, three months or even three years, but think 30 years into the future. The eighth wonder of the world is the law of compound interest, and by being an investor in a company that can prosper over 30 years, you can benefit from that compounding." This is another reason Davis particularly likes insurance stocks, which he calls "compounding machines."

The best investors, say Davis, not only have vision and patience, but focus on quality. These are characteristics any individual investor can develop. Davis explains, "To focus on quality means looking for major companies that have been around for 10 years or more. You can study how they've acted and reacted in certain situations. To have vision, you need to make sure that you invest in an industry where the lights aren't slowly going out, like the steel industry."

Individuals who want to be successful investors should make investing a habit, just like eating and sleeping, says Davis. "Do it every week or every year and don't worry about the day-to-day market. You'll be buying in the high markets and in the low markets and it will average out. Take a 30-year view. Set up a long-term investment program. Believe in the future and buy quality companies at good prices."

◆ ◆ ◆

73. Wait on the sidelines

There are times when making no decision is the best decision. The pros refer to it as going to the sidelines. Donald Cassidy, author of *It's When You Sell That Counts*, says that the decision to hold a stock is just as important as the decision to buy or sell. Cassidy says that holding is comfortable for many investors because when a stock is a winner, it proves that we are smart. When the stock is losing money, we are hopeful it will recover one day. It is only a paper loss when you hold. It is a real loss when you sell.

It takes an incredible amount of patience to sit on the sidelines. William O'Neil says the first couple of years of a bull market provide your best opportunity for profitable sitting. Sometimes you have to sit tight before you can achieve huge profits during one of these periods.

Most pros recommend that individual investors resist buying or selling at every opportunity. You don't need to act on every tip, rumor, or recommendation. Experienced investors can tell you stories of stepping into a position too quickly when doing nothing would have been best. Even professional traders occasionally step back from the market to sit on the sidelines. It gives them time to think and to evaluate what to do next. If you ever feel confused about what to do next in the stock market, remember that doing nothing is a decision, too.

74. Use stop and limit orders

Among the most effective ways to automatically protect your gains and limit your losses are using stop and limit orders. With a stop or limit order, you instruct your brokerage to buy or sell when your stock has reached a specific price. The advantage of using these orders is that it frees you from constantly monitoring your stocks. These orders are very effective in automating the buying or selling of stocks. Unfortunately, they can be quite confusing. You should not use them until you completely understand how they work.

When you buy or sell stocks, there are basically three types of orders:

1. Market order. A market order means you will buy or sell a stock at the best available price at the time. When you place a market order, it is executed immediately. It is the most common order and is used when you want to buy or sell a stock at the current price.

2. Limit order. When you place a limit order, you instruct the brokerage to buy or sell a stock at the price you want or better. For example, when you put in a limit order to buy a stock at $20 a share, if the stock drops to $20 or lower, the order is executed. You might get it at $19.50 or $19.25 or maybe at $20, but never higher than $20 a share.

When you put in a limit order to sell a stock at $30 a share, if the price goes to $30 or higher, the order is executed and your stock is sold automatically. The disadvantage of the limit order is that on one hand, it limits your gains, and on the other hand, it doesn't protect you if the stock suddenly drops in price. When you put in a limit order, you are telling the market the price you'd like to buy or sell. The problem is, the market doesn't care. The stock could rise from $30 to $40 a share but you might end up selling it at $31. For this reason, there is some controversy concerning the limit order. A number of experts don't advise using it at all.

3. Stop loss order. The stop loss order is primarily used to protect investors from major corrections or crashes. It is like an insurance policy for investors. On the sell side, you place the stop loss a few points below the current price. When it hits the designated price, it becomes a market order. For example, let's say a stock you bought at $35 rises to $40 a share. You're afraid to sell because you think it might go higher. You want to protect your profits but also don't want to miss out if the stock rises to $45 or $50 a share. The answer: Place a stop loss at $38 a share. If the stock drops to $38, the order becomes a market order and is immediately sold. You locked in your gains and protected yourself from a major loss if the stock falls even further. You could keep adjusting the stop loss upwards as the stock price rises.

Some experts like the idea of a stop loss for individual investors because it forces them to sell losing stocks. For instance, you could put in a stop loss order that is 8 to 10 percent lower than the price you paid for it. The stop loss will force you to sell the stock for a predetermined loss before it falls any further.

Not all experts agree with using the stop loss. Peter Lynch writes in *One Up on Wall Street* that although you limit your losses with this method, because of market volatility, your stop loss will probably execute too soon. A portfolio of 10-percent stop losses will be a portfolio that is destined to lose that exact amount, he says. In addition, when you use a stop loss, you are admitting you will sell the stock for less than its worth.

In summary, the advantage of stop and limit orders is that they free you from worrying about when to sell a stock. However, it is highly recommended that you study the different variations of stop and limit orders before you use them. It can take some time to truly understand how they work.

75. View trading as a business

People who apply sound business practices to their investments have a huge advantage over those who don't. You are fortunate if you can read and understand financial statements, value a business, and invest as if you were running your own company. Even if you don't have these skills, you can still make money, but you may have to depend on others to do the calculations.

Wade Cook, author of *Wall Street Money Machine*, writes that when you run your own company, you understand pricing, buying and selling, employee relations, taxes, competition, and market share. Cook says the same knowledge you have about running a successful business can be converted to the stock market. The bottom line, according to Cook, is to generate profits.

Benjamin Graham said that many capable business people invest in the stock market without following the same guidelines that made them successful in the first place. He wrote in *The Intelligent*

Investor that if you want to be successful in the stock market, you must use accepted business principles. These include:

◊ Know your business.

◊ Don't let anyone else run it.

◊ Don't enter into a business operation unless you can produce a reasonable profit.

◊ Have the courage to rely on your knowledge and experience.

There are several ways an individual investor can learn how to run a business. One idea is to take classes at a local college or university. Students taking business courses will likely have a better understanding of the stock market than students majoring in other fields. Too many people, as Peter Lynch says, fail to realize a share of stock is part ownership in a business, not a lottery ticket. The goal is to appreciate the connection between investing in the stock market and running your own business. You are truly fortunate if you can do both.

76. Don't catch a falling knife

Many of the pros I spoke to admitted they occasionally try to catch a falling knife—or buy a stock immediately after it plummets. It is hard for anyone to resist buying a favored stock that drops because of a temporary setback such as missed earnings or negative news. If you liked the stock at $55 a share, you'll love it at $30 a share. In the mind of many investors, it can't go much lower.

Richard Johnson, portfolio manager of the Columbia Small Cap Fund, bought FPA Medical after it suddenly dropped in price. He explains what happened next: "The stock started coming down a lot. I thought I had better knowledge than the rest of the Street, based on the work I had done and my conversations with analysts. I thought the stock price was very attractive. I thought I had an edge when I didn't have an edge. Looking back, I should have waited until all the bad news was out." Fortunately, Johnson quickly corrected his mistake by selling it as soon as he determined his edge was lost. Meanwhile, the stock kept falling.

Often, there are specific reasons why a stock keeps falling. Johnson explained the so-called cockroach theory: When you see one, there are likely to be others. "When a stock disappoints, nine times out of 10 they will miss the next quarter," Johnson says. He adds that it is futile to try and catch a falling stock at the bottom. "You don't have to be a hero."

Although a number of professional money managers have successfully bought on the way down to double their profits, most agree that this is an extremely risky strategy. As one pro says, averaging down is a good way to ensure miserable results. To make matters worse, some investors add to a losing position, or buy more shares when a stock drops in price. When you're right, and the stock starts to do well, it can be extremely profitable. Keep in mind that the pros who add to their losers spend a huge amount of time reexamining the stock until they are convinced they are making the right decision. However, when they're wrong, they end up compounding their losses. One pro called adding to losers financial suicide. Another called it buying at a discount. The consensus from the pros is to avoid adding to a losing position, especially if you are a novice investor.

When a stock starts to fall, most pros suggest that you wait until you know exactly what is happening in the company. Remember that no matter how low a stock goes, it can always go lower. You don't have to catch it at the bottom to make money.

77. Don't worry about the dollar price of a stock

The most appropriate comment about the obsession many investors have about stock prices comes from Oscar Wilde, as pointed out by The Motley Fool: "Nowadays people know the price of everything and the value of nothing." It is true that many investors focus too much on the price they pay per share for a stock. They believe it is easier for a $5 stock to go to $6 than for a $50 stock to go to $60. Amy Domini, president of the Domini Social Equity funds, says this just isn't true. The market, she observes, is moved by well-informed decision-makers. These portfolio managers are evaluating each share on the basis of underlying value per dollar invested. This is completely different from the price per share that many individuals worry about.

"Sophisticated investors don't care what the stock's price per share is," Domini says. "They are buying $20,000 worth of stocks and they don't care if they are getting 10 shares or 10,000 shares." The mistake many individuals make is to shop around for a low-priced stock so they can buy more shares. Domini adds, "The decision to buy 100 shares defaults you into a higher-risk environment."

Domini says you should focus on the valuation price, not the dollar price. "If you won't buy something unless it is selling at least 25 percent less than last year, that is a valuation decision," she says. "But if you won't buy a stock unless it is $20 is like saying it must start with the letters, JQ. It is a random decision—worse than random."

The experts say if you have $5,000 to spend, you should buy the stock you want without worrying about the number of shares or price per share you think you can buy. For example, America On-line might be a better purchase at $75 a share than a stock in a struggling company selling for $5. Even though you can buy more shares of the $5 stock, it means nothing if the stock goes down in price.

78. Don't forget about the stocks you sell

Many individual investors, after selling a stock for a loss, refuse to have anything to do with the stock again. They take the loss very personally. The stock brings back negative memories. Richard Johnson, portfolio manager of the Columbia Small Cap Fund, says it's common for investors to take disappointing stocks off their radar screen. He explains, "It's much easier psychologically, especially if a stock disappoints. They sell it and they never think twice about it. The stock goes in the penalty box and investors wash their hands of it. That's wrong. Everyone does it, even institutional people. You get rid of it, you lost money on it, you never want to see it again."

However, many pros suggest that there are valid reasons for keeping close track of the stocks you sell. Johnson says that some of his best investment ideas come from things he's owned in the past. He says it's much easier to keep track of stocks you are familiar with. "You are leveraging off that knowledge base. You can get back to speed on the stock very quickly. If you watch it, you can see that things are getting better and you can make money on it and get your revenge on it."

One way to track previously sold stocks is by creating a paper portfolio or spreadsheet. After selling a stock, you make detailed notes of the date, price, reason for selling, and potential profit or loss. This is also an ideal way to determine if you are selling stocks too early, a common mistake made by many investors.

PART 8

GETTING HELP

79. Hire an investment advisor

It's not easy to find a competent, experienced, and objective financial advisor who will create an investment plan that will meet your financial goals. It's not easy, but it is possible. In fact, many people have turned to financial advisors to help them with the intimidating task of managing their personal finances, including taxes, insurance, estate planning, budgeting, as well as investments.

The hard part is figuring out what kind of advice you need and who is the most qualified to give it. Anyone can legally say they are in the business of giving financial advice. With little or no credentials, people can call themselves financial advisors, financial planners, or financial consultants, among other titles. It's even possible that some of these people have no formal education, qualifications, or experience.

If you are looking for someone to design a customized individual portfolio, you should hire a registered investment advisor. At a minimum, you should look for advisors who have earned a CFP (certified financial planner) designation. The best advisors will rarely work for clients with less than $100,000. Some have higher minimums ranging from $500,000 up to $3 million. There is a tremendous demand for the top advisors. That is why the minimums keep getting higher.

The three most common pay structures for advisors are fee-only, fee-based, and commission. Many experts consider the fee-only pay structure the best for clients. Under this arrangement, an advisor recommends financial products that best meets the client's needs, especially no-load or no-sales-charge securities. Clients pay a flat fee, often 1 percent of assets under management. The downside is that fee-only advisors have the highest minimums. The pros say that if you do find a fee-only advisor who is willing to take on a smaller client, the advisor is either inexperienced or unable to give you personal attention.

If you have a smaller portfolio, your only option might be a commission-based or fee-based advisor. The advisors most hazardous to your wealth are advisors paid by commission. Instead of getting objective financial advice, you could be directed to products that generate the most commissions for the advisor.

In the worst-case scenario, you pay three times. First, you might pay a flat fee to the advisor for recommending a financial plan. This is the fee-based pay structure. Next, you pay a commission for buying the financial product. Third, the product might contain hidden sales charges. According to many financial experts, it makes more sense to avoid advisors who are paid a commission for recommending certain products.

Robert Levitt, an investment advisor and partner at Evensky, Brown, Katz & Levitt, explains how to find a competent financial advisor. "A starting point is a referral from other professionals. There are also several publications like *Worth* magazine that annually list what they consider the top financial advisors. You should always interview the advisor. Focus on the advisor's background, academic degrees, and professional designations. There are many career changers who enter the financial services industry with very diverse backgrounds. While they may be trustworthy, they may not be competent. You should look for advisors with many years of experience."

Levitt also suggests that you ask potential advisors questions about investment philosophy and style, if they will design a customized portfolio, and what they do to minimize risk. The advisor should give you a written investment policy statement, he adds. You should also ask to see the ADV (advisor registration form), which lists qualifications, experience, and any history of disciplinary problems.

When you hire an investment advisor, he or she will design a personalized investment policy for you. This policy will list specific financial goals and the best way to meet those goals. For example, the policy might include ways to rebalance the portfolio, how to select tax-deferred investments, which securities should be held long-term or short-term, and how to allocate assets. The investment advisor analyzes your need for money now and in the future. He or she also performs a risk-tolerance interview.

Levitt says that it is sometimes difficult to find competent investment advice. "If you're competent, you stand out as being extraordinary. But you aren't necessarily extraordinary; you're just competent." Levitt says that there is no rule of thumb as to who is competent and who is not. He says the best investment advisors are passionate about their work. They must not only be skilled technicians, but also have the ability to communicate well with their clients.

Finally, not all people should hire investment advisors. If you are the kind of person who hates letting others control your money, you might want to consider managing your own account. For instance, some people have successfully turned financial planning into a hobby. You could find out more about the CFP designation by contacting the CFP board. The Web site is www.cfp-board.org.

80. Join an investment club

Many people have discovered that one of the most enjoyable ways to learn about the stock market is to join an investment club. A couple of years ago, the reputation of investment clubs got tarnished a bit when the most well-known club in the United States, the Beardstown Ladies, inadvertently miscalculated their investment returns. Instead of the 23.4 percent annualized return they claimed to have made in a 10-year period, they actually made 9.1 percent, considerably less than the S&P 500 during the same period. In other words, millions of books and videos later, the Beardstown Ladies would have done just as well in an unmanaged index fund. (However, I am told the entertaining book contains some excellent recipes and shouldn't be dismissed outright.) It is my opinion that one excessively careless error shouldn't take away from the thousands of successful investment clubs operating throughout the world.

According to the National Association of Investors Corporation (NAIC), a not-for-profit educational organization, investment clubs are for groups of 12 to 20 people who get together for fun, education, and profit. The first investment club in the United States began in 1900. The NAIC was organized in 1951 to help people set up their own investment clubs by providing educational materials, a magazine, and financial reports on more than 100 companies.

The NAIC estimates there are over 35,000 clubs in the United States with more than 700,000 members. For approximately $40 a month, you not only learn about investing, but also get to share your stock ideas with people who love the market as much as you do. It is not only fun but can be financially rewarding if the club is successful. Because you are putting in a set amount of money each month, you are utilizing dollar cost averaging, one of the most effective ways to invest in the market. This means you invest equal amounts of money at set intervals without worrying how the market is doing day-to-day.

The discussions are one of the most valuable features of an investment club. Since members do intensive research on individual stocks and report to the group, you will learn a lot about individual companies just by listening to the presentations. The members give detailed reasons why they think the club should buy or sell certain stocks. Eventually, the entire club votes on the stocks. Even if you don't agree with the final decision of the club, you can always buy the stock on your own.

Although investment clubs do not promise to make you rich, some of the older clubs have boasted about spectacular returns. For example, the NAIC reported that some members of the Mutual Investment Club of Detroit, one of the NAIC's longest running clubs, ended up with $100,000 or more by the time they were ready to retire.

◆ **Profile** ◆

Spiros Segalas

President and Chief Investment Officer,
Jennison Associates
Portfolio Manager, Harbor Capital Appreciation Fund

Spiro Segalas says his introduction to the stock market started when he was a kid growing up in New York City. His father, an immigrant from Greece, was a carpenter who went into the restaurant construction business after arriving in the United States. "My father worked day and night, seven days a week," remembers Segalas. "It was very hard work." As the elder Segalas became more successful with his business, he began investing his hard-earned money into stocks. Because he had some difficulty with English, every evening, the elder Segalas would ask his son to read the stock prices in the newspaper. "Some stocks went up, some went down," he laughs. In thinking about his future, Segalas concluded that learning to pick stocks would be a lot more fun than chasing after subcontractors. While a student at Princeton, Segalas began subscribing to a number of financial magazines, and after graduating invested in RJ Reynolds stock. To his amazement, it went up 50 percent, and Segalas has been hooked on the stock market ever since.

Segalas says he's been a growth manager all his life and has always looked for growth companies at reasonable prices. He favors high-cap growth stocks, and tries to identify companies that have a defensible franchise. "What I mean by that," he explains, "is that the companies should have something unique about them, such as technological leadership, a unique marketing position or a great trade name. I look for companies that have above-average financial characteristics, high margins, and high returns. I like companies that not only have earnings growth, but also have above-average sales growth. I try to identify companies that will grow 15 percent or more over time."

As a growth investor, he suggests it's also important to buy into the future growth of a company rather than into the past. Segalas gravitates toward technology stocks because he feels that's where the growth is. However, there are some companies, such as HMOs, that he will stay away from no matter how good the story is, even though some investors have made a lot of money from them. Explains Segalas: "If you are sick, you don't want your doctor to cut corners because he has to beat earnings. You want him to give you the best medicine and treatment that you need. It can be politicized when you are dealing with health. I prefer pharmaceuticals."

In addition to doing fundamental financial research, Segalas also likes to visit with management. However, he doesn't make his decisions alone, but also relies on the opinions of his research staff. "I try to surround myself with people who are smarter than me," he explains. "And basically, I make a judgment based on them, not just on the company's story," he says. "I have a feel for who is hot or cold, who is more conservative in their estimates."

Although Segalas says it's tempting to buy a lot of stocks when you manage a mutual fund, he forces himself to hold only 65 stocks in his Harbor Fund. "I tend to be fully invested all the time," he says. "I assume that if the market goes down, it will eventually go back up. That has worked for the last 30 years." Segalas admits that the toughest part of investing is deciding when to sell. "When you first buy a stock, you are at the height of conviction. You can probably think of 15 reasons to buy a stock, but once you own it, your conviction won't be as high or the same. If the stock goes up, you're wondering when to sell, and when it goes down, you're wondering what went wrong." Segalas feels that limiting the number of stocks in his portfolio to 65 stocks forces him to be disciplined about the stocks he sells. "What that means, especially when you are fully invested, is that there are times you have to sell something to buy something you like more. And that is not an easy decision."

To minimize risk, Segalas holds a diversified portfolio, with no more than 5 percent in any one security. Segalas also deals primarily with larger companies, which usually tend to present lower risk than smaller ones. "In terms of beta," Segalas says, "the portfolios tend to gravitate between 1.15 and 1.20." Segalas explains that beta is a numerical measurement of market volatility. The S&P Index, for example, has a beta of 1. Although Segalas doesn't use beta, he points out that a beta between 1.15 and 1.20 is slightly more volatile than the S&P.

With a quarter of a century of investment experience behind him, Segalas admits to making his share of mistakes. "Sometimes what appears to be a growth company turns out not to be," he claims. "We are all trying to make judgments as to the future, which can be a humbling experience. By sticking to your disciplines, however, you should enhance the probabilities of being right."

If there is a secret to being a successful investor, Segalas says he'd like to know about it. "I learn something new every day," he admits. "A lot of people think they know it all and it gets them into trouble. To be successful, you have to know your strengths and weaknesses." In addition, he believes there are many ways to be successful in the market, even though people have different styles of investing. "You have to know your style and stick with it and not get shaken when it's not working."

According to Segalas, one of the biggest mistakes individuals make is buying stocks they know nothing about. "You have to understand why you are buying something. A broker might call you up about a hot stock and after you buy it, it collapses, and you wonder why you bought it." Individual investors also make the mistake of buying stocks after they have made a big move. "They come in after the fact," he says.

For the individual investor, Segalas recommends dollar cost averaging. "Very few people can call the market. It's tricky to try and catch the bottom or top of the market. The people who make money over time invest consistently what they can afford to invest, and do it on a systematic basis."

◆ ◆ ◆

81. Practice by making paper trades

An extremely effective way of trading stocks without risking real money is to make paper trades. Many professionals make paper trades to improve their skills, to relax, and to test new stock ideas. You could be committing financial suicide if you invested in the stock market without first practicing on paper a few times. It's like stepping up to the plate in the middle of the World Series without first taking a couple of practice hits. If you are serious about the stock market, you might not want to invest until you know exactly how the game is played. If you are trading online and press the wrong button, it could cost you hundreds of dollars.

There are several ways to create a paper portfolio. The cheapest way to keep track of your investments is to use notebook paper. You start with a set amount of money, say $50,000, $100,000, or $1 million. You buy the stocks you like, making detailed notes of the number of shares you bought, how much you paid for them and your profit or loss.

A more practical way to practice trading is to sign on with an online service provider such as America Online, Microsoft Investor, or Prodigy. These online companies provide sophisticated tracking programs that allow you to create dozens of play portfolios. You can also buy a software program that tracks investments—for example, Microsoft Money, or Quicken.

There are also a number of stock market simulation games at various Web sites, which have become popular with all age groups. Some of these games give cash and other prizes to the top-performing winners. For fun and prizes, you get to test your stock-picking ability against other investors across the country.

Similarly, I helped an eighth-grade teacher in Barrington, Illinois, teach his students about investments by using the well-publicized Stock Market Game. For the chance to test their stock-picking skills against students in classes all over the United States, each class forms six-member investment groups. The results are tallied each day and entered into a national computer database. Each group is given $100,000 in play money to buy and sell stocks in a paper portfolio. Using the *Investor's Business Daily* or *The Wall Street Journal*, the students spent hours researching and reporting on the stocks they want to buy. The group that made the most money wins the game. Adding to the excitement and competition, every day the teacher announced who was in first place. It is my guess that more than a few portfolio managers will look back one day and credit the Stock Market Game for leading them into a successful career.

There are other benefits to using a paper portfolio. For example, you could create a portfolio devoted only to stock tips. Whenever you get a tip, you can pretend to buy the stock. This way, you can enjoy looking at how much money you saved by *not* buying a stock based on a tip.

82. Attend classes or financial seminars

One relatively inexpensive way to learn investment basics is to attend a class at a local college or university. Many of the classes are offered at night for a modest fee as part of the continuing education program. You not only benefit from the expertise of a knowledgeable teacher, but you get to share your financial experiences with other novice investors—and this can be the most valuable part of the class. Hopefully, the teachers are primarily interested in your financial future, and not in finding new clients or promoting commission-based products. For many investors, attending school is the most practical way to learn how to invest in the stock market.

Another alternative is to attend one of dozens of financial seminars, workshops, shows, and conferences offered throughout the country. In the last few years, possibly because of intensive media coverage of the market and increased participation in 401(k) plans, attendance at these events has multiplied. The purpose of many of these events is to bring the paying customer in close contact with as many investment gurus as possible. At some events, dozens of experts participate, from newsletter publishers to portfolio managers to financial television personalities.

In an article published in *Bloomberg Personal Finance*, Marlys Harris says that thousands of individual investors are flocking to shows and conferences to hear first-hand presentations by the Wall Street experts. However, not all seminars are the same. The trick, says Harris, is to separate the product seminars from the educational seminars.

Although some conferences seem like lengthy infomercials, investors can't seem to get enough of them. The exhibition floor, lined with hundreds of vendors, is particularly popular with the paying public, says Harris. A few of the more exclusive seminars offer participants dinner and entertainment. Not surprisingly, some are combining the financial seminars with a week-long cruise.

There is little doubt that many people benefit from attending classes or financial seminars. However, before attending a seminar, compare prices, topics, and speakers. Harris mentioned a couple of the most popular conferences, such as InterShow's Money Show, which attracts as many as 10,000 investors. In addition, the American Association of Individual Investors (AAII), has full-day seminars on the most popular investment topics. Also, the National Association of Investors Corporation (NAIC) puts on investor workshops and seminars. You can also attend the Morningstar conference, which offers lessons from many of the top pros in the industry, some of whom are profiled in this book. Finally, if you want to attend a seminar close to home, look in the community affairs or business section of your local newspaper, or get a catalog from the nearest university or community college. Adult education classes at a local high school can be just as educational. There are lots of opportunities for you to learn about investing. They may take some effort on your part, but could be well worth your time.

PART 9

TRADING PITFALLS

83. Don't go on margin

Some people, in an attempt to increase their stock market profits, will go on margin—borrow from their stock brokerage—to continue trading. The margin rules allow you to borrow against your own stocks as collateral. For example, if you own $10,000 worth of stock, you have enough buying power to purchase an additional $10,000 worth of stock by borrowing from the brokerage. However, these are not hard and fast rules, depending on brokerage margin formulas.

The liberal use of margin was one of the reasons the market crashed in 1929. At the time, investors were allowed to go on margin by putting only 10 percent down. At the market peak, people with little or no assets were buying stocks 10 or 20 times their net worth. With nothing but paper backing up their stock purchases, it was inevitable that the market crashed. As the market began its free fall, investors scrambled for cash to cover their margin loans. Those who didn't have enough money were forced to sell their stocks at huge losses, causing the market to drop even further. After the crash, the government increased the margin requirements to 50 percent, but it was too late for thousands of investors who lost everything.

You don't need a market crash to get into trouble with margin. All it takes is one losing stock. If you get caught on the wrong side of a trade, that is, when the value of your securities are worth less than 30 percent, the brokerage will initiate the dreaded margin call, demanding you pay off the loan immediately. You know you're in trouble when the brokerage calls every day for more money. If you can't meet the margin requirements, the brokerage will immediately sell your stock at current prices.

The biggest advantage of margin is that you use other people's money to increase your profits. If the price of your stock rises faster than the amount of interest you pay to the brokerage, you will do well. This is called leveraging. A margin account is also convenient. Although you have to pay interest on the money you borrow, the rates are lower than a credit card.

As you read in the introduction of this book, I also got into trouble with margin. The lenient rules of borrowing and my lack of self-discipline combined to lure me into borrowing twice as much as I could afford. I focused on what I could have made, not on what I could lose if I was wrong. Now that I no longer have a margin account, I not only sleep better, I have no fear of market crashes or corrections.

Although a handful of professionals recommend that investors use margin to increase profits, most financial experts believe it's a bad idea. They say margin is a risky strategy that could be disastrous to your financial well-being. Try to imagine the consequences if, while on margin, your stock fell by 50 or 75 percent. When the unthinkable happens, a margin loan is guaranteed to double your pain.

84. Don't day trade

Some people can't resist the thrill of buying a stock in the morning, then selling it a few minutes or hours later for a quick profit. It's called day trading, the ultimate in stock market excitement for people who love to gamble. With a personal computer and an Internet account, you're in business. A few people use their corporate account to trade at work. Others get so addicted to the market they quit their jobs to trade at home. It sounds great on paper: Work in the privacy of your own home, be your own boss, make as much money in a day as you can in a month. Many people don't realize that living off the stock market is a highly stressful, unpredictable way to make a living.

According to many experts, few people actually make money trading for a living, especially when you add commissions and taxes. David and Tom Gardner, The Motley Fool and authors of *The Motley Fool Investment Guide*, say that if you make only 600 trades a year (approximately two trades a day), even with minimal trading fees, it will cost you $18,000 a year in commissions. Actually, the Gardners' estimates are quite conservative. Some day traders make as many as 1,500 trades a year.

Devin Leonard, a freelance writer, wrote an article for *Smart Money* about people quitting their day jobs to trade at home. With an array of quote services and electronic gadgets, some day traders concentrate so much on their work during market hours they avoid talking to other people. He wrote about one day trader who sat in front of his computer 18 hours a day. Another day trader lost $55,000 on a bad stock pick but couldn't admit he made a mistake. He was so determined to be successful at something he sold his townhouse for more trading money. "This industry is littered with bodies," a trading coach warns.

Many professional traders who trade for their own account are addicted to the emotional excitement. Dr. John Schott, a psychoanalyst and portfolio manager of Steinberg Global Asset, says that many day traders are only moderately successful. "I did a study asking a group of traders to estimate what they have returned over the last year," Dr. Schott says. "Their overestimation of their success was astonishing. More than 80 percent exaggerated their success. They remember their successful trades but suppressed the bad trades. Most traders, after they sit down with their three-year record and calculate their actual return, would have been far better off in a balanced mutual fund. Very few traders actually do very well."

Dr. Schott says it's difficult to draw sweeping conclusions from his study because he was only measuring people who came to him with problems. He admits that some traders have done extremely well in the market, especially over the last few years.

Before you quit your job to be a day trader, you might want to take a couple of weeks off to trade stocks at home. Find out if you can actually make money during that two-week period. Keep in mind that many experts say that people with strong gambling instincts are particularly attracted to day trading. Remember that the computer is a trading tool, not a slot machine. My advice: If you're not sure of the difference, stop trading, turn off the computer, and read every lesson in this book.

85. Don't short stocks

A lot of people make money shorting stocks, betting that the price of the stock will go down, not up. You short a stock by borrowing the shares from the brokerage and selling them, waiting for the price to go down, then buying the borrowed shares back at the lower price. Your profit is the difference between the selling price and what you bought it back for. It works great when the stock goes down. In fact, short sellers hope the company comes as close to bankruptcy as possible. Unfortunately for short sellers, things don't always work out the way they'd like.

The most you can make on a short trade is 100 percent of your money. For example, let's say you short 100 shares of a stock selling for $20 a share. You borrow 100 shares from the brokerage for a total cost of $2,000 plus commission. If you are right, the price of the stock falls, perhaps to $10 a share. If you decide to buy the 100 shares of stock back at $10 a share, it will cost you $1,000 plus commission. Your profit is $1,000, the difference between the $2,000 you sold short and the $1,000 you paid to buy it back. If the stock fell to under a dollar, the most you could make is $2,000, or 100 percent of your money.

Think of what would happen if you were wrong and the stock went higher. How much could you lose? 100 percent? Nope. 300 percent? Nope. The answer is your losses are unlimited. If you shorted Dell or America Online and held on, hoping that the shares drop to less than $1, you'd be the one that lost money. Adding insult to injury, you are also charged interest on the money you borrowed from the brokerage.

On the other hand, professional short sellers make money on overhyped, fraudulent companies that are ridiculously overvalued. If you can find a stock that is heading for trouble, you can do well if you short it.

To be a successful short seller, you need to be somewhat cynical. After all, according to the experts, the market goes up much more often than it goes down. Dr. Schott puts it this way: "Short sellers get gratification from outsmarting the market. They get pleasure in other people's losses. If that's the kind of personality you are, if you are a negative person, you can make money on the short side."

Surprisingly, The Motley Fool believes in shorting stocks. The Gardners say in their book, *The Motley Fool Investment Guide*, that the risks of shorting are overblown. In fact, they call it a low-risk investment approach. However, they do follow a strict set of rules. For example, if the shorted stock goes up by more than 20 percent, they will buy the stock back for a loss.

The last couple of years have been rough for the shorts. I have friends who shorted Amazon.com and Yahoo!, claiming that these Internet stocks were outrageously overvalued. By traditional valuation methods, my friends were probably right. However, the stocks still doubled and tripled. Although you can make money shorting stocks, most experts agree it is a speculative game best played by professionals.

86. Don't try to time the market

Market timing means that you try and predict where the market is headed, then move in and out of stocks, bonds, or cash at the most opportune time. For example, let's say I accurately predict the Fed is going to raise interest rates. The market would probably react to this news by sending stock prices lower. So, in anticipation of this event, I sell all my stocks and move to cash. If I'm right, the market falls, allowing me to buy back my favorite stocks at bargain prices.

To be a successful market timer, you have to successfully predict the future. Some use sophisticated charts or technical data to determine the direction of the Dow. If you ask Martin Whitman, CEO of Third Avenue Funds, what the market's going to do, he'll answer, "I have no clue." Nevertheless, every day we hear public predictions about where the Dow is headed. Most pros agree, however, that it is nearly impossible to consistently time the market.

John Montgomery, portfolio manager of the Bridgeway Funds, conducted his own study. He found that only one in 10 market timing newsletters beat the market. Starting six years ago, he pretended to follow the advice of the one newsletter that actually beat the market. His conclusion: The one-time winner didn't beat the market for the following six years. "It is so hard to do market timing," Montgomery concludes. "The track record is abysmal. The problem is that you have to make two great calls, not just one. Even if you sold at the peak in August, 1987, missing the October crash, you'd have missed out on one of the biggest bull markets in the next decade."

Other studies also prove the futility of market timing. In his book, *A Zebra in Lion Country*, Ralph Wanger talks about one University of Michigan study that showed that the 90 best trading days accounted for 95 percent of the market's gains. Another long-term study showed that if the best 54 monthly returns were eliminated from 1926 to 1990, your return after 64 years of investing would be zero. Zero! This means that if you were out of the market on the best trading days, just 7 percent of the last 64 years, you'd make nothing. That's a frightening statistic for people trying to time the market.

Most pros recommend that individuals buy and hold stocks for the long-term or use dollar cost averaging, especially through mutual funds. With dollar cost averaging, you invest equal amounts of money at set intervals. Research indicates that people who try and time the market end up buying at the top and selling at the bottom. If you are constantly flitting in and out of the market, trying to buy and sell at the best times, it appears the only one who will get rich is your brokerage company.

◆ Profile ◆

David N. Dreman

Chairman and Chief Investment Officer,
Dreman Value Management
Portfolio Manager, Kemper-Dreman High Return Equity fund
Author, *Psychology of the Stock Market* and
Contrarian Investment Strategies

If you were looking for someone to symbolize contrarian investing, it would be David Dreman. For more than 20 years, Dreman has been a pioneer of the contrarian investment strategy, and is well-known on Wall Street for being one of its strongest supporters. The premise of his strategy is simple: Buy the cheapest, most beaten down, out-of-favor stocks in any given industry.

The contrarian philosophy came to him very naturally, he says, because of the influence of his father. "My father, who is now 88 years old and still trading in commodities, was very much an instinctive contrarian," says Dreman. "He always tended to go against the crowd. When everyone was sure of one course of action, it usually turned out to be the wrong one." Dreman says he was taught from an early age to challenge the opinions and research of the experts to make sure they could back up their findings with hard data.

Even in college he questioned the popular investment theories of the day, such as the efficient market hypothesis, which suggested that all the information about a company, the stock market, and the economy are reflected in a stock's price. This theory concludes that because the stock market is rational, no one strategy can beat it. "A lot of the economic theories bothered me. I was a reasonably good student, but I just couldn't accept perfectly rational behavior, because it didn't make sense in view of the things we saw in the manic-depressive nature of the market."

Later, while researching his first book, *Psychology of the Stock Market*, Dreman says he became aware of the importance of emotion when investing in the stock market. He noticed that investors had fairly consistent and predictable behavior patterns. "People were either overly pessimistic or overly optimistic," he suggests. Dreman theorizes that these emotional overreactions were causing stocks to be overvalued or undervalued. He believes that if you could understand and manage these emotions, you could beat the stock market. He spent the last 20 years developing the contrarian strategies and pointing out holes in the efficient market hypothesis.

For example, Dreman points to the frenzy that often follows the introduction of an initial public offering (IPO). "We're in a bubbly IPO market now and people are paying ridiculous prices for some types of stocks. There have been studies that show that there have been four of these bubbles since World War II. And when each of them pops, the average decline is something like 80 or 90 percent. It's staggering how much money is lost using these strategies." In spite of the studies, Dreman believes people will make the same mistakes over and over again. Why? Because it's human nature for people to go along with whatever is popular at the time. "Memories are just so short," he muses.

Dreman singles out the Internet as another example of investor overreaction. He admits that many of the Internet companies are solid companies, but says some are enormously overpriced. "For instance," he explains, "America Online, a very successful company, has 13 million subscribers today. In order to justify its price earnings, they would have to increase something like 120,000 times that in the next 15 years. If they could do it, their subscribership would have to increase from 13 million to 18 billion, or three times the population of the world. Yes, it's a great company, but it's priced too high when you look at the numbers." These popular stocks don't tempt Dreman. "There has to be a distinct separation between companies that are good companies and those that are terribly overpriced. It doesn't matter how good a company's goods or services are, if it's terribly overpriced, there will probably be a major correction to it at some point."

Rather than buy the hottest or most popular stocks, Dreman looks for the stocks of large companies that are unattractive or out of favor to other investors. To find these stocks, he uses objective measurements such as a low price-to-earnings ratio, low price-to-book, low price-to-cash flow, and high-dividend yield. He then picks out the stocks with the lowest 20 percent of whatever measurement he's using.

The contrarian stocks that Dreman likes are usually out of favor because of a negative short-term reason but usually have good outlooks for the future. "We want low market multiples, but at the same time we want better than market earnings growth over time, better-than-market revenue growth, a higher yield in the market and faster-growing earnings per share. We won't get all of these characteristics on one stock, but a lot of them can be found in stocks that are out of favor at one point in time."

It's not easy to go against the flow, says Dreman. "It means going against expert advice, going against rising stock prices, going against the thinking of very, very bright people who are all in the most exciting areas, such as the Internet." Many investors can't handle the loneliness of being a contrarian investor and eventually abandon the strategy. Dreman, however, never deviates from his methodical, disciplined approach. "No strategy is going to work every quarter," he suggests. "There will be quarters, or months, or even years when contrarian strategies won't perform as well as growth strategies. Studies have shown that this systematic approach has consistently outperformed the market over time."

Dreman diversifies to minimize risk. He owns more than 20 to 30 stocks spread out over 15 industries, limiting how much he invests in any one stock. "Contrarian stocks go down less in bear markets," Dreman claims, "which also gives us more safety." And the fact that he steers clear of the most popular stocks also minimizes risk. "The concept stocks are much more vulnerable to sharp market reactions on the downside than contrarian stocks."

Like most professionals, Dreman believes that it is essential that investors develop a selling discipline. Although Dreman doesn't set up price targets for his stocks, he sells without hesitation when the stock hits the P/E of the market. He admits that few of his stocks will reach the market P/E, which could go as high as 29 or 30. Dreman has other reasons for selling, too. "We will also sell if there is a problem with the company or there are unanticipated economic circumstances."

Dreman says he didn't always have such clear-cut selling rules, but admits he has learned from past mistakes. "Early in our career, we didn't have these rules and it proved very costly." Another past mistake he admits to is not paying enough attention to a company's earnings. "Since then, we've found that if earnings go down, it doesn't matter how cheap a stock is, it will probably underperform."

If the entire market crashes, Dreman suggests that you just hold on. "Stocks have been the best financial class over time," he maintains. "The best advice anyone ever gave me besides buy low and sell high, was buy value and hold on. Have patience and have discipline." For individual investors interested in buying mutual funds, Dreman has two final pieces of advice: 1) Stick with funds that use strategies that have outperformed the market, such as the contrarian strategies and; 2) stick with fund managers who have proven long-term returns. "Many money management firms and mutual fund companies have long-term records, but they're made by people who are long-gone. You really want to look at the record and make sure the people who built the record are still there."

◆ ◆ ◆

87. Don't trade futures contracts

When I was living in Chicago, many of my friends worked at the Chicago Board of Trade (CBOT), or the "pit," as it was affectionately known. The futures exchange was created to provide a market for pork bellies, hogs, cattle, corn, wheat, oats, and soybean, among hundreds of other commodities. A futures contract is simply an agreement that requires the holder to buy or sell a commodity at a predetermined price during a specified period of time.

It is estimated that speculators trade half the futures contracts on the CBOT. For only 10 percent down, a speculator takes huge risks for the chance to make large profits. Francesca Taylor writes in *Mastering Derivative Markets* about what really happens in the futures exchange: Traders stand in a pit for the contract they are trading. They use a system called "open outcry," which means traders must verbally announce the order and price to everyone in the pit. This allows everyone equal access to the same information. Traders must shout an order and a price and keep shouting until the order is filled. They simultaneously use hand signals to communicate with other traders. To an outsider, it looks like pandemonium, hundreds of men and women continuously shouting and waving at each other.

Most financial experts recommend that individual investors completely avoid trading futures. Of all the investments mentioned in this book, futures are the riskiest. One of my co-workers studied the future markets for a year, then bought a $5,000 orange-juice futures contract through a brokerage company. Unfortunately, the exchange imposed a price limit on his contract because of an announcement that bad weather could have a negative impact on the orange-juice crop. This meant that all trading on the contract stopped while the news was digested by the traders. My co-worker suffered through three days of panic waiting for trading to resume. When he was finally allowed to sell, he learned that the price of his contract had plunged during the three-day period. Because of the rule governing futures, he closed out his contract with a $20,000 loss, owing considerably more than what he started with. My co-worker vowed never to dabble in the futures market again.

If you feel compelled to trade futures, you should first read everything about it. Although the rewards can be great, the risks are extremely high. I have known people who have made hundreds of thousands of dollars in a few days and others who lost everything.

One way of dabbling in futures without risking too much money is to invest in a mutual fund that specializes in futures trading. Although the record is spotty, it is a lot safer than trading on your own. If you want to make a fast buck in the market, most pros recommend that you look anywhere but the futures exchange. However, if you are interested in learning more about trading in futures, the Chicago Mercantile Exchange maintains a Web site at www.cme.com.

88. Don't buy penny stocks

It doesn't matter how many times the experts warn people not to buy low-priced, speculative stocks, as long as there is a stock market, people will be drawn to stocks that are selling for under $10 a share, the so-called penny stocks. Everyday, thousands of investors pour millions of dollars into these stocks, relying on luck, the assurances of stock promoters, and hope to make money. While other investors go on to make and lose fortunes, the penny stockholders still wait, dreaming that one day one of their stocks will turn to gold.

On occasion, some of these stocks do hit it big. Iomega went from $2 a share to $55. America Online went from $11 to $130. But hundreds more are sitting in a place Ralph Wanger calls a hospice. He says only a few of these stocks get out alive. Some people are under the mistaken belief that low-priced stocks have a better chance of going higher. The experts say that just isn't true. According to William O'Neil, "Of the best performing stocks over the last 45 years, the average per-share price before they went on to double or triple was $28 a share."

For investors who feel they cannot afford to buy Coca-Cola or Microsoft, the penny stock seems like a bargain. For $1,000, instead of buying 20 shares of a $50 stock, you can buy 500 shares of a $2 stock. Many people believe they are risking less money because the price is low. The truth is, you are risking all of your money. No matter how low a stock goes, it can always go lower, especially if its earnings continue to fall.

You have a better chance of winning the lottery, says O'Neil, than having one of your penny stocks double. He calls them fourth-rate, "nothing to write home about" stocks. O'Neil says it is impossible to buy the best-quality merchandise at the cheapest price. Like so many things in life, you get what you pay for.

Many pros suggest that you not buy a stock that sells for less than $10 or $15 a share. If your stockbroker tries to talk you into one of these inferior stocks, they recommend that you take your business elsewhere. If it's a friend or acquaintance, listen, but politely decline to buy. Even if they promise you it's going to be the next Wal-Mart, wait until there's proof the stock will go higher before you even think about buying.

89. Don't buy stocks solely based on tips

Most experts say one of the biggest mistake investors make is buying stocks based on tips from friends, relatives, and co-workers. It is so easy for the right people to lure you into buying the wrong stocks. It is extremely difficult to ignore tips when they come from people you know and trust, people who want you to be successful. Family and friends give out stock tips because they want to be helpful. It also makes them feel important and smart.

Unfortunately, there are some tips that seem too good to be true. At a cocktail party, you might be talking to the successful CEO of a company who hints his company might be a takeover target. A stockbroker friend tells you to buy as many shares as you can afford of a company that's coming out with a revolutionary new product. Sometimes the tipster will secretly reveal that a company is on the verge of solving the latest national calamity. Peter Lynch calls these "whisper stocks." If you buy the stock immediately, whispers the tipster, you will make a fortune. Sometimes the tips are disguised as telegrams or special announcements. A few stock promoters send e-mails.

The tipster most hazardous to your wealth is the cheerleader. After recommending a stock, cheerleaders call you on the phone, double-check that you actually bought the stock, and if you didn't, remind you how much money you supposedly lost by not making the investment. If you did buy the stock, the cheerleader encourages you to hold on to it with comments like, "This stock is going to make you rich." Although these people mean well, they are not being objective. Some cheerleaders are acquaintances who have lost money on a stock and want you to buy it at its new, bargain-basement price. Unfortunately, these stocks never seem to recover from the basement. One pro says that stocks do not rise on hope alone.

The pros have learned from experience to pay little attention to tips. John Montgomery, portfolio manager of the Bridgeway Funds, says that tips are rarely profitable. When someone calls him up with a tip on a hot stock, he calculates it as a negative variable. In fact, he has found that stocks based on tips tend to underperform the market. Nearly all the professionals prefer to find their own stocks and not rely on tips from uniformed acquaintances or pushy salespeople.

Like other investors, I've lost money because of tips. A close friend of mine told me about a biotech company that was about to get FDA approval. He told me he was personally buying 20,000 shares of this low-priced, speculative stock. I did some basic research on the company and discovered that a well-known drug company, Warner-Lambert, was a major investor. Even though I had my doubts, I still bought 1,000 shares based on my friend's recommendation. Two years later, the company was still waiting for FDA approval. Although I dumped my shares in frustration a year ago, the last time I looked, the stock was down more than 50 percent. Ironically, shares of Warner-Lambert climbed much higher.

The overwhelming advice from the experts is to avoid buying stocks based on tips. Order *Standard & Poor's Research Reports*, study *Value Line* at the public library, and check what the stock analysts say about the stock. Like a reporter, make sure you can find two independent sources to verify that the stock is worth buying. Otherwise, find another stock to buy.

90. Don't buy stocks from strangers

Every year, people buy millions of dollars worth of stock based on advice from cold-calling stock telemarketers. It is estimated that the securities industry makes billions of calls every year to individual investors. Sometimes the caller is a first-year stockbroker working at a legitimate brokerage company trying to solicit new business. Other times, however, it is someone calling from an illegal boiler-room operation attempting to pressure you to buy the latest penny stock.

Some telemarketers will say anything to get you buy their stock. You might hear statements such as:

◊ "I guarantee you will double your money in a week."

◊ "You have nothing to lose by buying this stock."

◊ "You are one of the lucky few who have been chosen to receive this call."

Fraudulent telemarketers will whisper in the telephone, hoping to convince you that they are letting you in on a big secret. If nothing else works, they'll say the magic words that will persuade you to take out your checkbook: "This stock is going to be the next Microsoft."

Some telemarketers will call you back on a regular basis, trying to establish a relationship with you. After a while, they might call you by your first name and ask how your family is doing. They will tell you how much money everyone else is making on the stock. The telemarketers who are working illegally don't care what they say as long as you buy the stock.

John Montgomery says, "I'd rather throw darts at *The Wall Street Journal* all day long before I'd listen to a broker who called me on the telephone." He explains that a legitimate broker doesn't need to call you to solicit business. It is also impossible to check credentials or years of experience.

A very common investment scheme is the "pump and dump." Telemarketers will call hundreds of people to convince them to buy the penny stock of the week. Because so many people are buying the stock at one time, the price rises. This is the pump. After a week or so, the stock reaches an all-time high. At this point, the stock promoters sell all of their shares, pulling in a huge profit. This is the dump. The stock starts falling, dropping back to less than what you paid. There is a good chance the company will fold up and disappear one day, leaving you with nothing but pennies.

Because telemarketers often target people over the age of 50, the American Association of Retired Persons (AARP) conducts an anti-fraud campaign to help people deal with sales solicitation calls. AARP's advice: First, don't feel like you have to make a decision. Many people are hesitant to be impolite to persistent telemarketers. Remember that the caller is intruding on your time. Second, never give your bank account number or credit card number to people or companies you don't know. Finally, AARP says the best advice is sometimes the simplest: Hang up the phone. The quicker you get off the phone with telemarketers, the better.

91. Don't invest in bubbles

As defined by Wall Street, a bubble is a phenomenon that causes people to buy stocks or other securities at such a feverish pitch that it becomes a mania. Burton Malkiel, author of *A Random Walk Down Wall Street*, calls them speculative binges. In their frenzy to make a killing in the market, says Malkiel, investors will disregard common sense and reason to build what he calls castles in the air. On occasion, entire nations have been swept up in the mania.

The problem with speculative bubbles is that most participants do not realize they're in one until it's too late. Ralph Wanger says it ends when people stop and look around and wonder how anyone in his or her right mind would pay that much for a stock.

One of the most spectacular bubbles occurred in Holland during the 17th century. According to John Train, author of *Famous Financial Fiascos*, it was called tulip madness or tulip mania. People were willing to pay almost anything to own a single tulip bulb. The most sought-after tulip bulbs were actually beautiful mutations, says Train, which the Dutch called "bizarres." Speculators would buy one, then sell it immediately for a much higher price. Put and call options were invented at this time, giving buyers the contractual right to buy the tulip bulbs for a designated price on a specific date. The contracts were bought and sold as rapidly as the actual tulips. Train says the Dutch had a name for it: *windhandel,* which means trading air.

As the mania increased, speculators pushed the prices higher. At the time, people thought the tulips were wise investments. Some mortgaged their estates to participate in the frenzy. One "Viceroy" tulip bulb, for example, sold for "four oxen, eight pigs, 12 sheep, four loads of rye and two of wheat, two hogs heads of wine and four barrels of beer, two barrels of butter, and a half ton of cheese together with a quantity of house furnishings," says Train.

Many people believed the mania for tulips would last forever. When it finally ended, however, family fortunes were wiped out, there was widespread panic, and the Dutch economy collapsed. Fortunately, says Train, there has never been a reoccurrence of tulip mania anywhere in the world.

Nevertheless, you have to be unusually astute to recognize a bubble or mania while it is occurring. To some investors, the Internet stocks are likely suspects. Some Internet stocks, America Online, and Amazon.com, for example, confounded the critics by doing spectacularly well and backing it up with solid earnings. Others didn't do so well. Although it is fair to say that the Internet has not quite made it to mania status, a few pros respectfully disagree.

Even if you correctly identify a bubble or mania, it takes an incredible amount of self-discipline to refuse to participate. When investor emotion moves stocks to unrealistic levels, the pros suggest that you think about selling or reducing your position.

92. Don't fall for investment scams

Some people are so desperate to make a fortune in the stock market they will literally plead with strangers to take their money.

Sophisticated scam artists are more than happy to help unin-formed people lose money in the market by investing in bogus stocks or fly-by-night investment schemes. These scams have been extremely lucrative for criminals, costing investors billions of dol-lars every year.

A recent boom-and-bust story involved a Canadian gold mining company, Bre-X Minerals. The company rose from pennies per share to more than $280, making thousands of people paper mil-lionaires. Investors drove up the price of the stock to unsustainable levels, believing the company's claims of being the world's richest gold site. Later, tests revealed the company's claims were false. Af-ter the scheme was uncovered, the stock price plummeted, taking $3 billion of investors' money with it. What made this scandal worse was that so many stockbrokers, fund managers, and ana-lysts believed the spectacular Bre-X rags-to-riches story and backed it up with clients' money.

Many of the most publicized scams involve low-priced stocks trading for less than $5 or $10 a share, the so-called penny stocks. Duff McDonald, in an article for *Money* magazine, advises how in-vestors can avoid becoming victims of investment ploys. McDonald identifies the four most common ploys:

Inside information. Scam artists will promise huge gains in a period of days or weeks because they claim to have inside informa-tion. One woman lost more than $50,000 to a rogue broker who asked her to wire money for a stock to his personal bank account. McDonald recommends you never invest with a broker who prom-ises spectacular returns in a short period of time. If the broker pressures you to buy these kind of stocks, call the firm's compliance department, the state securities regulator, or the NASD.

Bait and switch. In this classic ploy, the dishonest broker convinces you to invest a small amount of money so he or she can prove to you what a great broker he is. After making substantial profits on the first stock, the broker tells that you if you want to make some "real" money, invest even more on the next stock. After you invest more money on the second stock, most likely an inflated penny stock, the stock doesn't perform as expected. The broker gets a larger commission, perhaps extra fees for recommending the stock, and you end up with huge losses. McDonald says you should refuse to go along with brokers who start small and then ask for a much larger contribution.

Trading without permission. Because stockbrokers are paid by commissions and other fees, unethical brokers are encouraged to make unnecessary trades on your behalf. To protect yourself, McDonald recommends that you check the broker and the firm's record with state regulators and the NASD. If you feel that the broker is pressuring you to trade, after complaining to the compliance officer and state regulators, move your account to another firm.

Risky stocks. McDonald writes about a woman who, at the urging of her broker, lost more than $200,000 in the market investing in a questionable Canadian telecommunications company. All she wanted was a safe place to put her money during retirement. What she got was an extremely risky stock. The broker was subsequently fired from the brokerage, but not before defrauding four other clients over a six-year period. If the broker pressures you to invest in anything that makes you uncomfortable, immediately switch your account.

The best way to protect yourself from investment scams is to look for unusual trading activity. Criminals are getting more sophisticated, using the Internet and expensive computer equipment to separate you from your money. Criminal stockbrokers or financial advisors will change their names so you can't check their references or records. Others will send you false quarterly statements to fool you into believing your investments are actually making money.

To prevent these types of scams from succeeding, you should stick with reputable brokerage companies and stockbrokers. One of the most effective ways to foil scam artists is to do your homework. These criminals are often successful because their intended victims don't ask enough questions or read the fine print. Unethical stockbrokers or financial advisors will do anything to keep you in the dark and dependent on their advice. The less you know about the investment, the more likely the scam is to succeed. Remember, the remedy for "too-good-to-be-true" investments is a large dose of knowledge.

◆ Profile ◆

Louis Navellier

President and CEO,
Navellier & Associates
Editor and publisher, *MPT Review* newsletter

Louis Navellier is proud to call himself a *quant*, the nickname for quantitative analyst. This means he chooses stocks based upon an analysis of quantitative data using sophisticated computer models. In other words, he finds the best stocks by crunching numbers on his computer.

Navellier's interest in quantitative analysis began when he was a finance student in college. At the time, Dr. Harry Markowitz's Modern Portfolio Theory (MPT) was gaining in popularity. The idea behind this theory was to show investors how to maximize returns while minimizing risks. An intensive amount of analysis and experimentation was conducted on MPT beginning in the 1950s, with much of the research arriving at a similar conclusion: Because the markets were efficient, it was nearly impossible to use MPT to beat the market.

By the time Navellier graduated from college, he decided that the findings on MPT were unacceptable, so he began conducting his own research. He also had the good fortune to do some mainframe programming for one of his college professors who worked for Wells Fargo Bank. "The bank was trying to start their first index fund and they were trying to mirror the stock market." They couldn't manage to match the market; instead, they managed to beat the market. "We tried to figure out why we did better than the market," remembers Navellier. So Navellier developed a number of computer models to analyze the stocks included in the portfolio. It was then that he discovered *alpha*.

Alpha measures a stock's performance independent of the market. In other words, it is how much the stock would return if the market earned nothing. Alphas can be positive, negative, or zero. Navellier says his computer analysis showed that alpha was essential to identifying stocks that were likely to outperform the market. "High alphas are important for our long-term success," he says. "A lot of times if the market gets choppy, high alpha stocks will do better. They get more consistent performance regardless of what happens to the underlying market." To share his research findings with other investors, Navellier began writing and publishing the *MPT Review*, an investment newsletter devoted to finding high alpha stocks.

Navellier says his computer-generated model portfolios, which can be found in the 19-year-old *MPT Review*, have been proven successful at beating the market. "I can't say my philosophy is growth investing or value investing. But it is disciplined quantitative analysis. We're constantly testing what works on Wall Street, and we're constantly refining our models. What we do at our firm is build different models for stock-picking methodologies."

Although most subscribers to his newsletter are brokers, Navellier says that individual investors can also find it useful. "We recommend that people follow the model portfolios in our newsletter," he says. These model portfolios consist of stocks that have been thoroughly analyzed by Navellier and a team of analysts.

First, Navellier runs the stocks through a series of quantitative screens, with alpha as the primary return indicator. "The purpose of quantitative analysis," explains Navellier, "is to maximize return and minimize risk." To determine a stock's risk factor, he takes alpha and divides it by a stock's volatility to get the risk-adjusted alpha. "We call it the Risk-Reward Alpha," he adds. He also evaluates other fundamental data such as operating margins. "We only like stocks with expanding operating margins," says Navellier. "My average stock has shown 59 percent revenue growth in the past four quarters. Business is good if sales growth is up 59 percent."

Navellier recognizes that his computer-generated method of picking stocks might seem a little clinical, but he claims it's one of the reasons his newsletter has been so successful. "The way we like to describe it is this: If we were flying an airplane and it was a nice day outside, we wouldn't even look out the window. We'd fly by instruments. This is how we pick stocks and it is totally automated, totally unemotional and I think that's what made us successful."

The average investor, he says, gets too emotional about stocks. With his system, not only does a computer make the selections, it also decides the best mix of stocks for a particular portfolio by recommending specific weightings for each stock.

Although there is little room for human error with Navellier's system, it is possible for the computer to occasionally be fed bad data. "Sometimes the accounting data we receive from a company is bogus," he admits. As an example, he tells about a company that made a $100 million accounting error during a merger. "Fortunately, we didn't buy that stock because the company didn't reinvest in itself. Another one of our criteria is the internal reinvestment rate. When a company doesn't reinvest in itself, something is wrong," he says. He agrees that had the erroneous accounting data been entered into the computer, the results may have been different.

To minimize risk, Navellier says the first rule is to diversify. "When you diversify," he adds, "you have to be careful where you put your money. It is very rare for me to put more than 10 percent in any one group." The second rule is to try and mix strategies. "If you mix a growth strategy with a value strategy," claims Navellier, "risk goes down. If you mix a large-cap strategy with a small-cap strategy, risk goes down."

When it comes to selling stocks, Navellier again counts on computer analysis. "We use optimization models that tell us which are the best stocks and how many shares we should own. We also use our Risk-Reward analysis." When stocks become too risky, they will be sold. For example, Navellier says the computer indicated the tech stocks were becoming too frothy, so he trimmed back, removing the froth out of the portfolio. "We sold good stocks to buy better stocks," he says.

Many individual investors, he suggests, would do well to follow that strategy. "I think investors should constantly be selling good stocks to buy better stocks." When buying individual stocks, Navellier believes individual investors should begin with mutual funds because they are safer. "You don't want people to throw all their eggs in one basket and get burned. Start off with one mutual fund." Then, he says, as they gain more experience, they can move into individual stocks, following the model portfolios in his newsletter.

◆ ◆ ◆

93. Don't squander money windfalls

It is always surprising when you read about someone who wins the lottery and ends up bankrupt a couple of years later. You wonder how someone could receive so much money and end up losing it all. Sadly, the newspapers are filled with stories of hapless people who inadvertently lose huge sums of money to investment scams or speculative stocks.

My accountant told me about a married couple who inherited more than $100,000. They immediately bought 10,000 shares of a $9 computer software stock based on a tip from a knowledgeable friend. Within six months, the stock had risen to more than $20 a share. They sold the stock for a huge profit, doubling their inheritance to $200,000. The only lesson they learned is how easy it is to make money in the stock market. Later, they heard about an even better stock that was certain to double in six months. With an eye on becoming millionaires, these people went on margin (borrowed from the brokerage) to invest $300,000. Their entire net worth was tied up in this one stock. Unfortunately, this time they weren't so lucky. When the stock fell by more than 50 percent one day, they were left with more than $100,000 in debt. They ended up financially and emotionally devastated.

Humberto Cruz, a syndicated national financial columnist for Tribune Media Services, wrote an article about what he did with $75,000 in real estate profits. He began by asking his co-workers what he should do with the money. One guy suggested that Cruz should invest his money in stocks that will go up. Another suggested he use the windfall to pay off the mortgage. By the end of the column, Cruz concluded that individuals must decide on their own what to do with their money. By the way, Cruz wouldn't reveal what he did with the $75,000 because he was afraid his readers would blindly follow his lead.

If you unexpectedly receive an inheritance, lottery winnings, or other financial windfall, after you celebrate, you might want to consider a money market account or other cash vehicle until you have a sensible investment plan. Your goal is to put your money to work without risking your principal. If you receive a huge windfall, you could also consider hiring an experienced, competent fee-only investment advisor.

In addition, you shouldn't do anything sensational like quitting your job or buying a new house until you actually receive the money. Because of taxes and special arrangements, you may not receive as much money as you planned for. For example, a $300,000 windfall sounds great—until you learn it's distributed in equal payments over 10 years.

It is essential that you avoid investing directly in the stock market until you have taken the time to study all of your options. Remember, the stock market will still be there when you are ready to invest. The pros say you are most vulnerable to receiving bad advice when the check is in your hand. If you feel compelled to participate in the stock market but don't know what stocks to buy, put your money to work in a professionally managed mutual fund. This will buy you time until you have learned how to buy stocks on your own. If there is anything you should have learned from this book, it is that uninformed people with a lot of money could lose their shirts in the stock market.

94. Don't buy stocks that get too much publicity

All you have to do is look at history to see what happens to stocks that get too much publicity. In 1720, a group of British investors, with the blessing of the British government, issued stock in their company, the South Sea Company. John Train recounts what happened next in his book, *Famous Financial Fiascos*. The stock jumped from £129 to £160, instantly making a number of people paper millionaires. When members from the House of Commons began to buy shares, the stock rose as high as £390.

Poets were so taken by the South Sea Company that they wrote poetry about it. (Jim O'Shaughnessy, CEO of O'Shaughnessy Capital Management, jokingly says when they start writing poetry about your stock, you better think about selling.) Unfortunately for thousands of unlucky investors, including Isaac Newton, the stock collapsed. It fell from a high of £890 back to £135. Train quotes Newton: "I can calculate the motion of heavenly bodies but not the madness of people."

Many investors make the mistake of buying last year's hottest stock. Often, by the time they read about it in the newspaper or a book, it is old news. Even worse, they'll buy the stock at its all-time high. It's not just stocks that get too much publicity. Sometimes, mutual funds suffer from this affliction. If too much new money comes into their fund, especially from investors who have no idea what they're buying, there's a danger the fund will become a victim of its own success. Several of the year's hottest, most popular mutual funds crashed and burned after people rushed in to buy during the height of the bull market.

Sometimes the hottest mutual funds of the quarter or year are funds that invest in one small sector, for example, biotech stocks. Just because they performed well during one quarter doesn't mean they will do well in the future. As these funds begin to falter, some frantic investors immediately withdraw their money. To counteract this problem, a number of mutual fund companies close their doors to new investors before the fund gets too big.

Individual investors have to be especially careful when considering hot, overhyped stocks. Because the expectations of these stocks are so high, if one falls short of its earnings by even a penny, the stock could get hammered. Dr. John Schott agrees: "A lot of people's first investments are in stocks that are way too popular and they get killed for it. These stocks are most vulnerable to earnings disappointments."

95. Don't act on rumors

There is an old Wall Street saying that you should buy on the rumor and sell on the news. More than likely, people who try and follow this risky strategy get burned. "It's a loser's game," one fund manager says. Most pros insist that by the time the individual investor hears the news, it has already been reflected in the stock's price.

The biggest problem with this strategy is that it's extremely difficult to distinguish between a rumor and news. Some investors dig through the Internet chat rooms looking for juicy rumors or inside information. Some people believe the chat rooms are a useful way of getting an edge on Wall Street. Anyone who has spent more than a few minutes in a chat room knows this is a huge stretch. Although I can't prove it, I'm not convinced that many investors profit from chat room gossip. In fact, short sellers have been known to go online and spread destructive rumors about companies, hoping to drive the price of the stock down. If you're looking for legitimate news and information about your stocks, you might think twice before logging on to an equity chat room.

Sometimes the rumors begin on the floors of the stock exchanges. On November 16, 1996, the Dow was up more than 65 points and headed for another record close. A rumor circulated that Abby Joseph Cohen, a well-known strategist for Goldman, Sachs & Co., had reversed her previously bullish forecasts. On the rumor that Cohen was bearish, the Dow reversed course and dropped fast. By the time Cohen was notified about the circulating rumor, the Dow had fallen by over 60 points.

Cohen was pulled from a meeting and asked to speak by intercom to Wall Street traders and brokers to assure them that she was still bullish on the market. After Cohen made a few positive comments, the market reversed course again, ending the day up 35 points.

There are people who make a living out of spreading rumors on Wall Street. They will try every conceivable way to get false information into the media. Usually, they are unsuccessful in affecting the entire market but sometimes manage to snare a few unsuspecting individuals who don't have the discipline to stick to their strategy.

In general, the pros strongly recommend that individual investors leave rumors alone and focus on the facts. It's what Jim O'Shaughnessy calls the Joe Friday school of investing: "Just the facts." If you must have access to minute-by-minute news, watch CNBC, CNNfn, or stick with Internet news sites like Yahoo! and CBS MarketWatch, to name only a few.

96. Don't do anything illegal

A lot of people think the stock market is a rigged game that average people can't win. According to this theory, the only way to make money in the stock market is to cheat or become friends with people in the know, company insiders.

Unethical stock promoters take advantage of investors' greed by acting as if they have inside information, which happens to be illegal. For instance, someone might whisper that the FDA is going to approve a new drug, that a company is a takeover target, or the company's earnings report will be better than expected. Others might confess that they could get in trouble for telling company secrets but they will risk their jobs and jail time to tell *you*, a total stranger, how to make money. It is hard to resist buying a stock when someone tells you the information is secret.

J. Morton Davis, author of *From Hard Knocks to Hot Stocks*, writes about a Harvard Business School classmate who foolishly paid a stockbroker a fortune for what the classmate thought was insider information. The information was really just a collection of rumors. With every supposedly new inside tip, the classmate lost money. The stockbroker kept promising the classmate he would make it up on the next transaction. The broker urged the classmate to go on margin to make even more money. In the end, the classmate lost everything he invested. The moral of the story, according to Davis, is to do your own research and trust your own judgment.

The best advice for individual investors is to walk away from people who act like they know too much. The more they claim to know, the faster you should walk away. Wall Street is littered with hard luck stories of people who lost everything because they tried to rig the game in their favor. If you believe in yourself, if you are willing to work hard, it is possible for you to make money in the stock market without doing anything illegal or unethical.

97. Don't make stock deals with friends

I can speak from experience about how dumb it is to try to help your friends make money in the stock market. At first, I gave out free stock tips to my closest friends, thinking I was doing them a favor.

For example, I gave my first stock tip to a co-worker who needed the money to pay her bills. She reluctantly took out $2,500 from her emergency savings account to invest in the market. Although she would have been better off in a mutual fund, I mistakenly recommended that she put the entire amount in one highly aggressive computer stock. The stock went down, which made her extremely nervous. It was this woman's first experience with the market and she didn't know what to expect. Every day, she complained about how much money she was losing. Because I was uncomfortable with her complaints, I told her to sell the stock for a small loss. To relieve my feelings of guilt, I wrote her a check for the amount she lost and vowed never to give out a stock tip again. Ironically, the stock I recommended, Compaq, rebounded sharply after she sold all her shares.

I set up a more elaborate stock deal with a friend struggling to pay for college. I wanted to show her how quick and easy it is to make money in the market. Because she only had a few hundred dollars to invest, the only way I could quickly double or triple her money was to buy call options, a very risky and sophisticated investment. Options are not recommended unless you are extremely knowledgeable and experienced. As it turned out, the investment was successful. I doubled her money within a week. However, for a few hundred dollars profit, it cost me an incredible amount of time and energy. Because of the way options are traded, I was continuously monitoring her investment, making sure I sold it at the best price. In the end, although she doubled her money, she learned nothing about investing.

The best way to help others learn about the stock market is to teach them how to do it on their own. If you want to show your friends how to invest, teach them how to set up an account with a mutual fund company or discount broker. You can also recommend books to read or suggest that they join a local investment club. Most important, let them take personal responsibility for their financial affairs and not depend on others to make all their trading decisions.

◆ Profile ◆

Martin J. Whitman

CEO and Chief Operating Officer, Third Avenue Funds
Portfolio Manager, Third Avenue Value Fund
20-year member, Yale Graduate School of Management
Author, *Value Investing: A Balanced Approach*

Marty Whitman learned an important lesson when he was a stockbroker: People waste too much time trying to figure out what the stock market will do. According to Whitman, it makes more sense to master the financial side of the business rather than pay attention to the abnormal psychological side. After coming to this conclusion more than 20 years ago, he spent his career studying businesses, taking apart balance sheets and becoming an expert on mergers, acquisitions, and takeovers.

From Whitman's perspective, one of the first rules of investing is to buy good, safe companies at bargain prices. To find stocks that qualify, Whitman looks for companies that exhibit the following four characteristics.

First, he wants to see a company with an extremely strong financial position. Second, a company must be reasonably well-managed. Third, a company must have an understandable business. For Whitman this means, at a minimum, that the company must meet all SEC disclosure requirements and have issued audited financial statements. Whitman believes these documents provide reliable and objective financial information about a company. Finally, he doesn't like to pay more than 50 percent of what he thinks a business is worth.

To learn whether a company meets these four criteria, Whitman and his colleagues perform extensive trial-and-error research. They pay little attention to what the stock market is doing, but instead focus on the crucial elements of each business—what Whitman calls the fundamentals. As a value investor, Whitman believes that the cheaper you buy, the greater the reward and the less risk you take. Says Whitman, "We buy what is safe and cheap."

Although Whitman and his associates try to adhere to their established criteria when picking stocks, he admits it's sometimes hard to find companies that possess all four: "Take for example, the criteria that a company should be reasonably well-managed. This is usually the most difficult element for us to analyze. The way management entrenchment and compensation has grown in the past 20 to 30 years, there hardly exists management that doesn't have some conflict of interest with outside shareholders. If we didn't compromise a little on the criteria, we'd never buy anything. We have to be flexible." Rarely, however, will he buy companies that are undercapitalized.

Although many investors believe diversification minimizes risk, Whitman doesn't put much emphasis on it. "If you are running your own business, you're not going to diversify by buying common stocks. You will put all your resources, both financial and human, to try and make the business a success. That is one end of the pole. On the other end of the pole are academic, efficient market theorists who know nothing about the companies they're investing in. Certainly they should diversify. Diversification is a substitute for knowledge, control, and price-consciousness."

He also strenuously objects to the word "risk" without an adjective in front of it. Says Whitman: "We hope to avoid investment risk. We take huge market risk, but we don't pay attention to it. We only try to minimize investment risk. Right now, we're huge investors in Japan, but we don't take any currency risk because we hedge the currency. You have to know what you're doing," says Whitman. He believes that knowledge and extensive research—knowing the critical information about a company—is the best strategy for minimizing risk.

As a rule, Whitman prefers to buy and hold securities for long periods of time, which is why the average turnover of his fund averages 10 percent. Whitman will sell a stock, however, if he sees what he calls a permanent impairment of capital, or something that is going wrong with the business. "The most common permanent impairment of capital we found was dissipation of strong financial positions, loss of market position, or surprises from left field." He adds, "We don't see that too often, although in small cap stocks we see it a lot. It's hard to predict."

Whitman says there is a difference between a temporary loss and a company that has a permanent inability to rebound. If the underlying business and financial position of a company has deteriorated to the point where it is permanently damaged, Whitman will sell. "We never sell just because we think there might be unrealized market depreciation," he adds.

Safety and long-term performance should be important considerations when choosing investments, advises Whitman. The best investors, he adds, analyze a business—it's dynamics and value—and then stop. They don't carry the excess analytic baggage that most carry. "Dividend rate, gross national product, interest rates, stock market technical consideration, quarterly earnings—all that is excess baggage that has nothing to do with the underlying business. The very best investors focus on the business and don't try to figure out where a common stock will sell in the market."

That is why Whitman believes it is a mistake to pay too much attention to the market. "Most people are very short-term oriented and very much influenced by market prices. They play the market for the short-term. It's a casino game. Institutions sometimes make the same mistake that individuals do."

On a final note, Whitman firmly believes that the individual investor should invest in mutual funds. "Investment companies regulated under the act of 1940 are good for the individual investor because with these instruments he is not going to get ripped off as he has historically in some tax shelters and trading systems. There is great safety in investing with mutual funds," says Whitman. "You get an honest shake, low fees, the fund can't borrow a lot of money, and nobody can steal from you because you have a custodian."

◆ ◆ ◆

98. Don't invest in initial public offerings (IPOs)

Initial public offerings, also known as IPOs, refer to the process by which a private company converts to public ownership. The company first sells the stock to an underwriter, who then resells it to investors at a prearranged price. By going public, a company can raise large sums of money. This money is then used to help the company pay off debt, expand the business, and grow.

Many investors, hoping to uncover the next Microsoft success story, are lured into buying IPOs at whatever price they can get. However, a number of pros believe that IPOs can be dangerous for the individual investor. David Dreman writes in his book, *Contrarian Investment Strategies*, that investors are too eager to jump into new issues. "People are captivated by exciting new concepts," he says. "The lure of hitting a home run on a hot new idea overwhelms caution. The sizzle and glitz of a public offering like a Planet Hollywood at 140 times earnings and 13 times revenue is just too great." The truth is, says Dreman, studies show that for every Microsoft, there are many others that never make it.

If you cannot resist the excitement of investing in a risky but potentially lucrative start-up company, begin by doing your homework. This is essential if you're going to invest in an unknown company with no earnings history. To protect yourself, you should carefully read the prospectus, take apart the balance sheet, and find out everything you can about the people running the company.

Most important, don't buy an IPO based on the recommendation of a cold-calling stock promoter or novice stockbroker.

One way for you to check out the financial background of the IPO is to stop by Dun & Bradstreet's Companies Online Web site at www.companiesonline.com. Although registration is free, the report costs $20. If you'd like an updated list of IPOs, you can also look at a copy of *Investor's Business Daily* or *The Wall Street Journal.*

The most important question is: Are IPOs good investments? According to the experts, it is extremely difficult for individuals to make money on an IPO. The hottest new issues are usually allocated to well-connected customers or knowledgeable speculators. Often, they sell their shares after the first day, realizing a substantial profit. The bottom line from the experts: If you are an individual investor, you might want to find other places to put your money.

99. Don't ignore the warning signs

One of the mistakes that individuals make is thinking that a stock that is going down in price must be a bad stock. According to many pros, that is one of the least important indicators of a stock headed for trouble. Instead of looking at the stock price, experienced investors look within the company for warning signs that could lead to future problems. One of the reasons the pros spend so much time talking with management and looking at fundamental data is to try to uncover any accounting irregularities or unusual activities.

In particular, the pros get suspicious when they see any of the following warning signs, as pointed out by *The Stock Detective*, an online newsletter at www.stockdetective.com. These include:

◊ Weak fundamentals. The pros use fundamental analysis to take apart a balance sheet looking for high debt, exaggerated sales and earnings, excessive expenses, and high valuations.

◊ Suspicious backgrounds. *The Stock Detective* suggests you look closely at the prospectus, especially the backgrounds of company management. How much experience does the CEO have? Does this person have experience with turnaround situations? Is the company stacked with relatives of the CEO?

◊ Excessive executive compensation. The pros like to see manager salaries tied to performance. You should be alert, however, to managers who are excessively compensated; in other words, given millions of dollars and options even when the company isn't performing.

◊ Reverse stock splits. According to *The Stock Detective*, a reverse stock split is initiated to improve the public perception of a company. For example, with a 1-to-5 reverse stock split, a stock selling for $1 a share will now sell for $5 a share. Although this initially raises the price of the stock, after a reverse split, instead of owning 1,000 shares, you now own 200 shares. Unlike a normal stock split that usually occurs when everything is going well for a company, a reverse stock split is often based on weakness and marketing hype.

These are just a few of the warning signs the pros look for when evaluating a company. When pros uncover serious abuses overlooked by Wall Street, they might short the stock; that is, make a bet the stock will go down in price, not up. For most investors, however, the best advice is to be alert for any warning signs that could indicate a stock is headed for a fall.

100. Don't buy options

Whenever I'm in the mood to lose money, I buy options. To be fair, there are a number of option strategies that some pros call conservative, although I think that's stretching it a bit. Nevertheless, options are almost as exciting as trading futures contracts, without the same level of risk. With futures contracts, you can lose more money than you invested. With options, you can only lose all of your money.

The two most popular option strategies are the call and put. A call option gives you the right to buy a stock at a specified price. A put option allows you the right to sell a stock at a specified price. You have the right to buy or sell the stock, but most people don't exercise their right. They simply buy and sell the option. The fascinating part about options is you don't have to own the stocks to trade them.

For example, let's say that Cisco Systems is selling for $70 a share. You like Cisco a lot and think it will rise to $75 a share. So you decide to buy a call option with a strike price of $75. If Cisco does rise above $75, you will be "in the money." If it rises as high as $80 or $90, you could make a lot of money. But there's a catch: When you buy the option, you also have to specify a time period, usually three or four months from the date of purchase. What this means is Cisco must rise above the specified price before the expiration date or you lose your entire investment.

When you call your broker, you say: "I would like to buy five May contracts with a strike price of $75 a share." Each contract is worth 100 shares of stock. So Cisco has to rise to $75 or higher before the third Friday in May for you to make a profit. How much will this cost you? The later the target date, the more it costs. For example, the May contracts for Cisco cost $4 each. If you buy five contracts, that will cost you $2,000 (500 x $4). The August contracts cost more, perhaps $6 per contract.

So you buy the May contracts for Cisco at $4 each, which costs $2,000 plus transaction costs. Let's say Cisco rises to $75 immediately. You are now "at the money." By a stroke of luck, Cisco rises to $80 a share. You have nearly doubled your money. You also have the right, but not the obligation, to buy Cisco stock at $75 a share. Nevertheless, for only $2,000, you are controlling $35,000 worth of stock.

The downside is a lot of things have to go right for you to make money. First, if Cisco doesn't rise to $75 a share by the third Friday in May, you will lose the entire $2,000. The option will expire worthless. You should also know that, according to studies, 90 percent of option contracts expire worthless. After commissions and taxes, most individuals don't make a dime trading options.

The first time I heard about options was when I was in high school. One of my friends said the easiest way to legally make tons of money was to buy options. "How much do I need to get started?" I asked. "$5,000," he replied. Because I knew I could never come up with that kind of money, I passed on his offer, but I never forgot the conversation. A couple of years later, I found out my friend actually made millions in the options market. Apparently, he was one of the smartest traders in the business and taught dozens of his friends how to use his legendary techniques. Unfortunately, like many Wall Street stories, this one doesn't have a happy ending. A few years after making millions of dollars, he almost went broke when a couple of option trades went sour. That's the way it goes with options.

Generally speaking, though, most experts believe that options is a tough game to win. To make money on options, you have to be right both about the timing and the price direction of the stock. If you're wrong on either count, you will lose your entire investment.

However, if you're still fascinated by options and want to learn more, there are dozens of books written about various strategies. Ask your broker for the brochure, "Characteristics and Risks of Standardized Options." This explains in detail exactly how options work and the risks you take by trading them.

101. It's never too late to make money in the market

This is perhaps the most important lesson, told to me from a very wise acquaintance of mine. No matter how many mistakes you may have made in the past, no matter how much money you might have lost, nothing should stop you from using what you've learned in this book and others like it to make a fortune on Wall Street.

With the right tools, a positive attitude, and quality information, you can be a successful investor. It doesn't matter if you're young or old, the stock market is one of the most fascinating and potentially lucrative places to invest your money. In addition to making money, you can also use the stock market to learn economics, psychology, history, mathematics, and financial planning. No one said the journey was easy, but the financial and educational rewards of investing are immeasurable.

It is up to you to make the next move. With the information you have learned in the previous 100 lessons, you can succeed as an investor in the 21st century. The stock market will be there when you're ready.

THE LESSONS I LEARNED

You might wonder what I learned after talking with some of the sharpest investment experts on Wall Street. To tell you truth, if I told you everything I learned, I'd have to write another book. Therefore, I'll only focus on the lessons that helped me the most.

First, I learned that the first three lessons are most important—adopt a strategy, develop a set of rules, and practice the self-discipline to follow the rules. Like many people, I thought I could win in the stock market by playing it by ear and relying on my instincts and experience. Maybe some people can make money that way, but I can't. I've learned that it is essential to protect myself from *myself*—and the best way to do that is to follow the first three lessons without exception.

As a result of talking with the pros, I have taken a longer-term, more philosophical approach to the market. Although I still hate to lose money, I am now more confident that the stocks I buy will eventually outperform the market over time. I learned from the pros to pay less attention to what the market is doing each day and more attention to the quality of the companies I invest in. Because

I'm buying what I consider the best companies, the schizophrenic movement of the market doesn't bother me as much as it used to.

Nevertheless, the hardest lesson for me to follow is to cut my losses. Like many investors, I don't like selling my stocks, even when they start to drop in price. After spending so much time researching and analyzing the company, it's difficult for me to believe I could be wrong. I did my homework, now I expect to be rewarded. Yet, even the top pros don't expect to be right all the time. At best, they expect 65 or 75 percent of their stock picks to be right. With that in mind, I learned that you have to sell the stocks that are losing and add to the stocks that are winning. It seems so simple, yet it is so hard to do.

While doing my research, I discovered that everyone has a psychological comfort level, or as the pros say, a risk tolerance. For me, this means keeping a portion of my portfolio in a money market account. It not only makes me feel comfortable, it also gives me the opportunity to buy when everyone else is selling. Speaking of risk tolerance, one of the oft-repeated sayings on Wall Street is that the greater the risk you take, the bigger your potential reward. Maybe it's true if you want to make a lot of money fast, but I believe it's still possible to make money in the market without taking huge risks. If I'm going to take chances, I'd rather do it with less of my money.

One surprisingly important lesson for me is how easy it is for emotions to play havoc with my portfolio. I believe that too many people underestimate the importance of psychology in determining how they will do in the market. What I have learned is that no matter how much I know, if I don't have control over my emotions, the market will beat me. I have learned to look honestly at my strengths and weaknesses before I commit any money to the market. As a result of this self-analysis, I avoid many of the most common trading pitfalls—such as penny stocks, day-trading, going on margin, "hot" tips, and IPOs. Before, I was a gambler using the market like a casino to make bets on stocks. Now I am an investor, patiently buying high-quality stocks that have excellent long-term prospects.

As it turns out, patience is one of the most important characteristics of the top investors. When the pros talk of patience, they usually mean that you should give your investments time to work. For me, this also means having the patience to sit on the sidelines until the right opportunity comes along. Before, especially during bull markets, I'd buy anything that looked like it was going up. Not anymore. I learned from the pros to be choosy about the stocks I invest in.

Like many investors, I underestimated the importance of doing my own research. Today, if I don't have the time to thoroughly research a company, then I won't buy its stock. Fortunately, the Internet has made it extremely easy to get access to important financial data. This means that I don't have to rely primarily on stockbrokers or acquaintances to tell me what to buy. Doing my homework also means visiting the company and finding out how it is being run.

It is also fascinating to me that so many pros got interested in the stock market when they were children. All it took was a helpful parent to explain how the market worked. What I've learned is that if you want your children to be successful investors, it makes sense to encourage them to use part of their allowance to buy a few shares of stock or a mutual fund. You never know how it will change their life. It changed my life. When I was younger, my father taught me everything he knew about the inner workings of the stock market. As a special treat, I was allowed to spend the day watching him work as a stockbroker at his Chicago brokerage company. Like the pros I interviewed, my early exposure to the market helped instill in me a deep appreciation and passion for investing that will remain with me forever.

Now that our journey is nearly over, I'd like to let you know how much I enjoyed sharing what I learned. If, after reading this book, your lives have been enriched in even the smallest way, my efforts have been worthwhile. Finally, if for any reason, you have any thoughts or suggestions about this book, you'll find my e-mail address on page 249. I would be delighted to hear from you.

APPENDIX

Popular Financial Websites:

www.aol.com	research and financial news
www.barrons.com	research and financial news
www.bloomberg.com	research and financial news
www.briefing.com	market analysis and quotes
www.businessweek.com	research and financial news
www.cnbc.com	research and financial news
www.cnnfn.com	research and financial news
www.dailystocks.com	charts, quotes and financial news
www.financenter.com	100 financial calculators
www.firstcall.com	research
www.fool.com	financial news and advice
www.forbes.com	research and financial news
www.hoovers.com	company profiles and financial news
www.investorama.com	Internet directory
www.imet.com	news and market commentary
www.kiplinger.com	research and financial news
www.marketguide.com	company reports and analysis
www.marketwatch.com	minute-by-minute market news
www.money.com	research and financial news
www.morningstar.net	research and financial news
www.prars.com	order company annual reports
www.quicken.com	research and financial news
www.quote.com	research and quotes
www.sec.gov	EDGAR database
www.smartmoney.com	research and financial news

www.securities.stanford.edu	listing of class action lawsuits
www.stockpoint.com	research and financial news
www.thestreet.com	research and market analysis
www.worth.com	research and financial news
www.yahoo.com	research and financial news
www.zachs.com	earnings estimates
www.zdii.com	research and financial news
investor.msn.com	research and financial news
quote.yahoo.com	minute-by-minute market news and research

FOR FURTHER READING

Future Edge, Joel Barker, William Morrow & Company, 1992

Bogle on Mutual Funds, John Bogle, Dell, 1993

Free Lunch on Wall Street, Charles B. Carlson, McGraw-Hill, 1993

Big Blues, Paul Carroll, Crown Publishers, 1993

It's When You Sell That Counts, Donald L. Cassidy, McGraw-Hill Companies, 1997

From Hard Knocks to Hot Stocks, J. Morton Davis, William Morrow & Company, 1998

Contrarian Investment Strategies, David Dreman, Simon & Schuster, 1998

The Motley Fool Investment Guide, David and Tom Gardner, Simon & Schuster, 1996

You Have More Than You Think, David and Tom Gardner, Simon & Schuster, 1998

The Intelligent Investor, Benjamin Graham, HarperCollins, Revised Edition, 1997

Beating the Street, Peter Lynch, Simon & Schuster, 1993

One Up on Wall Street, Peter Lynch, Simon & Schuster, 1989

A Random Walk Down Wall Street, Burton G. Malkiel, W. W. Norton & Company, 1973

Beating the Dow, Michael O'Higgins, HarperCollins, 1992

How to Make Money in Stocks, William J. O'Neil, McGraw-Hill, Inc., 1988

What Works on Wall Street, James P. O'Shaughnessy, McGraw-Hill, 1997

Investment Psychology Explained, Martin J. Pring, John Wiley & Sons, 1993

Mind Over Money, John W. Schott, M.D., Little Brown and Company, 1998

Market Wizards, Jack D. Schwager, Simon & Schuster, 1990

The New Market Wizards, Jack D. Schwager, HarperCollins Publishers, 1992

The Unemotional Investor, Robert Sheard, Simon & Schuster, 1998

Investing Online for Dummies, Kathleen Sindell, IDG Books, 1998

Mastering Derivative Markets, Francesca Taylor, Pitman, 1996

Famous Financial Fiascos, John Train, Fraser Pub, 1995

A Zebra in Lion Country, Ralph Wanger, Simon & Schuster, 1997

About the Author

Michael Sincere is a third-generation investor, his grandfather having founded Sincere and Company, one of the early stock brokerage companies in Chicago. He is an experienced corporate trainer, currently employed as an adjunct instructor at Florida Atlantic University in Boca Raton, Florida. If you have any suggestions or thoughts about this book, feel free to contact Michael Sincere directly at mike1456@msn.com.

INDEX